EPIPHANY
AND THE
SHOPPING
TROLLEY

**Monologues about the mundane
and the miraculous**

CATHERINE BRADSHAW

ILLUSTRATOR: PAULINE ZUFFEREY

Paperback ISBN: **978-1-923650-01-5**
Author: **Catherine Bradshaw**
Editor: **Lynette Reurts**
Cover Graphics: **Mylen Carascal**

A catalogue record for this book is available from the National Library of Australia.

DISCLAIMER

The information contained in this book is for general informational purposes only. The author and publisher are not offering any medical, legal or professional advice. While every effort has been made to ensure the accuracy and completeness of the information provided, the author and publisher assume no responsibility for errors or omissions or any outcomes or consequences resulting from using this book's content.

COPYRIGHT

All original material in this book is the sole property of the author and Morpheus Publishing.

DISTRIBUTION

This book is distributed by Morpheus Publishing and is available through authorised distributors, booksellers, Morpheus Publishing website.

COPYRIGHT PERMISSIONS

For copyright permissions or any other inquiries, please contact:

PUBLISHER: Morpheus Publishing
www.morpheuspublishing.com.au |
hello@justinemartin.com.au | +61403 564 942 |

AUTHOR: Catherine Bradshaw
https://www.morpheuspublishing.com.au/authors/catherine-bradshaw

To my Three Cherubs.
And their Nanny Annie.

AUTHOR'S NOTE

I need to be very honest with you as you pick up this book. I believe in God. More specifically, I believe in Jesus. And I pray. I hope that won't make you put this book straight back down again. I did warn Justine before she read my manuscript that I had a Christian faith and that most of my monologues were about God and my experience of faith. She took it on face value. And I thank her for her open mind and heart.

Those who know me, know that I love people. I remain interested in what others think and believe. I believe that authentic relationships ask us to stay curious and to value the individual's quest for meaning and purpose. I suppose that is what writers and philosophers have called 'the human condition'. This collection of monologues is my messy attempt to make sense of my 'condition' in more ways than one. But being human is not my only condition. I live with another one called Multiple Sclerosis.

When I started writing these monologues, MS was a readathon and had nothing to do with me. I now recognise that so many of the symptoms which I lived with as annoyances were part of my immune system's self-sabotage. So, when diagnosis came, I had to drill down very deep into the reservoir of my humanity. However, I recognised that I was not drawing from my own reservoir. That well had already run dry. Instinctively, I was reaching out to something over and beyond myself to help me keep moving, to help me stay hopeful and to help me extrapolate something meaningful from the depths of my despair.

Why monologues? Blame it on Shakespeare, Browning and T.S.Eliot, masters of the genre who I have studied and loved. They used the monologue to give voice to the life we live beneath the surface. I could call my scribblings internal ruminations, clumsy ways to outwork and make sense of my experiences. But really, they are my prayers, the outpourings of a bewildered soul longing for clarity. And every so often, they become duologues as another voice breaks in and over mine to reveal the treasure in this jar of clay.

I started writing *Epiphany and the Shopping Trolley* in my head while I was on maternity leave with newborn twins. Part of it was to keep my sleep deprived mind from falling asleep at the wheel. Part of it was to keep me in constant conversation with God as I wrestled with the brave new world of motherhood. These were fraught times. I had spent 10 weeks on bedrest and in and out of hospital to stem the tide of premature labour. These little ones were very precious and worth fighting for. At 8 weeks pregnant, I had started to bleed. The obstetrician saw no signs of life on the scan in his surgery but decided to let nature take its course. He would scan me again in a week.

And that is when they found 'them.' Thinking I had lost a baby, the radiographer, after much searching, alerted my husband and my attention to two little twinkling lights on the screen. The heartbeats of our twins.

In the week leading up to the scan, I learned a lot about praying. I knew it was not a vending machine where I deposited a coin and retrieved my purchase. I learnt it was conversation of the deepest kind. It was a conversation of absolute trust, honesty and vulnerability. I knew I was in safe hands, despite the outcome. The lessons learned in that week have sustained me ever since.

My outcome on this occasion was a good one but I know for many who have prayed, been disappointed and subsequently lost their faith, prayer is anathema. I hope in reading my stories, you may start to talk to God again as with a friend who knows and loves you. I hope some of my stories will make you feel less alone. I hope they make you laugh in solidarity, embarrassment (for me!) or recognition. We are, after all, in this ramshackle roller coaster ride of life together.

And at this point, I must thank Rebekah, Hannah and James for being the inspiration behind most of these monologues. Thanks for the stretch marks. You are literally etched onto my body. And you are eternally etched onto my heart.

I also thank my long-suffering husband, Richard. The best of men, a champion of women who has modelled for our children what an equal, respectful and honouring partnership looks like.

And I thank my parents Frank and Anne. I open this volume with a tribute to my mother who died before this work was published. I then share my father's story in the monologue called 'The Arrival'. Both my parents were victims of abuse, and it broke them in ways I will never understand. I do not know how they endured but they did. And to my sister, Angela, a champion who also lives with MS.

Love covers a multitude.

Thank you also to my dear friend and colleague Lisa Neale who edited my work and encouraged me to keep going.

And thank you to PZUFFY aka Pauline Zufferey, my talented and inspiring friend who has added her images to my words. She was diagnosed with breast cancer at about the same time I was diagnosed with MS. We both know what it is like to be blindsided by life's curveballs. This little collaboration was a dream spoken aloud around her dining room table. Dreaming and creating kindled hope in the face of uncertainty and fear. I know she would love to thank her beloved Camille, Michelle and Joshua.

Catherine Bradshaw

May 2025

CONTENTS

IN
MEMORIAM

BIALETTI

In memory of my mother

And so now the manuscript that has been languishing in my desk
drawer since the Covid 19 Pandemic might finally see the light of
day.
Have the waters broken on a five-decade gestation?
But before I sit to prepare the final draft for editing,
I make coffee.
For me, an objective correlative.
My brain, a Bialetti percolating on the stove top.
57 years bubbling away inside my head.
My ruminations like steam
increasing the pressure to distil something aromatic from the beans
of memory.

I begin to research coffee.
Google.
A procrastinator's kryptonite.

Apparently, there are ten steps from coffee seed to coffee cup.
Beans are milled and roasted
then ground by
burr or blade,
pulverised or chopped.
Either way, it is an
aggressive,
necessary
process
to produce
the inky nectar.

I start to measure out my life in coffee spoons.
Prufrock-like with
*Ragged claws**
I try *to squeeze my universe into a ball…**
I hear the Bialetti
*Bubble, bubble, toil and trouble.***
The internal monologue in my head crescendos in unison.
Wearisome…
  *more than one can say.****

I feel well and truly roasted.

It has been brewing.
This grief is now at boiling point.
A year since I buried my mother.
A year since I packed her beautiful, blue Country Road knitwear
into a garbage bag

and sent it to Vinnies.
She would have approved.
For her,
there was a time to buy
a time to wear
a time to send to Vinnies.
Sustainable fashion by Anne.
I wonder if someone has bought her clothes.
It comforts me to think that her elegance
may still be walking the streets of Sydney.
The wool has taken her shape.
Its weft and weave tell her story.
Part of the garment's history.
And if it could speak,
it would be a sad and lyrical tale.
Of a beautiful soul, trapped in a jar of clay.
A delicate mind, in an ungentle world.
Of unrelenting pain, and unyielding faith.

I pour myself a cup.

This is a dark roast.
I taste in it the notes of loss.
They are bitter, but earthy, bold and rich.
Death, a harsh, inevitable process
has taken something from me.
But it has also distilled something through me.
My love for my mother has grown richer, deeper and more intense.
And, as if for the first time,

I see.
I see her.
I understand.
She treasured and she pondered.
Much was stored up in her thoughtful heart.
Until it broke.

And yet,
She lived as one with absolute reliance.
Confident in the One who can make sense
of this ephemeral mystery.
Assured that He would carry her over its chasm
into the divine and eternal.

I know she is there.
Her legacy,
My belief.
And though the shadow of the shroud has now moved closer to me,
it bears the imprint of a human God,
whose solidarity with mortality,
restores the years eaten as if they had been a dream.

I cling to a Hope beyond human comprehension.
One that answers my overwhelming questions.
And I know
My Redeemer lives
And in my flesh
I will see Him.
My mother, alongside him.

Outstretched arms.
Whole and at
Peace.

*A reference to 'The Love Song of J.Alfred Prufrock' by T.S.Eliot.

**A reference to *Macbeth* by William Shakespeare.

*** A reference to Ecclesiastes 1:8.

MOTHERHOOD

This is the beginning of my relationship with the shopping trolley, my call to ministry and my profound, beautiful and terrifying journey into motherhood. This was a departure from my known world into the bottomless crevasse that is the love a mother has for her children; a subterranean world that ignites both fear and wonder. No woman should take this journey alone. It will require the light of a supernatural torch.

This is for all mothers. But Jane, Michelle and Adeline, my fellow twin mothers, it is especially for you.

WORSHIP, TWIN STYLE

2.00am: A child's cry pierces the suburban silence.

2.01am: Another child's cry pierces the suburban silence.

It's feeding time again at the Bradshaws'.

I perform psychological gymnastics to make my feet and the floorboards meet.
Two screaming babies are manoeuvred downstairs.
Nappies are changed on automatic pilot.
Is this to be my ministry?
At times like this, I wish God had sent me to outer Mongolia instead.

2.30am: The lamentations begin.

"O Lord, deliver me from the vale of sleep deprivation
The valley of wet nappies
The weeping and wailing and gnashing of hungry gums.
For how long must this be endured?"

A voice louder than crying startles me from my disgruntled reverie:
"*For how long?*" it repeats, and then replies.
"*For as long as it takes you to do this with love in your heart.*"

I recognise a divine rebuke when I hear one.
A cold face washer no longer required,
I am awake, being refined in the crucible of motherhood.

3.15am: Battling two premature babies who have forgotten how to suck.

Like the wheels on a recalcitrant shopping trolley, they keep rolling off the breast in opposite directions.
My pile of supporting pillows implodes.
I am a sea of cushions, babies, tears, perspiration and post-natal fury.

And I think of a young Jewish girl who gave birth in a stable.
No obstetrician.
No epidural.
No Nursing Mothers' Association.
No disposable nappies.

Did she struggle as I am struggling now?
What were the things she pondered in her heart?
Moments such as these?

"*Keep persevering,*" the voice tells me.
"*Be patient; be persistent as I have been and will be with you.*"

And I see in my babies an image of myself;
An image of how God sees me;
An image of humanity;
Tiny babies, too immature for food richer than milk;
Struggling to digest even that.
Being weaned, gradually, into the deeper mysteries of faith.

And I think of Jesus:
Once a tiny baby, like my Hannah, my Rebekah.
And I think of the destiny of that baby in the barn.
A glimpse, in the sacrifice of sleep,
Of a greater sacrifice,
A greater love.

Words sung in the fervent, first days of conversion
Resonate with empowered meaning,
An old chorus exhorting me
To worship the Lord in the heavens,
Worship the Lord all the earth,
Worship the Lord in this temple.

And this is my 3.00am act of worship.
Head bent forward over my children,
I bow down before my God as He teaches me to shepherd His flock;
To serve Him with infinite patience
In the simple act of feeding His two little lambs.

4.00am: My prayer vigil is now complete.

I carry one
and then another sleeping child up the stairs.
Fatigue makes me pause under the skylight.
Two shut eyes open again.
I almost miss the perfect moment for fear she will cry again.
But she smiles!
Her first real smile of recognition—
An affirmation of God's purposes and plans for me,
For out of the lips of children and infants
He has ordained
His praise.

On a cold May morning,
through the ministry of motherhood,
I become ambitious for the higher gifts.
And I am in awe of the God of all creation.

BOXING DAY TEST

(or What they didn't tell you in prenatal classes)

I went into labour with my son on Day 5 of the Boxing Day cricket
test.

The obstetrician almost didn't make it

but when he finally arrived, in the nick of time, he looked first at the
TV screen above the bed and then at my husband to enquire how
we were going.

In the grip of a violent contraction, it took me a minute to realise he
wasn't asking about me but Australia's performance at the crease.

Try as I might, I couldn't remember the breathing exercises they
showed me in prenatal class because I just wanted to hit both men
for 6.

This was my second labour.

I must admit, I had sat through my prenatal classes the first time
around the way most indifferent travellers sit through the safety
procedure talk on an aeroplane

… a look of polite boredom on your face, an occasional smile and
nod …

Most of us are only interested in when the drinks trolley is going to
make it up the aisle; either that, or we are too interested in the
inflight magazine and choosing the entertainment channels for our
headphones.
But really, in the event of an aeroplane crash, who could remember
what to do other than scream and assume crash positions?

It was a bit like that for me in childbirth.
And what they didn't tell me in prenatal class was that by giving
birth
I would be in for the ride of my life.

The birth …
that was just the plane taxiing down the runway.
Taking the babies home …
that was when we hit turbulence.

And I didn't have an airline hostess pointing me to the emergency
exits
because
there
were
none.

This was it.
This was a long haul flight.
I was now a mother.

I'd had 2 years of preschool to prepare me for primary school
6 years of primary school to prepare me for high school

6 years of high school to prepare me for university
and 7 years of undergraduate and postgraduate study to prepare me
for my future employment
but only 2 hours at the Mater Hospital, with a midwife, a
whiteboard, a Scotch Finger biscuit and a cup of decaf tea to prepare
me for the role of a lifetime.

What they didn't tell me at prenatal class was that I would one day
lock my keys, the shopping and my six-month-old twins in the car
by accident
and that breathing deeply would help me
not to pass out before the NRMA arrived to smash the windscreen.

They didn't tell me that I would listen incredulously to a young
work colleague apologise for being late because she slept through
her alarm clock.
(You try to remember what an alarm clock is. You used to have one
of those,
but now you have children.
You are also aware as she is speaking that you are obsessing over her
words as they float like bubbles around her head …
You hear the words 'slept through … slept in … late night … only
six hours sleep'
and you want
to kill her.
Sleep has become your obsession.)

And they didn't tell you that you will never stand still again.
You will catch yourself even now standing in the checkout queue,

rocking your trolley backwards and forwards, backwards and forwards, as if the frozen peas need to be put to sleep.

They didn't tell you that you will never drink a cappuccino in peace again because every one of your children will want some of the froth.
If you hadn't wanted the froth you would have ordered a latte!

They didn't tell you that a Sydney urban professional woman would become obsessed with whatever goes into a child's mouth and comes out the other end.

Changing a nappy becomes an episode of CSI; a forensic investigation as you look for that missing piece of Lego you suspect got swallowed along with the play dough.

They didn't tell you that the phone is an electromagnetic device that seems to draw children to it only when the mother is talking on it.

They also didn't tell you that you would take your child to the doctor with suspected conjunctivitis only to be told it was dried Weet-Bix.

They didn't tell you that you will be on call 24 hours a day and that when all your children have gastro you will develop X-Men-like skills as you anticipate by listening to the way your child is breathing who is going to vomit next.

(With supernatural dexterity you leap from room to room with your ice cream bucket and wet face washer landing beside the bed just in time to catch it when it falls and you've only missed once.

They could make this an Olympic event.)

They didn't tell you that it would all go by so fast
and that one day you will wake up and find that they can get their
own Band-Aids
and that you actually miss watching Thomas the Tank Engine.

They didn't tell you that one day they will stop wanting you to walk
them into school and that they won't want to kiss you goodbye.
They run in the gate and don't look back.

And you remember then the mornings when they held onto your
neck and wouldn't let you go
and through their tears begged you not to leave them.
And they didn't tell you in prenatal classes that at that moment your
heart would break
the way it is now when you realise that your children are releasing
themselves from you and that you have to let them go.

At that moment, you will take the turbulence back in a second.

They don't tell you that even when they sleep through the night, you
will still wake up thinking about them.
You will lie awake and worry about the things you know are
troubling them and pray for God to let this cup pass from them
knowing full well that they must drink of life as you yourself have
drunk,
the bitter with the sweet,
and that you with a new agility must help them negotiate their way
into becoming the people they were created to be,
must watch them make choices that only they can make,

must let them walk into each stage of their lives the way you
watched them take their first steps,
holding fast to your hand at first, shaky, tentative, prone to falls,
but then the grip loosens, and they stand alone,
you stand behind, hands outstretched, ready to catch them …
and that often they will fall,
and that sometimes you will miss.

It is at these times you realise that in this you are only the caretaker
and that they have another parent who broods over His creation like
a mother hen around her chicks,
One who perceives their thoughts from afar,
who has known them before I even knew they were there being
formed, finger by finger, in the dark of my womb.
They heard His voice first calling them into being
and they felt His breath breathing into their lungs the substance of
life.

They could never have told me in prenatal classes
that the love I feel for my three
is a shadow, a hint of the love He feels for the 8.2 billion* children
He created all over this world
and that He never sleeps, watching over them, listening to their
prayers, waiting for many of them to turn around and wave to Him
as they go on with their lives,
feeling the pain as many of them no longer speak with Him or
acknowledge He is there,
watching them stumble and fall as they try to walk on their own,
making choices He wishes they wouldn't make,
releasing them into these choices

but loving them just the same
day in, day out,
year in and year out,
calling their names over and over and over again
so that they may one day recognise again the voice that first called
them into being.
He can do no less because
He is love.

And because of Him
I must try to do no less
for the rest of my life.
He has called me to be a mother.
From that I can take no holiday, no long service leave.
The marks of my children are etched onto my body
and into my heart.
I have laid a part of my life down for them and I can never again
take it up.

But any sacrifice I have made can only ever be possible because
He laid it all down for us first
and on His body and in His heart are the birthmarks for the
salvation of all humanity;
the blueprint of His love of which we are all caretakers.

We love because He first loved us
and we cannot be indifferent travellers now.

*as of 2023

MI5 INTELLIGENCE AGENT

Like an MI5 intelligence agent from *Spooks*,

I am about to come in from the cold.

I have insider information about a Special Operations Unit active within Australia and the world.

For years now, I have been part of an international Tactical Response Unit otherwise known as TRU.

Its all-female officers sign up for life, motivated by a primordial sense of devotion and duty; often with no formal qualifications or experience.

There is no training manual.

It is all field work, requiring a high level of intuition, adaptation, improvisation and the distillation of conflicting information to find the best strategic plan for their operation … often with not a second to lose.

Their mission, should they choose to accept it, is to secure Australia's future.

While out on the grid, a TRU officer is referred to as a Multi-

tasking, Ultra-efficient Matriarch—
MUM for short.

They can never take long service leave or resign their positions.
They are a not-for-profit organisation.
Their dividends are tied up in a long-term investment called KIDS.

The MUM missions are carried out in solitude, in the dark, the early
hours of the morning, or peak hour traffic.
They are on call 24/7.
As they attempt to underpin the strategic and governance
framework of the average suburban home, they are continually at
risk of emotional and physical meltdown.
Operationally, this is called 'losing it'.
When this happens, they must attend a debrief with other MUMs
and often relocate to a Safe House during this time.

MUMs often work undercover disguised as ruthless, unfeeling,
unreasonable and unfair.
It appears that they just don't understand anything, deliberately
humiliating and embarrassing the KIDS.

MUMS can stretch themselves to be in six places within the space of
minutes.
For this reason, they often double as jugglers, contortionists and
event coordinators.
Many have successfully auditioned for Cirque du Soleil.
The unexpected and unpredictable nature of their missions requires
MUMs to shower and eat breakfast simultaneously.

The most commonly anticipated time for a domestic crisis is the minute a MUM closes the bathroom door and gets into the bath.

MUMs must learn to drive with one hand on the steering wheel while holding a car sick bag in the other.
Driving a manual car increases the risk factor of the operation.
Under the Official Secrets Act, I can now disclose that the Stig is not Michael Schumacher; he is in fact a MUM.

MUMs are also unofficial members of the UN Peacekeeping Forces. Trying to work out whose turn it is to sit in the front seat of the car has averted many an international incident.

Every MUM is also expected to work within the Counter Terrorism and Special Tactics Unit and will at some time in her career defuse a toddler tantrum in the Macquarie Centre carpark, remove a hysterically screaming child from a doctor's surgery, and try to negotiate with a monosyllabic adolescent to get out of bed and onto the school bus before graduation.

One of their most difficult operations as part of the Special Tactics Unit is to try to make broccoli appetising for the KIDS to eat.

Intelligence just received indicates that there is still a cold war being waged over the consumption of vegetables.

Regrettably, despite the MUMs' best surveillance, the whereabouts of every pair of school socks in the house has not been identified.

Some MUMs report that they have finally located the floor in a teenager's bedroom.

It is hoped that this piece of intelligence will reveal the whereabouts of the socks.

As part of the Forensic Services group, MUMs may need to locate and identify missing pieces of Lego while changing a nappy.

They can smell a squashed banana in the bottom of a school bag from at least 8 kms.

MUMs are also the chiefs of Operational Communications and Information Commands.

They are expected to know the exact movement of everyone on the grid and the whereabouts of all apparatus pertaining to the smooth operation of the domestic front.

In the event of the KIDS returning home from school with an assignment, it is expected that the MUM will have a thorough working knowledge of all aspects of the NSW Department of Education Syllabus including the Gold Rush, The Reproductive Life of Plants and The Quantum Theory of Mechanics.

Contrary to popular opinion, MUMs do not have an easy access account with a Swiss Bank.

So how do these special agents manage to fulfil this mission, day in, day out?

The remarkable thing about them is that although there is no training manual for each specific assignment there is a blueprint for all operations in the hands of the TRU Controller.

MUMS are not asked to do or be anything that He has not been or done.

Everything they need
for every mission
is embodied in
specific code names
that He has been using since
His spirit hovered over the face of the water
and He revealed Himself as
Jehovah-Elohim—
the creator of the heavens and earth,
the actively present, faithful, loving and unchangeable God.
Yahweh.
The Great I Am.
And this is the starting point, the strongest frame of reference
that any MUM can have when embarking on her TRU mission.

When she needs
encouragement,
rest,
financial resources,
she calls on
Jehovah-Jireh—
the one who provides.

And when the MUM fails in her mission,
El Shaddai is enough

to cover the multitude of her sins and sorrows
And make them His own.

When her KIDS are sick
and she herself is overwhelmed
and sick in heart
she can call on
Jehovah-Rophe—
the God who heals.

When the KIDS need cover, she calls on
Jehovah-Nissi—
the Lord as their Banner, their covering, their protection.

When chaos reigns and the house is in uproar she can call on
Jehovah-Shalom—
the God of peace.

And ultimately, when she must guide and lead
and go all out to bring her children safely home, there is one who
has gone before her and continues to lead her—Jehovah-Rohe—the
Lord our Shepherd.

He reminds her that with
Jehovah-Shammah
she will never be alone
but will always have a table prepared for her
in the presence of any enemy.

The MUM is indeed on a Mission from God,
Daunting, at times frightening, exhausting, inescapable,
And she does it all with a love that is over and beyond human
capabilities
because
the way, the truth, the life
is Jesus—
Jehovah saves.

DIODRAMA

There are some words I dread hearing when my children come
home from school.
They aren't "There's an outbreak of head lice"
They aren't "The kid next to me has scabies"
Or even "I've been expelled"
They are "Mum, I've got a project, and we have to make a diorama"
A diorama—or more appropriately a DIODRAMA—
When your kids are sent home with the task of making a three-
dimensional model, maybe of the Pyramids, the Harbour Bridge,
Taronga Zoo or the life cycle of a bee.

Dioramas are the boomerangs of education
They just keep coming back
And this is my conspiracy theory:
Everyone knows the diorama becomes a family affair
It takes over the dining room table
Involves trips to hardware shops and recycled garbage
Glue that won't stick, paint that won't dry
It involves weeping and wailing and gnashing of teeth
Recriminations for *leaving everything to the last minute*

And bewilderment as you, the parent, find yourself still awake at midnight trying to put the finishing touches on your *child's* model of the Great Wall of China.

You'll be really ticked if you don't get a good mark for this one!
And you sincerely hope you beat that other parent this time
You are still smarting over your model of Circular Quay being trumped by their model of Warner Bros. Movie World.

Through the diorama, the sins of the fathers are visited upon the sons
Because if you escaped making one as a child
You will not escape making one as a parent
The education department is determined to make sure that everyone at some time in their life will eventually have to make a diorama
Diorama … even the name sounds apocalyptic
A disaster film in 3D without the popcorn
And this is my point:

In the 21st century, the humble diorama has been transformed into Pandora's Box.

I call this The Avatar Effect
Gone are the days when you could make your model out of paddle pop sticks, alfoil, toilet rolls and shoeboxes
If you had really keen parents, they might have made a papier-mâché model out of balloons and wet newspaper
But dioramas these days need James Cameron's Performance Capture Technology

Because there is a high-tech battle going on out there in our
playgrounds
And our children's reputations are at stake!

A model of Jenolan Caves can't have playdough stalactites just
hanging there anymore
They need ones that glow and drip.

Making a model of a volcano?
Crumpled up red and black cellophane just doesn't cut it anymore.
And forget the bi-carb and vinegar to simulate volcanic activity
A committed parent will consult a geophysicist as to how we can
sample some real Icelandic volcanic ash and lava.

Making a lighthouse? You'll need halogen lights and fibre optic
cables
A degree in architecture, engineering and marine biology.

And don't think you can just put your child's model in a plastic bag
You'll have to hire Kennards to transport it to school
And when all these dioramas finally make it back home, your living
room will look like something out of *Night at the Museum*.

I can't recall it ever being this difficult or competitive when I was a
kid
Or maybe I have selective amnesia
The result of the blissful ignorance of childhood
I am sure I never fully appreciated or understood the sacrifices that
were being made on my behalf
Of a devoted mother who just manoeuvred us through life

A conductor of a large unruly orchestra
Trying so hard to keep us all in tune
All to time
While trying to draw out our own unique voices.

Now that I am a mother
I am in awe of all who have gone before me
Of my mother and the mothers throughout history
Who laid down their lives
The minute their newborn infants were taken up into their arms
Did they realise the enormity of their divine assignment?
That this was a 3D construction project of epic proportions
Life given into their hands to mould and shape
Praying that love would cover a multitude of their failings?

And so to mothers everywhere
I salute you
For enduring morning sickness, labour pains and mastitis
For sacrificing a flat stomach to stretch marks
For all those sleepless nights
And three-hourly feeds
And visits to Casualty.

I salute you
For all those cold winter mornings when you stood on the sidelines
at Saturday sport with the oranges and the drink bottles
For uneaten dinners that took you all afternoon to prepare
For making over two-and-a-half thousand lunches per child
For PE uniforms washed at midnight because apparently it's sport

tomorrow
For countless loads of washing taken out and brought in
For sheets changed and beds made.

I salute you
For withstanding supermarket tantrums
And broken curfews
For signing excursion forms
And balancing budgets
Juggling baths, homework, dinner and a working life
For being on call 24/7.

I salute you
For asking 'Are you warm enough?'
And 'Have you brushed your teeth?'
For teaching us to wash our hands and use the toilet
For house training the puppy
And holding the funeral service for the goldfish.

I salute you
For being the taxi service, the acrobat and the UN peacekeeping
force
A living GPS system because apparently you know the location of
every single item belonging to everyone in the house at all times
Because after all you must have moved it or thrown it away!
For being grunted at in the morning
For being given the silent treatment
For having to say no sometimes
For the times you felt misunderstood and unappreciated

I salute you
For wiping away tears
And being there when we didn't make the team
For carrying in your heart the past, present and future of your children.

Today, we will arise and call you blessed.

BMW SMILE

I have just paid off a BMW.
It's a red Series 3 sedan
Billed as the ultimate driving machine
It promises life, unique features and exhilarating times.

The only problem is
It isn't mine
It's my children's orthodontist's.

I remember the dental nurse brought me a chair, smelling salts and
a glass of water when I was told how much braces would cost for the
twins.
The orthodontist suggested I start one twin now and the other later.
I asked him had he seen Meryl Streep in *Sophie's Choice*?
He said he hadn't.
I said he should
Because then he'd never ask a mother to choose
Because then I'd be paying for a psychoanalyst as well as an
orthodontist.

No.
We would have to start at the same time
But did he have a two-for-one offer going?
Buy one get one free?
50% off the second pair?
A free set of steak knives, perhaps?
Or a year's supply of dental floss?
I detected a slight curl of his upper lip
But no other emotion registered.

It was then I realised the poor man had lost his sense of humour
It had receded with the years like gums …
A little humour removed with every extraction.

And so I paid the deposit on the braces
And sat in the waiting room while at the first visit he put the
equivalent of four alloy wheels, some shock absorbers and cruise
control and air conditioning onto my daughters' teeth.
For the next 18 months, they had what I called The BMW Smile.

The great poet T. S. Eliot said that we measure life out in coffee
spoons
But we don't.
We measure it out in dental bills.
Each stage of life seems to be dominated by teeth.
Every childhood ailment is put down to it—
A bad night's sleep
A runny nappy
A pink cheek

A supermarket tantrum
An acute dislike of puréed broccoli
Has to be teething … can't possibly be the broccoli.
But genetically, my ancestors took their time getting teeth
And so I looked into my children's mouths
The way a shipwrecked Crusoe looks to the horizon for the white
sails of a rescue ship—
Wondering if teeth would ever appear.
After all, I was up against a unique breed of mothers at the
Community Health Centre.
They had given birth to infants with full sets of teeth,
At six months old they weren't gumming rusks,
They were chewing on T-bone steaks …

But years later I recognise one of these mothers one afternoon in the
orthodontist's waiting room
Those T-bone munching milk teeth all fell out and an overbite took
their place.
So now we are on the level playing field of braces, O-rings, elastics,
power chains and retainers.
We share a laugh at our own expense and wonder if the next round
of dental bills will be our own.
Next stop: root canal therapy.
Or dentures.

But as my son so reassuringly told me, I should not worry about the
future.
He had seen an ad on TV selling Seniors' Insurance and apparently,
I'm almost eligible to apply …

I remember when the only thing I waited for to pop out of his mouth were little white teeth, not pearls of adolescent wisdom.

But here I am, entering a new stage of motherhood and of life.
I am now the mother of high school students
And I am now a netball mum.
It is a life stage that has taken me by surprise.
I used to play netball in the most spectacular yellow cotton box pleat tunic a respectable Catholic girl could wear. One-inch-above-the-knee-regulation hem. Sr Mary Edwards had a tape measure.
Now the netball courts look like a superhero convention:
I've never seen so many daring shades of lycra in my life with costume designs straight out of International Figure Skating competitions.
I half expect Sr Mary Edwards to come flapping out from behind the trees waving her tape measure although I think she'd find that on these uniforms there's not enough hem to measure. In fact, there's not enough of any material to measure.
There is also the risk the girls will get hypothermia in the winter.

Once, netball mothers would sit on the side in plastic fold-out chairs with bags of oranges and their knitting or a book. A very organised netball mum would bring a thermos filled with tea.
The general motherly approach was a supportive but disengaged nod and smile.
There might be the occasional wave if you scored a goal.
But I seem to be part of a new generation of netballing mothers.
Now it's *Alien Versus Predator*.
Benign mothers with bags of oranges?

This is *Call of Duty* played out for real … in lycra.
These women have PS3 controllers concealed inside their tracksuits
to maneuver their children into killer positions.
It's dark. It's dangerous.
It's 21st century Saturday sport.
I look around at these grown women, women I would have played
netball against as a teenager
And I can't believe that life has led me to this moment.
I see myself start to pace up and down the sideline like a caged lion.
I hear myself calling out battle strategies
And woohooing with the best of them.
And I wonder if I am having a midlife crisis.

It had never crossed my mind to have one, actually, but I realise its
seeds were sown by my osteopath.
One visit she recommended a few lifestyle changes to help me
navigate through perimenopause.
Peri who? I asked.
I'd watched *Friends* in the 90s and knew Matthew Perry was an
actor, Alex Perry a fashion designer who wears sunglasses on top of
his head, and Katy Perry a singer with changeable hair colour … but
Perimenopause?
He just sounds like a bad stand-up comedian.
But no, this is the name given to women in my stage of life—the
ones five years off Seniors' Insurance.

So as I look around the netball courts, I wonder how many other
mothers are feeling the same pressure.
How many women here are trying to come to terms with yet

another change in their lives?
Trying to reposition themselves the way the coach switches Wing
Defence and Goal Attack at half time?
And the pace of life gives us no time to pause.
No time to reflect on the momentous stage of life we have just lived
through.
We just lurch from birth to weaning to playgroup to preschool,
We give them over to school for six hours every day, our primary
influence gone,
And now that we have 'all that time back', we are expected to segue
back into the mainstream as if it was just a temporary break in the
transmission of our lives.

But our lives, like our bodies after nine months of being inextricably
connected to our children, are changed forever.
For so long, our children have relied on us for the bare necessities of
life;
Their wishes are our commands.
And as we take them on the journey from interdependence to
independence,
We begin to feel their grip on our hands loosen
Until they walk unaided into their futures
As they should.

But you will grieve—imperceptibly,
And there will be moments when you feel bereft of purpose.
But then you hear a voice say to you,
'Well done, good and faithful servant.
Well done for doing what I have asked you to do,

Well done in laying down your life for another.
And here is the surprise.
Rejoice O barren woman.
I am doing a new thing.
See how it springs up.
See how the kingdom of God is never finished.
See how time for me is not linear or defined by stages.
See how it has no use by date,
How it never perishes but flows on and builds what was and is and
is to come.
See that it is eternal and your purpose in it is endless.
While you have breath in your body,
Sing to me
And prepare yourself knowing that the most fruitful years are yet to
come.
The seeds you have planted will grow
And you will see a harvest before your very eyes.'

Caleb, an old man, entered the Promised Land with Jacob,
But for him there was no Seniors' Insurance.
He just cried, 'Give me my mountain.' And kept building.
So maybe the world tells us our best years are gone,
Like Samuel Beckett, I don't want them back, not with the fire
within me now.
I belong to God. The journey secure.
And with Him is the promise of life, unique features and
exhilarating times.

– 41 –

THE SHOPPING TROLLEY SERIES PARTS I-IV

THE SHOPPING TROLLEY SERIES, PART I

The shopping trolley and I have a co-dependent relationship. It is a recurring image in many of my monologues. I didn't realise how significant an impact it had made on my domestic life and my experiences as a mother until I sat down to piece together the last 30 years of my life. And there it was, looming large in the forefront of my daily activities: a metaphor for breastfeeding, an unfortunate connection with long-lost adolescent love, a symbol of rebellion, avarice, escape, and even faith. At times, the trolley has lurked quietly in the background, obscured from my line of vision by the smudges on my rear-view mirror. It is usually at these times that I have collected one or two of them under the back wheels of my car as I have tried to reverse out of the shopping centre.

But as a mother who had three children under three, there were times when a pram just didn't cut it. I needed that trolley as a supermarket paddy wagon. Throw in a box of Tiny Teddies and you might get the shopping done without too much carnage. My very own Chariot of Fire!

The simplest, most mundane exercises of life are often the portals through which the voice of God speaks. And for me, a sojourn with a shopping trolley has facilitated moments of clarity and understanding.

So, what are the 'unidentified items' that I have been carrying around with me over the last 30 or more years? What items have been placed into my emotional shopping trolley without me being aware that they are there until the checkout? And even then, do I try to make an unauthorised or alternative payment for them anyway? Or has it already been paid for by a higher purchase?

Just some thoughts …

UNIDENTIFIED ITEMS IN THE BAGGING AREA OF LIFE

Tonight, I am a finalist in my own MasterChef challenge. It is 6.45pm and dinner is not on the table. The family is hungry, like starved lions in the dens of the Colosseum, ravenous and ready to pounce.

I can hear Matt Preston telling me that it's all up to the dish I cook tonight.
In my imagination, he is a cravatted Caligula waiting to give me the thumbs up or down on this ultimate invention test.
Maximus walking out into the arena, I open the pantry door.
I hear the crowd chanting my name and the hungry lions' growls.
It's worse than I thought.

Does the *Take Four Ingredients* cookbook have a recipe for Weet-Bix, tinned salmon, wasabi and chives?

How am I going to plate this one up without facing elimination?
The fact is, I'm not.
I'm off to get a BBQ chook.

It's my fault really.

I did stop at the shops on the way home but I have difficulty navigating my way around the modern supermarket; the bright lights, everything chrome and shiny.

It feels like the Starship Enterprise with me pushing my trolley down aisle after endless aisle into the unbounded realm of choice; each manufacturer trying to boldly go where no other manufacturer has gone before.

But as I survey the vast open plains of retail, I develop the shopping trolley equivalent of driver fatigue.

I need to Stop, Revive, Survive.

I see a product test going on in the dairy aisle; it is to the weary shopper what a McDonald's drive-through is to the long-distance driver.

I feign interest in the newest line of fruit yoghurt—apparently this one has real fruit pieces. Makes me wonder what it is that has been masquerading as a blueberry in the yoghurt I've been eating. I notice there are four flavours from which to choose. I help myself to the Berry Bliss and plan another circuit so I can try the Citrus Passion Swirl and the Vanilla Pine Crush.

I dare not go back one final time for the Nectarine Peach Parfait as I am starting to look suspicious.

I reorient myself by looking at my shopping list.

We need toothpaste.

I feel my equanimity starting to waver as I am confronted with:
Mint Stripe, 12-hour Total Protection, Whitening Baking Soda

Paste, Triple Stripe Gel, Sensitive Teeth Cavity Protection with Refreshment Beads and Dora the Explorer Fruity Fun Flavour.

It is the same with pantyhose.

I am made to choose from noir, ebony, midnight, nearly midnight, ink, jet, onyx and charcoal when all I really want is black. I am drowning in a sea of Nylon so I move on to the biscuit aisle and lament that even the iconic Tim Tam has not escaped diversification.

I pick up two packets of Original in protest.

I head for the checkout.

There is only one person serving today and there is a queue a mile long for her so I settle for the self-service option. I scan my Tim Tams and try to place them in the plastic bag. The static electricity has sealed the bag opening together like superglue. This is indeed a test of my fine motor skills.

The automated voice tells me to *Please place the item in the bagging area.*

I tell it I could if I could get the bag to open, to which she replies, *Please place the item in the bagging area.*

The voice sounds cultured, English, dispassionate and icy calm, unlike mine, which is starting to sound rustic, heated and unapologetically Australian. I finally get the bag open only to be told that there is an *Unidentified item in the bagging area.*

I try scanning my Tim Tams again.

The machine speaks. *Unidentified item in the bagging area.*

The queues are swelling, impatient eyes are on me.
I feel guilty of a shoplifting crime I haven't committed.
I swipe again. *Unidentified item in the bagging area.*

I realise that I have started talking back to a machine by telling it that of course Tim Tams are unidentifiable to her. They are an Australian biscuit. Would she prefer I scan a packet of Digestives instead?
To which she replies, *Unidentified item in the bagging area.*

Is it my imagination, or is the computerised voice starting to sound sinister?
I almost expect it to start screaming, *Exterminate, Exterminate,* but the shop assistant finally makes it over to my machine.
She has been circling the self-service machines like a seagull at the beach waiting for someone to drop their fish and chips. She flaps her way over to me looking flustered and overworked.

It takes a couple of swipes of the special ID card to get my Original Tim Tams recognised. It is then that I realise how late I am for school pick-up. If this was the Star Ship Enterprise, I could ask Scottie to beam me up and transport me straight there.
But it's Ermington Woolies and I am at the mercy of Victoria Road.
I hastily scan the rest of my items. I threaten the faceless voice in the machine that I don't have any more time to be unidentified. She tells me to select my method of payment, calmly, like we are old friends.
I enter my Mastercard and she takes her final revenge by telling me

that I have an *Unauthorised card*
And need *an alternative payment method.*

I look at my watch.
I look at my items in the bagging area and decide
to just walk away
from the Tim Tams
the toothpaste
the dinner
the lot.

And so I leave Ermington Woolies, leave my automated checkout
chick who is repeatedly asking me to *remove* my items from the
bagging area. She is welcome to them.

I have much time to think as I drive down Victoria Road. The lights
are out and traffic is banked back to McDonald's West Ryde.
At this rate, I might make pick-up in time for my son's high school
graduation in 2017. I am wondering whether the overworked
seagull girl will now have to put my shopping away. All those
unidentified items.

And I think of our brave new world that has so many brands in it;
The tyranny of the choices that have made us forget what it was we
really wanted in the first place;
The human soul that has become an unidentified item in the
bagging area of life.
And hearts like shopping baskets overloaded with stuff they don't
need, always struggling to find alternative methods of payment to
satisfy their primal cry for significance.

The 21st century may have opened up our lives to unparalleled choices but it has also closed us down from essential truth.
Because really in the end, despite the machine, a human being will have to sort through the unidentified items and put them all away …

And God knew this.
Knew to send a child to be born in a barn;
an act so profound in its complete simplicity that it still confounds those who think they are wise.
For this child was the invisible God made visible here to open up the doors of eternity;
to give us freedom not marked by a barcode.
An opportunity to choose life!
The birth of this child would purchase for us all that we could ever hope for or imagine.
For in the stable, wrapped in swaddling clothes and lying in a manger,
was God's assurance that
no one in Christ would ever be
unidentifiable to God.

THE SHOPPING TROLLEY SERIES, PART II

An out-of-control shopping trolley, Christmas, and trying to find a parking spot. The minutiae of life can often expose the underlying motives of our lives. For me, it was a revelation of just how far I had removed myself from what I thought I valued.

We can often float upon the surface of things, buoyed up on a life raft of unidentified items. Often it is a thin veil of propriety, religion, denial, guilt, bravado, self-deprecation, fear, or self-sufficiency that stops us plunging headfirst into the murky depths of what Yeats called "the foul rag and bone shop of the heart". This is a place far removed from the ideal vision I have of myself. But it is a real place. It exists. And its daily undertow threatens to pull me into it.

But for the grace of God. But for His vision of me. But for the baby in the barn.

Do you fear what lies beneath the surface of things? What is keeping you afloat?

EPIPHANY AND THE SHOPPING TROLLEY

Shopper exits Woolies with an over-full and structurally unsound shopping trolley—an engineering anomaly if ever there were one.

This trolley and the architect of the carpark have conspired together to ruin this woman's day. I can see that she is anxiously contemplating the steep descent to her car. Will she get there without the trolley careering into the BMW parked at the bottom of the perilous slope we called the old Top Ryde carpark?

Woolies for lower prices—
because what you save on your toilet rolls you can put toward the panel beating.

I watch this woman in anticipation. As she takes the keys out of her handbag, they are the scent of blood to the car-parking sharks circling these concrete waters in search of the rarest of creatures: a parking spot at Christmas.

I came in search of Christmas cards. Simple ones with the message,
Peace on Earth and Goodwill to all …
But not, it seems, in the carpark.

It is the survival of the fittest, and I saw her first.
Because in the opposite direction I see him.
Mr Black Pajero—shiny hubcaps.
And we begin our pursuit.

Like synchronized swimmers without the smile, we round our
respective corners simultaneously,
facing each other headlight to headlight, ready for the fight of our
lives.
I am a gunfighter at the O.K. Corral but my hand isn't on my gun
belt.
It's on the indicator and I am ready to flick.
Mr Pajero might have a big black shiny car but I've got Lazarus: the
1998 silver Camry that just keeps rising from the dead.
Together we're the fastest indicators in the west.
I raise my eyebrow, Clint Eastwood style.
There is no sign of the good here at the moment, just the bad, and
things could get pretty ugly.

My eyes are looking into the steely eyes of my opponent. I'm
waiting for the tumbleweed to drift across the carpark in this tinned
spaghetti western. So intent are we on this brinkmanship that we fail
to notice that the woman has now lost complete control of her
trolley and its contents. An aerodynamic Christmas pudding has
taken flight out of its green enviro bag and is hurtling into space.

But still we don't move. This is a stakeout and we are taking no prisoners.
Let alone flying cake.
We watch her wrestle with the trolley the way that Steve Irwin used to wrestle a croc.

When the trolley is finally pacified and the shopping contained in the sanctuary of the car boot, the woman tries in vain to get our attention. Waving her arms wildly and shaking her head, she mouths apologetically the words no desperate shopper wants to hear.
"I'm not going yet."

All that for nothing.

Opposite us, an unobtrusive blue Hyundai has just peacefully negotiated a parking spot with a white Toyota Corolla.
The meek shall inherit the earth
And so, it seems, the parking spots …

Mr Black Pajero drives past me snarling. The poor woman manoeuvres her shopping trolley back up Mount Everest. My kids in the back seat have digested the stress like a candy cane and at the moment it is as brittle
but not as sweet.
Didn't I want them to inherit a portion of my spirit?
And what spirit have they inherited from me today?

Mr Black Pajero has driven away my adversary.
How will my face through the windscreen be remembered?

What imprint of Christmas have I left on his heart? For a few moments we became sworn enemies over an insignificant piece of territory belonging to the god of retail.
Bethlehem seems such a long way from Top Ryde.
And in the geography of the human soul, it has been left off the map.

A still, internal voice speaks into my darkness.
Comfort, yes comfort,
Though people may still live in the blackout
The light has already come.
While we search for the meaning of life in the catalogues, long ago the answer was a gift wrapped in swaddling clothes and placed in a manger.
While we cry that in Sydney this year there are not enough reindeer or decorations for the children to see,
God Himself walked this earth with outstretched hands saying,
"Let the little children come to me."
And though all of this may seem so far removed from Him
He is anything but removed from us.
For God so loved this place that He gave us a Son.
And the weight of what has been, what is, and what is to come will always be upon His shoulders.
And on this sloping piece of asphalt the crooked has been made straight
and the rough places made smooth.

Jesus—the highway to our God.

THE SHOPPING TROLLEY SERIES, PART III

Vanity: all is vanity.

Why is it you always run into people you really don't want to see when you are looking like crap?

Why is our self-esteem contingent upon how we look or what we do? Motherhood and a shopping trolley taught me a liberating life lesson.

What makes you feel significant?

ANY RESEMBLANCE TO PERSONS LIVING OR DEAD IS PURELY COINCIDENTAL

It was one of those days when …

every decent piece of clothing I owned was in the wash—
including underpants
the only ones left in the drawer were emergency knickers—
the kind your mother told you never to wear out in public in case

you had an accident and they had to call a doctor who would be appalled at the state of your underwear and pity you for being the victim of bad parenting …

Bad parenting …

It all came unstuck before breakfast when
the Godzilla school of mothering won out over the Mother Teresa school of mothering.
We'd run out of Fruity Bites
and the weeping and wailing and gnashing of teeth on the kitchen floor would have made Job look like a stand-up comedian …

And now it's 5pm and we are out of nappies.

Pile three kids into the car for an emergency trip to Woolworths. Dressed in an ensemble that would make inner city feral look like Prada, I pray I will not be discovered.
Scurrying across Macquarie Centre carpark with children in tow, I look like a fugitive from justice.

While looking furtively along the nappy aisle (and musing as to the marketing reasoning for putting baby food on the shelves next to pet care), I spy him putting gourmet cat food into his trolley.
An instant flashback momentarily blocks out the sight of my twin daughters rolling cans of *My Dog* down the aisle,
one scuttling dangerously towards the wheel of his trolley.
No hope of a quick exit now.

In just seconds, his eyes will wander from trolley wheel to dog food to my children to me …

Me …
Remembering 1984 …
Formals that were a sea of turquoise taffeta, thin leather ties, straight-leg black jeans, red converse (and Gen Y, you thought it was your idea) hair gel … shoulder pads … big hair.

Someone working at Franklins is an 80s tragic because our eyes meet … just as Bonnie Tyler's *Total Eclipse of the Heart* begins playing over the loud speaker …

Turn around, bright eyes …

And I couldn't agree more!
Turn around and run away …
just leave the children, they can fend for themselves, because this is my worst nightmare.
This is Mr Fabulous … an old high school crush.

His eyes begin to blink faster than a police speed camera.
A congenial façade of vacuous pleasantries cannot hide the horror as his stare gravitates toward my left shoulder.
It is then that I notice it too.
There is baby puke all over it.

I am beyond humiliation.

As I try to navigate my wounded pride toward a checkout laden with beauty magazines and gossip (telling me about all the celebrity

mums who got their figures back three minutes after giving birth),
Mr Fabulous breathes a sigh of relief that I'm the one that got away.
I try to tell myself that it doesn't matter.

And so, I begin a process of re-evaluation.

Is this where I imagined myself to be twenty years ago?
A momentary flicker … a wavering flame
Reignites …

No, of course it isn't.
Instead …

*I have come to Mount Zion, to the heavenly Jerusalem, the city of
God, to thousands upon thousands of angels in joyful assembly to the
Church of the firstborn whose names have been written in heaven.*

*I have come to God, the judge of all men, to the spirits of righteous
men made perfect,*

To Jesus the mediator of a new covenant.

Even as I stand with my trolley in Woolworths feeling
misrepresented, embarrassed, unsuccessful,
my spirit tells me that I am standing firm with God
And that now I really live.

As my past walks out the door with his gourmet cat food,
I look down into the faces of my children now contentedly eating
their way through a box of Tiny Teddies.

And I see them as God's arrows pointing brilliantly into the future.
They are sharpening me as iron sharpens iron.

They are teaching me to be ambitious for the higher gifts.

The girl of twenty years ago may have gone
But a child of the living God has taken her place.
And everything I ever was,
wanted to be, and am
has been reconciled and transformed by God's unfailing love.

Iron sharpens iron. People sharpen people. Different personalities teach us different things about ourselves and perhaps make us understand different ways of seeing; different ways of being human. I am sure that is why God is one substance and three persons: Father, Son and Holy Spirit. The very model of interdependent, inter-supportive, interconnected relationship.

MARTHA AND MARY GO TO IKEA

For my sister

(A modern reading of a story in the Gospel of Luke, with references to Revelation, Galatians and Isaiah)

It has been said that the ancient world built civilisations
and the modern world builds shopping malls—
vast retail empires more detailed than The Hanging Gardens of
Babylon
with underground parking stations more complex than the lost city
of Atlantis

where human beings, like wide-eyed hobbits, join the fellowship of
the shopping trolley on a mysterious and epic quest across concrete
Middle Earth in search of the cars they know are parked somewhere
on this level.

But for Martha there was no greater symbol of civilisation at its
height than the 21st century's very own Colossus of Rhodes …
The largest of its kind in the southern hemisphere:
The IKEA Super Centre.

For Martha, Rome could have been built in a day if it had come in a
flat pack.
And the Great Wall of China would never have taken 12 centuries
to build if the Chinese had used an allen key.
And Alexander the Great could have conquered over 34 countries of
the world without violence or dysentery if he had taken out an
IKEA franchise.
Martha loved the Swedish mind.
The systems, the strategies, the design concepts, the order, the
practicality.
Where else could you redesign your kitchen, bathroom and
bedroom, buy ready-to-heat Swedish meatballs for your dinner
while having a coffee after putting the children into play group, and
buy obscure European biscuits for $1 a pack?

And this year, IKEA was putting out its very own brand of
Christmas turkey—with no assembly required.
Everything under one brand, under one roof.

What efficiency! What economy!
Such organisation …

But for Mary, her sister, it was different.
In her mind, Sweden would be best remembered for giving the
world ABBA and the Volvo.
And the greatest achievement of the Roman Empire was surely the
cappuccino.
She had an Italian mind as unstructured as a bowl of spaghetti;
thoughts, ideas, relationships, connecting and interconnecting
going in all sorts of different directions
but always in search of a destination.
And somehow she had a knack of twirling onto the fork of her mind
all these contrary strands into her own unique vision of the world …

It drove Martha nuts.
And their worlds often collided …
particularly while shopping
particularly at Christmas.

Mary knew she had ADHD—"Attention Deficit around Home
Decorating Disorder"—
she watched helplessly on the sidelines as Martha and her shopping
trolley took no prisoners,
for every year Martha launched into IKEA like a paratrooper into
Normandy on D-Day.
With the stealth of a mine sweeper, she cleared aisles of available
specials and sniffed out undetected bargains with the skill of a UN
weapons inspector.

It was shock and awe.
It was too much for Mary.
She would retreat to the IKEA café for her $2 coffee, free refill and muffin,
And write the family Christmas cards.

Once upon a time this would have created a problem …
Martha, overworked, stressed and resentful, would accuse Mary of "doing nothing to help".
Mary, on the other hand, would refuse to take the blame for her sister's "constant activity and perfectionism"—
always distracted by the preparations and worried by all the little things, she felt that Martha had "lost the ability to enjoy the very moment she had worked towards …"

But this Christmas something had changed.
Someone had changed them.

It had been quite a year … their brother's sudden illness, his death
And then the miracle—
Lazarus called back from the grave by the voice of one man they called Lord.
Martha had heard about Him first and invited Him into their home, so eager to be hospitable, she didn't see it at first.
Mary did.
And she listened.
His voice the sound of rushing waters …
And in it she heard The Word made flesh living and breathing …
She saw in Him salvation prepared in the sight of all the people.

Light in the darkness
And glory to a tarnished humanity …
And in His presence the thoughts of all their hearts were revealed …
He knew everything about them
But nothing about them could ever separate them from His love.

He looked at them with eyes not of this world but with compassion
and understanding—
the eyes of eternity.
And then He asked them to look at each other through His eyes and
not their own.
He asked them to forgive each other,
to love because He first loved them,
to extend to others His grace
for it is sufficient and will cover a multitude of wrongs …

Then in their corner of the world there could be peace on earth;
a peace He has already established for us:
the incarnate God.

As they unloaded the trolley into the car, Mary marvelled at her
competent sister who understood how things can be put together;
her meticulous sister who loved to serve and loved to give.
Her language of love was one without words but one of actions.
She had unknowingly invited Jesus into their lives because she loved
to do things for others …

And Martha was thankful that the Christmas cards were written
because words were not her strength
and Mary had such a way of listening to people and affirming

others.
She had a way of seeing the possible in everything;
of calming the storm;
of bringing joy.

Her intuitive mind had first embraced the revelation …
Jesus Christ is God with us …
The reconciler of opposites.
The Alpha and the Omega.
The beginning and the end.
The king and the servant.
The one who is and always was
And always will be.

So Martha left IKEA this year mindful that everything we could ever
accomplish, even through Swedish ingenuity,
He has already done for us.

IDENTITY

I had my mid-life crisis in my 30s. I realise it was about all the expectations I had placed upon myself and all the expectations I felt had been unhelpfully thrust upon me by others. I needed to do some identity filtration. I needed to tap into what Imago Dei really means and reconcile how I viewed myself with how I was viewed by God.

I recommend making this a vital part of your daily self-talk. Brush your teeth, look in the mirror and say, 'I am fearfully and wonderfully made!' Work in progress.

LIFE'S LONG
LINOLEUM CORRIDORS
(On Turning 40)

There is something large looming in the distance …
It reminds me of the way Sister Teresita (or 'Terror' as we called her) used to stand at the end of the long linoleum corridor at Our Lady of Dolours Convent of Mercy waiting for her piano students to arrive.

She was not a *Sound of Music* kind of nun.
She would have willingly handed me over to the Nazis for my failure

to do piano practice.
Either that, or she would wallop me over the knuckles with her
yardstick every time I played a wrong note.

I think in those days this was called
incentive.

But now other billowy, shadowy figures wait for me at the other end
of another corridor in my life—
the corridor of my 30s.
And at the end of it I see the number 40 and the cast of *Desperate
Housewives*.
I don't know who is more terrifying to me now,
Sister Terror or the Kardashians.

I was prepared to sail calmly into the oceans of 40;
to embrace the biblical themes of this decade.
39 years in the wilderness and now here is the Promised Land.

I imagined myself hitting 40 and mellowing into it like a good bottle
of cab sav …
velvety, smooth, oaky but with a touch of spice.
Only, as the reality grew closer, I was feeling
slightly corked.

I blame Wisteria Lane and all that talk of the 40s being the new 30s.

I ushered in the previous decade of my life in a labour ward
delivering twins.

I was as enormous as one of those mutant pumpkins on display in
the Agricultural Pavilion at the Easter Show.

Do I really want to go back there?

But how do I move forward without being walloped by
yet another big yardstick …
the yardstick of what popular culture perceives to be womanly at
any given time?

As the day grew closer
I capitulated.
I decided I needed an overhaul,
a complete grease and oil change,
starting from the bottom up.

I made an appointment to see the podiatrist first.
She pronounced rather sympathetically that my arches had fallen
and I should start wearing more sensible shoes.

Not off to a good start, then.

My next appointment, with my gynaecologist,
was like reading a naughty student's report card:
"Incompetent cervix, with irregular periods and a uterus that is
always out of place…"
Leaving the consulting room was like surviving an interview with
the Principal.
I wanted to snap, "Well, you should try giving birth to three
children in three years"

but I thought he would just put me on detention.
I accepted my behaviour modification contract,
promising to do my pelvic floor exercises every day.

I went straight to the physiotherapist.
After an initial consultation, I decided not to go there again.
How can you work with someone who likens your abdominal
muscles to perforated underpant elastic?

So here I am staring down the linoleum corridor of 40 with faulty
infrastructure.
I contemplate liposuction and a tummy tuck but think Bridget Jones
underpants would be cheaper and less painful.

I decide to buy a new dress.
I need a new image, a new definition, a new look.
The boutique next to the beautician looks promising.
It is owned by either Trude or Prue who, after initial disinterest in
me,
says that it would be *Fine* to try on some of the garments.
I try on a series of chic, sleek and minimalist creations ...
fabrics that suggest confidence, daring, future adventure,
but with price tags that suggest bankruptcy.
Trude or Prue has perhaps sensed that some credit card blood may
be spilt today and so she hovers around the change room curtain,
a Vuitton vulture.
I am not sure whether I can make it out of here alive.
I don't have enough time to dig my way out like in *The Great
Escape.*

I long at this moment to be in the inconspicuous world of Target
where I believe no one has been served by a human being since
1976.
I need an exit strategy.
I decide on the *Oh my goodness, is that the time, I am so late for my
appointment, I'll come back when it's finished* routine.
But We are not amused.
By the way she flares her nostrils and purses her lips
you'd think I'd farted
and in one fell swoop she snatches the garments out of my hands,
looks at me distastefully, and says
FINE!
I leave feeling guilty and ashamed like Oliver Twist after
pickpocketing.

I seek refuge in the candlelit rooms of the beautician.
The music filtering through the sound system is the sound of
trickling water over bamboo.
It is supposed to make me relax.
It just makes me want to go to the toilet.
I lie there thinking that this facial and scrub will be like a quick
vacuum around the house before guests arrive
But then it becomes more like a spring clean.
My face is being pummelled with oils and lotions, the steamer and
laser lights;
I'm marinating
and there is a strange tingling sensation all over my face.
My lips begin to expand like bicycle tyres being pumped up with air,
my forehead feels like it has been superglued to my scalp.

I casually mention this to the beautician

who casually answers that it's just the collagen doing its work.

Collagen?

Well yes … didn't it tingle last time? she says.

Last time? There's never been a last time.

I try to explain that there must have been some kind of mistake but

I can't make my mouth move.

I am pinned to this table with the certainty that I will leave looking

like either Scarlett Johansson or Joan Rivers.

Next I am at the basin having

a revitalising treatment and intense moisture therapy with a keratin

infusion.

Apparently my hair is stressed.

Of course it's stressed.

It's living on *my* head!

I try to explain that my hair is a little wayward and needs to be

handled with care.

It is in fact Bonnie Tyler trying to be Jennifer Aniston.

No amount of smoothing products, refining serums and GHDs can

take the 1980s out of it.

All explanations are of course useless because my mouth still won't

work.

My face is fixed in a permanent, kind of demented smirk so it looks

like I am agreeing with everything they say.

I leave loaded up with dehumidifying restructuring gloss, flattening

shampoo and a molecular reconstruction conditioner, a

rejuvenating day repair cream containing acacia micro pearls and

green coffee extracts and a juniper berry purifying serum to

diminish the appearance of wrinkles, fine lines and enlarged pores.
I walk to the car like I have whiplash,
sucked into the beauty myth again.
It's okay, I tell myself.
I will just go home and make a nice cup of tea
and then I will ring the accountant and refinance the loan to pay for
my attempt to defy gravity.

But reality tends to bite the ankle of our best-laid plans in the way
the neighbourhood dog chases the unsuspecting postman up the
street …

There is a parking ticket under my windscreen wiper.
At that moment, I really do become a desperate housewife.
I begin unravelling then and there on the footpath.
Well, Happy Birthday to Me, I wail in full view of the world.

And then my mobile rings.
It's the ophthalmologist confirming my appointment.
I make it just in time.

The collagen has made my eyes looks as wide as Frodo Baggins'
but it doesn't seem to concern my eye specialist.
After much observation he declares my optic nerves to be
magnificent

and my retina, he says, is
beautiful.
I am overwhelmed at this simplicity.

The eyes—the windows to my soul— are
magnificent and beautiful.

My soul …
the neglected part of today's renovation rescue plan.
My soul …
How has it negotiated its way through 40 years of life?
How is it preparing itself for what is to come?

Man may look at the outward appearance
but today God is looking at my heart.

Podiatrists, gynaecologists, physiotherapists, ophthalmologists …
can any of them lead me beside quiet waters to be restored?

I no longer feel quite so desperate.
As I sit a moment longer before starting the ignition,
I do what I should have done hours before.

I speak to the one person I know has been with me down every one
of life's long linoleum corridors.

How am I doing, God?

And I hear the words
You are magnificent and beautiful.

And by the way, I paid a price for you far more expensive than any
accidental collagen facial
and in my eyes
and in all the days to come

you will be
just
FINE.

HARI'S 50TH

(Or to quote the Talking Heads, 'How did I get here?')

When you turn 100, you get a letter from the Queen
But when you turn 50, the Australian Government sends you a big
white envelope.
Part community service
Part blackly humorous reminder
that the creaky hinge on the door of your life is about to swing open
into another room
A room you will now need multifocals to see into.

As I opened the white envelope on the day of my 50th birthday,
I stared philosophically at my bowel testing kit,
complete with sample bag and pre-paid return envelope
and I remember thinking …
"Just because I think the government is crap doesn't mean I have to
send them some."
And then I thought about the poor, unsuspecting Australian postal
worker sorting through the mail …
I put the pack in the recycling, took a Prepkit-C and had a
colonoscopy instead.

But that white envelope is a magnet, Hari.
You will start receiving all sorts of flyers in your letterbox from
various 'Lifestyle' Retirement Resorts for the over-50s—
It seems that turning 50 ushers in a new life of tennis clubs, walking
tours, laughing by the jacuzzi, glass in hand, walking a caramel-
coloured retriever along a windswept beach, wearing crisp linen
trousers and a pastel-coloured knit … everything you need to
transition to retirement.
I received a "10% off your next packet of Poise" discount voucher
from Priceline,
an advertisement for "Anna's All Natural Wild Yam Cream"
formulated to alleviate hot flushes,
and a free consultation at The Australian Menopause Centre.
Going to the letterbox—this was more fun than unwrapping a layer
in pass-the-parcel.
But then there was the invitation to join the FiftyUp Club.
(I was brought up to be suspicious of clubs, secret societies, aprons
and handshakes;
my mother never let me join Brownies because she thought it was a
cult.
An elegant woman in a twinset and pearls, I just think she could not
stand the thought of me wearing a yellow skivvy with brown slacks
…)
I decided to google it
And what I found was a revelation—
Ita Buttrose and I were now in the same demographic.
The concertina of time had folded and the one-time Editor in Chief
of the *Australian Women's Weekly* was now my contemporary.

And here she was offering me a cheaper deal on my Opal Card because I was now Over 50.

I continued scrolling down the "Services for the Over 50s" page and discovered that I was eligible for bulk-billed health checks, discounted premiums on my car and travel insurance, telecommunications deals …
I could even pre-pay for my funeral.
And I could join Australia's biggest lobby group— the National Seniors.

But then I found it.
The FiftyUp Club (or "The Club" as they like to call themselves).
The Club, whose mission in life is to capitalise on the buying power of the fiftyups.
And they wanted me.
I was apparently "low risk" but "high value".
"The best possible customer that a company could hope for."
If I joined the FiftyUp Club, I could capitalise on the combined buying power of over 200,000 members to help me unlock discounts, exclusive products and services specifically released for FiftyUp Customers.
I would also get special access to the information and influence that I, as a FiftyUp, deserved.
It was sounding like *The Da Vinci Code*.

With all these flyers scattered over my kitchen bench, I began having an existential crisis.
Yet another one.

But this one was different.
This one was like the scales had finally fallen from my eyes and I
was seeing life as it really was meant to be lived.
With gusto, with relish, without fear.
And the basis of all of these flyers was fear—
Of the unknown, of being ripped off, of being left out, of being
incontinent, washed up, unemployable.
I do not want to retire, thank you. Not just yet. I feel like I am just
getting going and just getting the hang of this thing called life. I do
not want to be pigeonholed.

Yes I am 50.
Bloody brilliant.
I have made half a century. Better than most cricket players.
But there is more in me than a number, a demographic.
FiftyUp Club, you got one thing right:
I am of high value
but I am not low risk.
The Spirit of the living God lives in me
and every day is a resurrection …
Don't give me a discount Zimmer frame;
give me my mountain!

Hari, let's go back to the beginning and that bowel test kit.
Let's bring it back to crap.
You have had your fair share,
Life has dealt you some wild cards
And thrown you the odd curveball.
But you have played them both.

You, my friend, have turned crap into Dynamic Lifter.

It has made you courageous, compassionate, resilient and wise.

This is a new beginning.

Walk into it in the most outrageous Peter Sheppard shoes you can find.

Let's grab this 50th thing in our teeth and chew it so darn hard that our dentures fall out!

MR DARCY

Mary Shelley is not the only author to have created a monster.
Jane Austen also created one but she called him—
Mr Darcy.

Mr Darcy has cast his overblown romantic shadow over centuries of
unsuspecting men:
Men who managed to avoid reading Jane Austen's 19th century
classic *Pride and Prejudice* at school but have been secretly
measured up against the Mr Darcy Yardstick and been found
wanting for years!
Just when it looked like Mr Darcy could sink into the oblivion of
post-modernism,
Along came the BBC and their 360-minute-long adaptation of Jane
Austen's classic
and rubbed salt into the wound.
Jane Austen's word has been made flesh.
And the actor Colin Firth has become its incarnation.

When Colin Firth's Darcy dived into *that* lake in his puffy shirt and
pantaloons

Women around the world swooned—
I confess, I did too.
But not any longer.
I have seen the light and in an act of inverted feminism—
menimism—
I plan to liberate all captive men from the chains of Mr Darcy and
the myth of the so-called 'ideal man'.

Somehow we have interpreted Darcy's 'haughty and aloof'
behaviour as aristocratic charm and magnetism.
But when 'Darcy looks haughty and aloof,' is Colin Firth's only stage
direction in 100 pages of screenplay, he isn't really looking
charismatic and mysterious, but constipated and in need of a
chiropractic adjustment.

And what woman really wants to sit across a dinner table from a
man who looks 'haughty and aloof' anyway; who badmouths your
mother, won't dance and can't express his emotions, who belittles
his friends and is intolerant of any company other than the select
circle that he has chosen?
(And he doesn't seem to like them much either!)
Hello Lizzie, I would be getting up from the table, paying my share
of the bill and getting a taxi home!
This guy has issues
and I'd be thinking NPD:
Narcissistic Personality Disorder.
And you think all of this will be resolved after the credits roll?
So he has lots of money and an estate in the country but face it,

ladies,
this is one high-maintenance man!

But even if we free the average male from the shackles of Mr Darcy,
Other images of perfection will only take his place
And the 21st century is no exception—
Only this time the average Australian male will have a difficult time
fitting the criteria for Hollywood's latest ideal man: *Twilight*'s
Edward Cullen.

Few Australian men can really aspire to being a vegetarian vampire;
it could make you a little out-of-place at a traditional Aussie BBQ
And what does a vegetarian vampire do anyway?
Suck blood out of a lentil?
Women, don't be fooled by descriptions of Edward as enigmatic
and brooding!
He just looks bored and in need of deliverance.
Since when has the word 'smouldering' been defined as someone
who looks like they have conjunctivitis, iron deficiency and
insomnia?
In most of the photos, he just looks like a sulky little kid who's just
dropped his Vegemite sandwich in the dirt at lunch time.

But even if your search for the perfect male ended a long time ago
with
Brad Pitt or George Clooney, I bet they still leave the toilet seat up
and their dirty socks on the floor.
They have all had their wrinkles and imperfections
photoshopped or Botoxed away.

In the 21st century,
Seeing is not necessarily believing.

And this also goes for women.
We too are taunted by the cult of celebrity and its unending quest
for perfection.
Magazines are constantly analysing Nicole Kidman's waistline for a
baby bump.
Well, I am proud to announce
I still have one.
The twins may have grown up but I have heritage listed my
abdominals as
the site of my children's first home.
A permanent reminder of the structural ingenuity of childbirth.

And yes, I got back to my pre-pregnancy weight—
ten *years* after the birth of my son because every woman knows that
the Tim Tam is survival food!
Where is the joy in life if you can only eat macrobiotic sushi
to have the complexion of a movie star?

I am Italian and I eat carbohydrates!

And I do not want the 40s to be the new 30s.
For me, 42 is the new 42 because I have never been here before
and I should celebrate making it this far!
Every part of me is the sum of these years
The lines, the bumps, the visible and invisible scars
are testimony to it.

Why should I hide them away and defy gravity?
Gravity keeps the earth and the other planets revolving around the
sun.
It keeps the moon in its orbit around the earth
The ebb and flow of the tides
Part of the natural phenomena
That make up this life.

In ancient times, they said that the pagan gods would never walk the
earth,
Would never mix with mere mortals.
They observed humanity with disdain from a distance,
Untouchable, capricious, remote, impersonal,
Yet we spend our lives making mortals into gods to satisfy the
hunger in our hearts for
The God we have defied.

Cut off from the author of our lives
we have built alternative altars on which to worship—
The new moon of counterfeit spirituality.
And in this we are all like Dr Frankenstein.
Making gods in our own image,
We run the risk of creating a monster.

And these gods will never satisfy,
They neither see, nor hear, nor walk,
They can never place eternity in our hearts
They cannot go before us
To make the crooked paths straight and the rough places plain.

God's Word has been made flesh
In Jesus Christ:
Fully human,
Fully divine,
A body, a soul, a mind, a spirit—
God embracing, entering into and embodying complete humanity
To help us understand what perfect humanity can be:
Loved, forgiven, restored, redeemed,
The best of ourselves
Already spoken into our being
Since before the world began
Because our humanity has been birthed out of who He is.
In Him is reflected the face of God
In whose image we are made.

The Alpha and Omega
Born of a woman
Knows the vulnerability of our condition
Because He has lived it
As God supreme
He is not far from any of us
But love incarnate,
Mighty to save.

Our feeble imaginations
Could never invent a God so magnificent
Or a human being so beautiful
A love so wonderful
And tender in its mercies.

God has walked the earth,
He has lived among His people
To be the gravity that draws all things to him.

The search for perfection is over.
He has found us
And will perfect us
Because He is alive
And lives in us
If we will but enter through the stable door
And worship
At the altar of
Emmanuel,
God with us.

MR MAGOO
(for Richard)

My friends at school called me Mr Magoo
after the short-sighted cartoon character of the same name.
It took two visits to two different ophthalmologists to find out what
they already knew:
I needed glasses.

Yes, I am the woman who without her glasses sprayed half a can of
Baygon over a Pluravit multivitamin capsule after mistaking it for a
cockroach.
I am the woman who dunked dog biscuits into her coffee after
mistaking a jar of canine treats for a jar of cottage cookies.
And I am the woman who has washed her hair with moisturiser
because without your glasses a pump pack of shampoo looks
identical to Sorbolene cream.

At the beach, I always tried to stay swimming directly in front of my
belongings because when you are as short-sighted as I am, it is
sometimes difficult to find your towel after a dip. But sometimes
the current would drift you off course and you'd emerge from the

surf bleary-eyed and disoriented.

I'd always wanted a drive in a surf life-saving beach buggy. How very *Baywatch*.

But somehow driving in one up and down a North Coast beach with a jocular life-saver looking for your towel, thongs and beach bag wasn't quite what I had in mind.

At first, I would only wear my glasses at school so I could see the blackboard—

my myopia a closely-guarded secret.

It wasn't until Mr Perfect Prefect from a reputable boys' school in Sydney asked me out to a movie that I realised the extent of my ocular deception.

Vanity getting the better of me, I resolved not to wear my glasses.

Contact lenses were not quite cutting-edge technology when I was at school

So trying to put a pair of them in your eyes was like a car being fitted by Windscreens O'Brien.

So I sat through the entire movie looking at the screen like it was a kaleidoscope.

Swirls, shapes, dots and beads of colour but not an identifiable actor in sight.

I bluffed my way through the movie but couldn't bluff my way out of not being able to locate my date in the foyer afterwards.

I should have fitted him with a tracking device.

There was no chance of us being like Romeo and Juliet—

star-crossed lovers whose eyes meet across a crowded room—

no, in this case it was more like cross-eyed and squinting

with me just trying to figure out who I was looking for by the shape

of his head.
But if my memory serves me correctly
Mr Prefect only had eyes for one person
And that was for himself.
I located him in front of the glass doors
Admiring his reflection.
The train carriage on the way home wasn't big enough for the both
of us.
Between him, me and his ego, things were getting a little crowded.

Of course, I couldn't see it at first (and not just literally).
I was blinded by the Prefect Badge
the Oxbridge Haircut
the Blazer
the Private School Tie.
My parents had sanctioned co-curricular debating as a sensible
intellectual pursuit for a daughter who in her senior years should
focus only on her studies,
and I had an Italian Father:
it was study or the convent.
But what he didn't realise was that inter-school debating was a
cross-cultural field trip for us regional Catholic School girls.
It was an anthropological study,
a socio-economic index.
We had learnt to discern this from the biscuits served at supper.
There were no Arnott's Family Assorted served in GPS schools
And no watered-down cordial either.
Slices were baked in the refectory
And tea served not in polystyrene but in monogrammed china cups.

You could say the success had gone to our heads.
Our little school had made it into the debating big league quarter
finals
And we were living the high life.
These boys knew what deodorant was,
unlike our male counterparts across the road.
Familiarity had bred contempt for the local Christian Brothers
school.
Holding dance practice after sport in a sealed room in February
did nothing to facilitate a positive working relationship between the
two.
Death by asphyxiation seemed inevitable.
Because if the boy's BO didn't kill you, the excessive use of Impulse
Musk spray by the girls would.
And then there was the humiliation of trying to make conversation
with your partners during the progressive barn dance.
Attempts at civilised communication were met with monosyllabic
grunts.
On one occasion, when the music stopped my partner just turned
his back on me.
I realised at this point that I could never believe in Charles Darwin's
Theory of Evolution.
Dance practice was de-volution before my very eyes,
Proof that we could not have possibly evolved from simple to more
complex life forms.

Yes, the grass had to be greener on the other side of the railway
tracks.
And so that is why I found myself coming home from a movie I

couldn't quite see with Mr Not-so-perfect Prefect.

In a lovely ironic twist,

I married one of those monosyllabic boys from dance practice instead.

In fact, I married the one who had turned his back on me without even saying a word.

How could I, in that stuffy hall, ever have envisaged the way my life was going to turn out?

How, at 17, could I have known that the grass with Mr Dance Practice would definitely be greener?

Often what we think we are looking for is not what we expect to find.

And often we keep looking when what we are searching for has already been found.

So, the people walking in darkness would see a great light;

an unsuspecting Middle Eastern child would become the lens through which the world could see and know God.

A child called Yeshua—Jesus—would be God's salvation,

the lens through which the world could understand and interpret life with meaning, purpose, and hope.

And who would have thought that a child born in a stable would have the power to make sense of what we see and know.

And often of what we can't see and don't understand.

Anna was 84 when she saw Him,

A frail widow, alone in the world, eyesight probably failing,

Yet what she couldn't see in the natural, she saw with the eyes of her heart.

She knew that this child was the long-awaited consolation of the
Lord,
the redemption promised by God
and spoken about through the prophets.
She knew that this child was love in its most pure form.
God giving us Himself,
an unprecedented relationship in the history of the world.

Yet how often do we choose to stay short-sighted,
choose to leave our spectacles in the case
while we, cross-eyed and squinting, try to search for something we
know is missing?
How often do we muddle through life only seeing it in part;
conscious only of shapes, blurry and undefined.
How often do we try to find our way alone
distracted by voices telling us that our way is lost,
that God doesn't exist and cannot be proved?

But do you not know and have you not heard—
Your way is not hidden by our God.
Your cause is not disregarded.
His eyes are always searching for you across a crowded life
And He waits for those who wait for Him,
so they'll rise up with wings like eagles.

Christmas means that, like Anna, our wait for Him is over.
In our flesh we can see God.
And what is to come through Him and in Him
is greener than any grass we could ever imagine.

We can taste and see that He is good.
For if we but seek
We will surely find him.

REUNION

This monologue was inspired by attending my 30-year school reunion in October 2014. Someone told me I was the best-preserved person in the room. I told them that formaldehyde was an essential part of my beauty routine.

But it got me thinking about the last 30 years and asking myself how well preserved was I, really? How well-preserved were any of us in that room? We were all in various stages of disrepair and repair physically; but how was the preservation of our souls, our spirits?

How has TIME impacted us?

Two significant things were happening in November 1984:
In England, Bob Geldof was forming Band Aid and trying to record "Do They Know It's Christmas?"
In Australia, I was about to finish my last HSC exam—3 Unit Ancient History—while planning to head straight out that afternoon to buy my dress for the formal.
Bob was oblivious of my plight, as I was equally oblivious of Bob's humanitarian campaign to draw the world's attention to the famine

in Ethiopia.

But being a self-obsessed teenager cocooned in the bubble wrap of her final year of school, I had yet to fully appreciate the incongruity of life beyond the convent walls …

My dilemma was whether to go with the flow of electric blue taffeta with the tight bodice and ruching, or the dark teal taffeta with the long black lace puffy sleeves.

Or should I go the dropped-waist red velvet and black taffeta dress with the enormous shoulder pads—like a straitjacket up the top and a parachute down the bottom?

Or should I break out of the mould and go with the iridescent orange strapless pleat dress with asymmetrical neck and hem?

Regardless of the dress, the hair would have to be big, the shoes pointy and the earrings enormous … fashion had never been so remarkable.

These were extraordinary times …

But before any of that, I had to get Julius Caesar across the Rubicon so I could get across to Chatswood Chase and buy the outfit that would signify the end of one stage of life and the beginning of another.

Within two hours, Caesar's immortal words would also be true of me:

Iacta alea est—the die is cast!

120 minutes away from throwing in my lot with the rest of humanity to begin forging a career, a life, a destiny.

There was no turning back.

It had to be the iridescent orange!

Common sense got the better of me and I chose the frock that was
more *Brideshead Revisited* than *Bride of Frankenstein*
And it was, thanks to the advice of my mother, an elegant and
understated affair.
Not at all like the formal itself.
The 40 degree heat was melting everyone's hair product,
The static electricity coming off the taffeta would have powered a
small rural substation,
And there was a bag snatcher in the carpark.
A fight broke out in the girls' toilet,
And there was murder on the dance floor—
The cover band found guilty of killing anything remotely
resembling music.

And the cuisine …
A prawn cocktail without a prawn but with an abundance of
Thousand Island dressing over the humble and much-maligned
iceberg lettuce leaf.
There was no such thing as arugula, mizuna and mesclun,
And wasn't Kale a character from an American soap opera?
The main course was the house speciality: Chicken Maryland with a
twist, the twist being the raw chicken underneath the breadcrumbs.
And the fruit cocktail came straight out of a tin, with a dollop of
Streets vanilla ice cream and a maraschino cherry floating above the
tide of SPC syrup like a lone surfer riding a wave.

I surveyed the room and wondered what would become of us all …

Cuisine would not be the only thing that would change over the next 30 years.

We would live history, not just study it …

Within five years, the Communist Bloc would crumble and a piece of the Berlin Wall would adorn my bookshelf.

Chinese students would stage a rebellion in Tiananmen Square

And Hong Kong would be handed back to China.

Nelson Mandela would be released from prison and become President of South Africa.

The fairy-tale wedding of Prince Charles and Lady Diana would end tragically in a tunnel in Paris.

There would be wars in Iraq and Bosnia, and genocide in Rwanda.

And an ongoing war against Terror.

There would be Osama Bin Laden, 9/11, the Taliban and then ISIS.

A tsunami would hit the Indian Ocean affecting 228,000 people in 14 countries.

I'd see three Popes elected,

America elect its first black President,

Australia elect its first female Prime Minister.

There would be talk of climate change and global warming,

And the cloning of a sheep.

AIDS would affect 78 million of the world's population

And our insatiable quest for information, for knowledge, for answers, for invincibility would begin once again with an Apple.

A new millennium with new technologies—

iCloud, iPod, iPad, iPhone,

Facebook, X, Influencers, the Selfie.

People creating online virtual worlds but bringing them closer to

reality.
A world getting smaller but still searching for intimacy and true
connection.
Old certainties challenged,
Truth becoming whatever we want to make it.

And all of this is circling about me while I:
Graduate from University,
Travel to Europe, getting caught up in the first Gulf War,
Marry the guy I sat talking to in the small hours of the morning on
Trisha Crampton's front steps after the formal,
Buy a house,
Raise three children,
And do about 105,485 loads of washing …
And I see that girl from 1984 with her *Brideshead Revisited* dress
and short bobbed hair standing by the dance floor.
This is her very own *Interstellar*.
She is about to launch into the great unknown
And I'm looking at her from behind the bookcase trying to give her
the coordinates to help her navigate her way into a new place and
time.
I want to reach my hand out from my present, which is her future,
into our past;
To travel with her across the different dimensions in time
To help her sustain life.

Many of the people on this dance floor will, in 30 years' time, still be
looking for some new life out there.
They will keep exploring, attempting to seek refuge in some new

galaxy in an effort to buy Time, to stop it or to turn it back because they feel they have wasted it.

But we are all on borrowed Time. None of us knows the day or the hour.

Life is not about the what if;

It's about the what now.

In this finite dimension, anyway.

But there is a place where the laws of place and time become infinite;

where 1000 days are like a day and one day is like 1000;

where finite time is redeemed by the one who holds our times in His hands.

There is one who cuts across the dimensions of space and time

And enters this dimension

From eternity

And places it in our hearts.

The Kingdom of God makes us permanent time travellers as the Holy Spirit works in us and through us to make all things new.

The great science of an omniscient God who breaks through the dimensions of relative time and communicates with us in the only way we can understand.

Gravity can be made visible by three-dimensional objects back on earth.

And this is the Quantum Physics of Christmas.

The great Source of light.

The Word became flesh and dwelt among us,

Emmanuel, God with us

In the here and now,

Eternity transforming the moment.
A Saviour has been born to you:
Christ the Lord.

And this is the only certainty.
We are loved unconditionally—
In time, through time, beyond time.
And He is born to repay the years the locusts have eaten,
To give beauty for ashes,
The oil of joy for mourning,
And He is hope—the physical reality for all of us.
The invisible God made visible.

PROVERBS 31 AND THE DOMESTIC CRISIS

I see her standing before me

My nemesis.

She is clothed in fine linen and purple

I'm wearing tracksuit pants and an oversized shirt.

She is clothed in strength and dignity

I'm covered in yoghurt and pureed vegetables.

She can laugh at the days to come

I'm just trying to get through them standing up.

She does not eat the bread of idleness.

Well, can I have her slice?

Because it's 2.20pm and I still haven't had my breakfast.

She is the Proverbs 31 woman.

"A wife of noble character who can find?"

After reading her job description, I am not surprised they are asking that question …

There she is buying and selling a field
And I am just trying to clean the toilet.
There she is making coverings for the bed
I'd just like to sleep in mine.
There she is supplying merchants with sashes
While I struggle to get my box of 88 disposable nappies, a twin
stroller, two babies and a nappy bag from the car.
She is this gargantuan figure looming large over the piles of washing
I still have not put away
A kind of Old Testament amalgamation of Carol Brady, Mother
Teresa, Nigella Lawson and Coco Chanel.

I am being beaten to death by this Biblical yardstick.

I bet she never had a bad hair day.
I bet she didn't even get stretch marks.
Did she ever say a great many unwise things before the faithful
instruction was on her tongue or did it all just fall into the
uncreased folds of her lap?

What is your secret O perfect wife and mother?
Voiceless paragon, speak!

She speaks.

Ah, my modern friend. Try to stop seeing everything through the
eyes of a 21st century superwoman.
There's nothing incredible about me.
I only did what I was asked to do.
I learnt long ago that there was no point trying to be who God knew

that I wasn't.

I learnt long ago not to focus on what I could not achieve but on the heart that could achieve it.

My own strength was never enough

And before comparing yourself with me, remember the most important thing:

I was never asked to be the mother of your Hannah, your Rebekah, your James.

No one else was trusted with them as you have been.

No one as perfect for them as you are.

He believed in you enough to place them in your care

And He can give you the resources to complete the work He has chosen for you.

It will then be a privilege to do anything great or small that can bring glory to His name.

Time and another culture may have separated us
but I understand.
Unless the Lord asks us to build we often labour in vain.
And if my story can teach you anything it is this:
Allow our God to show you, in this exacting life of ours, places of
His simplicity and peace
For when we go there with Him,
We will find
That even a dirty nappy can be made perfect in love.

CONNECTION

So many more ways to communicate in the 21st century but so much disconnection and misinformation! I find myself guilty of doom scrolling, of going down the rabbit hole of social media, of wasting so much of my time in a detached online world, fighting battles from my keyboard instead of fighting them on my knees in prayer.

Nothing replaces human connection.
How can we keep being human?

TRAFFIC LIGHTS

It has been said that the average person spends two weeks of their life waiting at traffic lights
I think I've just spent what seems like ten years of mine on hold to a telecommunications company about an incorrect mobile phone bill
Yes: and I've just been served a debt collection notice of $560 for a supposedly free upgrade
After six months and twelve phone calls
My phone bill has become an international incident
I have spoken with call centres in India, the Philippines, Canada and the USA
I have just been transferred to Perth via Melbourne via Brisbane

An automated voice tells me I have been placed in a short queue
It seems no one knows what to do with me
I am an anomaly in their system
And once again I am put on hold

I wonder what Beethoven and Mozart would have said if someone
had told them that their famous compositions would be used as
electronic hold music in the 21st century
Far from pacifying irate customers, the sound of Für Elise and Eine
Kleine Nachtmusik played on a computer-generated glockenspiel is
enough to make even the most reasonable of people slightly
demented after half an hour
I think at that moment Beethoven would be grateful that he went
deaf

Another automated voice then gives me a sequence of numbers to
choose from
But none of them seems to match my particular inquiry
Another one of life's ironies—
Telecommunications:
But no one will actually speak with me
I try to respond to the mechanical voice
I would like to speak to a human being please
But she tells me she didn't quite get that and would I mind choosing
from the options again
I tell her there is no option for my problem
I would like to hear a real person
But I am told politely and dispassionately to please choose again
from one of the options

Maybe this is *The Matrix* after all
And I am waging a war against the machines

I begin by ordering three large ham and pineapple pizzas and a
garlic bread
the voice tells me that she is sorry
but she didn't quite catch that and asks me to select from the
options
So I order a medium supreme pizza without anchovies and then ask
for a small pizza bianca with gorgonzola and a diet coke
she says she's sorry she didn't quite catch that
and asks me again to hold while she puts me through to the first
available operator
I feel like Neo hacking his way into the system
I've found a way to reprogram the agent

When I finally get through to a human being, I've been put through
to the wrong department
This is corporate sales and not bill enquiries
I am redirected and put on hold again
Trapped inside this fibre optic Tower of Babel
I fear I may never escape
That no one will ever reach me
That my voice will reverberate in cyberspace without ever being
heard

Words have been my life
but they serve me no purpose here
there is no one listening

no one to hear my case
It seems in this brave new world of technology
The human condition is still the same

The eternity placed in the human heart cries out for a connection
more primal than any social networking system can deliver
yet humanity has muted the one voice we most need to hear
and filtered its truth through too many channels
we let its message go through to a voicemail we never retrieve
we tune into alternative signals
virtual communities
online intimacy
And the more information superhighways we construct
the greater the potential for disconnection
unless we build them to make straight in the deserts a highway for
our God.

And God, the ultimate communicator, who spoke and it was,
signposted the way, the truth, the life
through the cries of the Word made flesh

'Eloi Eloi lama sabachthani'
My God My God why have you abandoned me
Cut off from His own Father
The Son chose to be abandoned on our behalf
Chose isolation, alienation and disconnection
So that we would never be abandoned
Never separated from the love of God

There was no network coverage for Him on Calvary
He had to listen to God's silence
Have His cries unanswered
So that humanity could once again hear the voice of God
And have connection restored
He stretched out His arms on a cross and created a flat earth
drawing all things unto Himself So that the
World could be united through space and time
A communication system so finely tuned that no one need ever cry
out to God and be unanswered again

He endured silence and held death in His hands
So that we may speak with anointed tongues
And be welcomed into the presence of God
And those witnesses who heard His voice
Knew of the ancient scripture from which He cried
And those with ears to hear would know
Its promised end
Posterity shall serve Him
Future generations will be told about the Lord
They will proclaim His righteousness
To a people yet unborn
For He has done it.

GRACE

I meet her in the bathroom at the Children's Hospital, Westmead …
Two mothers trying to toilet train their toddler sons.

And as we stand at the basin teaching our children to wash their
hands,
we share through the reflection of the mirrors a quick glance of
unspoken understanding …
The universal language of motherhood.
It's been a long day and we are both a bit frayed around the edges.

I view the electric hand dryer with suspicion.
I still remember the Year 11 dance at the Lane Cove Town Hall …
drying my sweaty face and armpits under the hand dryer in the
bathroom
thinking I was Madonna from *Desperately Seeking Susan* …
until a cockroach flew out of the nozzle and down the front of my
dress.

Apparently, my screams could be heard across the carpark …

So I hesitate before waving my hand under the sensor
but my toddler son beats me to it.
He runs excitedly underneath it and activates a sudden gush of
warm air.
The machine unexpectedly roars in his tiny ear like a 747 leaving the
runway …
As he wails in terror, I try to comfort him, wondering if having a
negative experience with a hand dryer could be genetic.

But my child's terror has terrified hers
and here we are, two strangers united over the mutual comforting of
our sons.

Two women worlds apart.
I am in jeans.
She is in a hijab.
I a descendant of Sarah.
She a descendant of Hagar.

When the chaos is over and order has been restored to our little
worlds,
I gather up the nappy bag and the contents that have been displaced
all over the floor.
All the tension has gone to my hair.
I look like a Muppet.
As I feebly attempt to reassemble myself, our eyes meet again
through the mirror.
We smile.
She has finished washing her child's face and hands, but she

continues to wash her own face, hands and then her arms.
She apologises to me and asks that I not think her strange.
She must wash for prayers.

I tell her it is not strange.
It is beautiful.

I leave the bathroom admiring her commitment,
feeling conflicted about my own lack of zeal, the irregularity of my
devotions,
my Western indifference and obsession with appearance.
I even envy her the hijab.
I could do with one now as my bad hair day has just got worse.

I push the stroller to the car, distracted and unsettled by this
Muslim woman in black.

I buckle my son into his seat thinking about her
and wanting to know her name.

Call her Grace,
I hear that familiar inaudible voice breaking in over the disjointed
rabble of my thoughts.

Call her Grace and pray that she will know it
Because it is sufficient.

Two daughters drawn together by your sons
are now drawn together by mine.

Pray for her here
On the seat of your car.
My Son has already washed on your behalf
And His power rests on those who know Him.

Pray that she may know and that you will remember
that though sins be scarlet, through Him they are as white as snow;
that nothing can ever separate us from the love of God that is in
Christ Jesus;
that though you are weak, He is strong
and His power is made perfect in your weakness.
No more anxious striving
All is forgiven
And it is finished.

There is nothing more for you to do but believe in the one whom I
have sent
and love on His behalf.

So for Grace, my covered sister,
You are justified freely
the law through Moses
but truth and grace through Jesus Christ …
the universal language of God.

And through God's son I pray that one day I may see you face to
face
not as a poor reflection in a bathroom mirror
but we shall know each other fully
even as we are fully known.

A NEW COMMANDMENT

Reflections after a Good Friday service.
For Bill and Denise.

I hear them over the back fence,
Same time every night.

I can set my watch by them.
At the third stroke it will be six o'clock precisely—
The "Punch and Judy Show" is about to begin …

She—a screaming harridan on the back deck.
He—a muffled voice of inebriation inside in front of the telly.

My three-year-old learnt her first four letter word from them.
I did a double take over the breakfast cereal as she enunciated it
with the proud wonder of an innocent child learning new
expressions.
Anger wells up inside of me every time I have to haul my children
inside when the tirade begins.

They have, however, provided entertainment for our dinner parties.
Friends, standing incredulous at the back door, have listened
intently for the latest instalment of an ongoing domestic feud.
We have laughed at their expense,
revelled in their secrets, accusation,
Waited for more … better than Ricki Lake.
We've wondered if it has all gone too far this time,
and whether in the best interests of neighbourhood safety we should
perhaps call the police
Before it's too late.

Definite voices but invisible bodies.
Until the day …

My husband, chopping privet along the fence line,
Hears an all too familiar voice attempting to make contact.
I nearly trip down the back stairs—
Desperate to catch a glimpse …
To satisfy a perverse feeling of curiosity.

Peering through the bushes through the holes in the fence,
I am face to face with the gorgon; my very own urban myth.

She tells me her name.
A tiny vestige of her humanity—
And something within me breaks.

It is too small a withered body to contain such a twisted, angry rage.
There is too much pain in the face of this monster.

And now she leans over her back deck attempting to make contact
with her neighbour,
The Christian.
Who having just come straight from church has already judged her.

When I look at her and we talk of trees,
I want to ask her forgiveness for not loving her as myself.

As my three-year-olds rant and rave with expressionistic tantrums,
I think of her, my neighbour—
In God's eyes, this angry woman is still a screaming toddler,
Confused; unsure of limits, boundaries; bewildered; lost.

I think of leaving a note in her letterbox saying,
"There must be a better way than this!"
I want her to know about the Tree of Life,
To know that the old branches can be cut off and thrown into the
fire,
The pruning painful, but ah, the fruit!

My husband discusses his gardening plans with her.
"Chop down the whole damn lot!" she cries. "I don't mind.
Don't get much sun in my backyard with all those in the way
And I get such bad asthma I can hardly breathe."

"Cut the old trees down," I say to my husband.
"Clear all the way along the fence. Let the sun shine into her
garden."

I walk away carrying the image of her lonely face in my heart.

At 6.00pm tonight when Punch and Judy start,
I won't scoff.
I will stop.
I will pray that the Son will also shine into her heart,
I will pray for the Son to breathe new life into the asthma of her
lungs.

On this Good Friday,
I'll remember.
Christ has died,
Christ is risen,
For moments, for people, for chains such as these.

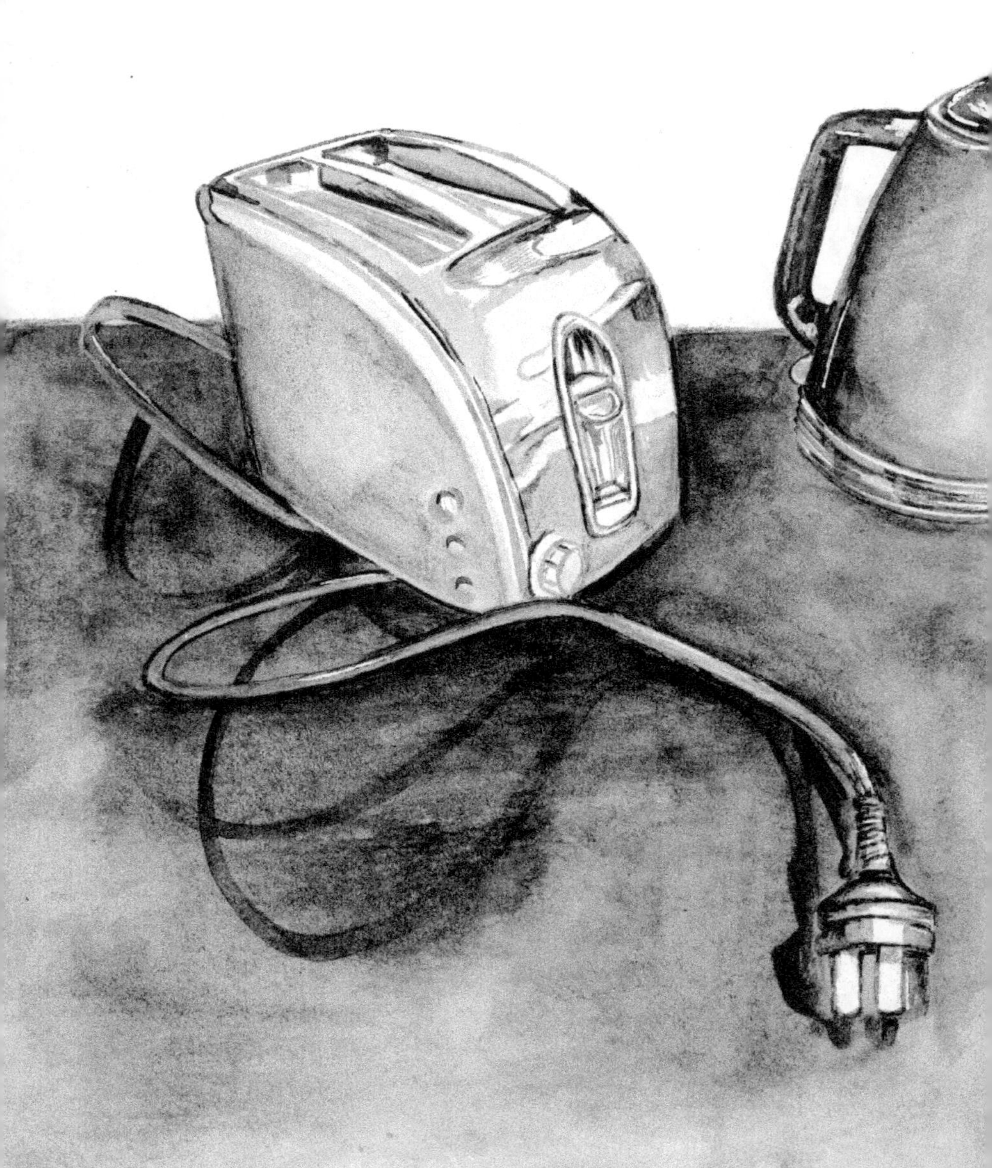

UNEXPECTED ITEMS IN BAGGING AREA: THE COVID SERIES

UNCOORDINATED

My crisis started the day I went to the urologist, and she told me I had an uncoordinated bladder …

Now before you think this is too much information let me preface this by saying I have Multiple Sclerosis
And this means that my nervous system is like the cord of an old toaster—
Frayed around the edges with the occasional spark which ends up short circuiting all the other electrical appliances in the house.
And there are these little spots in my brain that act like a fuse box,
And this leads me to another question …

Why are fuse boxes always in the worst location?
Around the side of the house, through the foliage and the spider webs,
And blackouts always happen at night and in the rain
When the battery has gone flat in your ironically named Eveready Torch—
And so, with the trepidation of a bomb disposal unit, you risk

electrocution, and the huntsman spider you know lives in there, to reset the safety switch.

You get the picture.

MS wreaks havoc with your sensory processing,
And so, it seems, with my bladder.
But I am okay with that.

It just means that I have had to install an app on my phone which tells me the exact location of any public convenience within a 50m radius of where I am …
This has led to some interesting experiences when travelling overseas,
Particularly with the unethical system called the coin operated pay toilet,
Because, let's face it, all occasions conspire against you when you try to scramble together 80 euro in change when you are busting to pee.
And there is always a queue and a turnstile …

At times like this you understand Brexit as you pole vault over both queue and turnstile in defiance of the European public lavatory system.
And after you have negotiated a move that would qualify you for an Olympic track and field event, you get inside to find you have to pay another 80 euro for toilet paper …

So, forgive me if I replied to my urologist's diagnosis with an icy cold stare that communicated a terse "How dare you!"
She obviously has no idea who I am.

I won a Friday night Nutbush competition at North Sydney
Leagues' Club in 1985.
The only thing uncoordinated about me on that dance floor were
my colour combinations,
And that, my friends, was an act of pure defiance against the 1970s
and the generation that gave us beige slacks and the brown safari
suit.

For the 1980s was my decade.
It started innocently in January with the release of the Rubik's cube,
And ended with David Hasselhoff singing in a flashing black leather
jacket in front of the Berlin Wall as it and the Eastern Bloc
collapsed.
In what other decade could that have been possible?
(Not so much the collapse of communism,
But *David Hasselhoff*?)

I walked back to the car that day from my appointment via
Nostalgia Avenue
My head a synthesised drum beat of memories of a time when the
bigger the hair,
The bigger my dreams …

Back then MS was a readathon.
It was Betty Cuthbert.
It wasn't me.

To learn that I had it was slightly surreal,
It was as if someone had attached me to a defibrillator
And with a sudden shock, jump-started me back into life in an
alternate universe.

I walked in as one person but came out as someone who was now
standing on an uncertain precipice
Surveying the new terrain of living with a body at war with itself,
The ultimate example of friendly fire.
My immune system hell bent on destroying itself
One bodily function at a time.
The Collateral Damage Estimation was uncertain and the variables
uncontrolled.

In the *Grand Designs* of diseases, Kevin McLeod would call this one
'bespoke'
As it came with a plethora of possible additions unique to my own
central nervous system
From slight tingling in the hands and feet and fatigue to
paraesthesia, neuropathy, blindness, asphyxiation, paralysis and
complete organ failure …

Perhaps my fuse box analogy was too benign.
I was negotiating with a terrorist who had strapped an undetonated
load of explosives to my chest.
There was no way of knowing how this thing would play out.

And so I began thrashing my way through the undergrowth of fear
Headfirst into webs of panic,
The winds of doubt wailing and moaning in my ears
like King Lear in his storm.
I felt the icy shards of despair threatening to smash my unprotected
head
And I wanted to cry out into the perilous night
*'Oh, fool I shall go mad …'**

And then the miracle happened.
A quiet, unobtrusive, velvet revolution in my soul.

I wrestled with the demon of fear
And was gifted a shawl of peace.
Gossamer-like it landed on my shoulders
And promised a way forward,
A minute-by-minute revelation of the grace that sustains us all.
All I have is this day,
This breath,
This vapour,
This mystery.

Once terrified at the ephemeral nature of my existence,

I felt strangely liberated by the sudden realisation that this was
beyond my control.
I was at the mercy of something greater than a disease.
And in another one of life's glorious ironies, I found that although
the damage in my nervous system was disrupting the
communication between my brain and my body,
It could never destroy the communication between my soul and its
creator.
Nothing could separate me from His love.
The myelin sheath had broken down along my spinal cord
But the cord of Father, Son and Holy Spirit was not so easily broken.

And so I sat with my memories, my fears and my dreams
And I used what free will I had to give them away.
I wanted to be nothing—
Not the nothing of emptiness and futility

But the nothing that leaves space to be refilled with lasting treasure
That moths and rust, thieves and disease cannot destroy or steal.

I accepted that this cup may not pass from me.
I accepted because I knew I had someone who could show me how
to drink it.
I sat in my nothing with the one who had gone before me in
everything,
Calvary the fulcrum upon which all our stories turn,
Where all our sicknesses and all our diseases are actualised and
redeemed.

For Jesus knows what it is like to have MS.
His broken body has experienced every configuration of this
disease,
Of exhaustion caused by carrying a cross far too big for one man to
bear,
And He has stumbled, crushed under the weight of the wood
So that His bones were shattered and broken on impact every time
He fell.
He knows the paraesthesia and paralysis this will cause,
Of nerves raw and exposed from skin flayed so that He would feel
sensations akin to electrocution,
Of heart, renal and pulmonary failure,
Of suffocation and choking,
Of every part of His mortal body disfigured beyond human likeness.
His death, bespoke,
For me.
For you.

For a world hell-bent on destroying itself.
And for that He endured a nightmare.
He knew how it must play out.
He went onto that cross as a tortured human being
And came out the other side of death having transformed broken
life into a glorious Eternity.

Was there ever a greater empathy with my condition?
With our condition?

And as the cycle of our history goes around and around
And the mistakes of the past seem to be replicating themselves in
the present
I must graft myself onto the vine,
My body coordinated and organised in Christ,
Joined and held together,
Every supporting ligament
Building itself up in love.

And so here I stand in another act of pure defiance,
Not to dissemble or rebel
But with a willingness to contend for Christ
As He contends for me;
Knowing that in Him, all things,
Even the tyranny sent to destroy me,
Can work together for
Good.

*A reference to Shakespeare's King Lear.

CURVE BALLS

My mother used to drop me off at school and then go home and
wait by the phone.
Usually before recess, she would have to come and pick me up
again.

Either I had tripped over a shoelace in the playground almost
knocking out my teeth
and giving me a black eye
or I had slid down a bannister flat onto my face.
On that occasion, Sr Mary Edwards was more worried about my
broken nose
than the multiple fractures in my arm.
'Just keep moving it up and down,' she said
as she practised her unique version of amateur physiotherapy on it
in sick bay.

And then there was the time I tried to perform stunts on my bike
down Mrs Greening's driveway and flew headfirst over the
handlebars onto my face.

I am not sure how long I lay concussed in the gravel before the ambulance arrived.

Or the time we went on a family outing to Skippy National Park and I was attacked by a kangaroo.
"What's up, Skip,
A crazy little kid tried to pull your tail?
And you socked her one in the face missing her right eye by a millimetre?
And now she has a 10 centimetre scar down her face?"
I was almost disembowelled, but remember my father beating the kangaroo off me with a black umbrella.

Thank the Lord it rained that day.

But I also remember punching the lady in the First Aid room for putting iodine on my face.
It stung.
And I was embarrassed.

They closed the interactive kangaroo enclosure shortly after …

So at an early age I got used to life throwing me curve balls.
Quite literally on occasions, as a short-sighted child I squinted bravely as the tennis ball came hurtling towards me to find my face as the racquet …

But what do you do when you are knocked out cold by the unexpected spin of life?

How do you learn to play a life that deviates from the straight path,
Hits you right between the eyes
And leaves you bleeding in the gravel as you hear the ambulance
whirring up the street?

If, in that moment, someone tells me that this is all part of God's
plan or that I am being tested
They will suffer the same fate as the poor First Aid nurse at Skippy
National Park who tried to put iodine on my cuts.
Because maybe it is and maybe it isn't …

For who am I to know the mind of God?
And why must I explain Him anyway,
Constraining Him within the confines of inadequate theologies?
If any of these circumstances are of my doing, then I repent in dust
and ashes.
But we can't distil the mystery of life into a
Cup of cold comfort
Or contort scripture into a
Bumper sticker aphorism.

The collateral damage will be our hearts
Bruised and
Confused about the character of God,
A God we say is Love.

No amount of theology can immunise you against the
Storm and
Stress and
Mess of our humanity.

For the long dark night of the soul is like
Going on a bear hunt …
You can't go over it, you can't go under it,
You just have to go through it.

And so these thoughts came to me the night I watched my mother
wrestle with her sanity
in a psychiatric ward,
Dementia creeping into her mind like poison ivy
Choking what years of depression and anxiety had left vulnerable
And I sat alongside her that night in the miry clay
And watched her writhing in the agony of her despair
Calling on the name of Jesus
And why, oh why God have you abandoned her?
I thought
Incline and hear our cry
Reach into this pit
Into this unweeded garden of our pain.

And then I saw Gethsemane
And my mother was in it with
Jesus in a state of mental anguish
Enough to draw the blood through His pores,
A terror unimaginable,
The brink of madness.

Let this cup pass …

And in that moment, I saw a fully human Jesus
Experience a fully human trauma

In the pit, alongside and with my mother,
But the cup was at His lips and not hers.
It was His to drink
In this agonising moment.

When you think things could not get any worse
You realise they could …

We could be in this alone,
Left to the fate of impersonal and capricious gods
Or the survival of the fittest
In a savage and random universe …

But we are not.

When you hit rock bottom there is nowhere else to dig.
You have to look up
To the rock that is higher
And you need to wait
To be lifted out of the pit
By hands that bear the scars of the human condition.

And in that moment of suffocating grief
you realise the only thing holding your head above the water
Are those hands of empathy,
Empathy with a face and a body,
A body bruised, torn, beaten and flayed
And in all of those marks is an eternal understanding of suffering,
A validation of it as a lived experience.

I can put my finger into the holes that testify to a place where deep,
deep despair was met with the promise of deep, deep hope.
A hope
That we will enter Zion with singing,
Everlasting joy will crown our heads,
Gladness and joy will overtake us
And sorrow and sighing will flee away.

The now, but not yet;
But the yet
Can keep my feet from stumbling
Over a precipice of despair
Because it declares over every shattered dream
and every broken street
Restoration.

THE HEART
OF THE MATTER

This week I had to teach Philippians 3 to Year 9,
not just the verses about pressing on towards the goal;
the full chapter—
including the bit about confidence in the flesh.

Now, this led to a very interesting discussion about male
circumcision in my co-ed class.

My mother-in-law, who gave birth to three boys in the 1960s, once
told me that she had no say in the matter.
On the eighth day, the boys were taken away and the delicate
procedure was performed …

But by the time it came for me to deliver my own son, my
obstetrician refused to have any confidence in the removal of any
male flesh.
And so, by the 21st century, such a procedure was now shrouded in
controversy.
I was not about to inquire as to how many male students in the class

had been subject to the procedure,
but there was much sniggering and the crossing of legs in an
exaggerated fashion by the adolescent gentile males in the class,
while my delicate Year 9 girls cast bewildered glances around the
room to each other and to me.

I realised a sensitive exegesis of the passage was required …
I took a deep breath and anticipated phone calls from parents—
after all, this was Christian Studies and not PDHPE.
Surely, I just had to teach them to memorise the Ten
Commandments, the books of the Bible and the Lord's Prayer …

And so I launched into my explanation.
It did involve a whiteboard marker and a diagram.
And the enunciating of certain words pertaining to the male
anatomy
And a glossary of medical terms
And cultural practices …

But in navigating my way through some difficult verses in a safe,
urban, middle-class classroom
I learnt something, as if for the first time.

The Bible really is gritty and edgy.

It contains awkward stories, unsettling incidents and visceral details.
And sometimes we cannot sanitise it in the way we can our hands
during Covid
or muffle its more dissonant and confronting voices behind a face
mask.

Because the Bible is not a safe book.

It tells the story of the first pandemic—
when a thought, like a virus, lodged itself in the human mind,
spoken by a counterfeit voice whose deceit
replicated itself into every cell of our mortality.
This thought was highly contagious, opportunistic, and structured
to mutate.
A thought designed to destroy us from within.
And to complicate matters, this thought was actually a lie—
a lie that told us that the possession of divine knowledge was our
right—
for if we were to possess it, it would mean that we too would have
power and control.
And could become as gods.

There was a profound wisdom in withholding from us the fruit of
any such tree.
It was not the action of a despot
but of a father, ancient of days, who knew:
It is dangerous to gain knowledge unethically and without love.

For when Truth is exchanged for a lie,
the fruit of it is poison.
And it will kill us, in waves, with each wave making us sicker and
sicker.
And it is this wave we read about in the pages of our scriptures,
and of all the fruitless endeavours to flatten its curve
through laws and sacrifices,

kings and dominions,
politics and war,
exploitation and injustice.
An endless, historical cycle resisting closure,
offering symptomatic relief for systemic disease.

And so, Year 9, I must do my best to explain to you
the graphic image of a circumcised heart;
a heart in which Eternity has already been placed,
despite our best attempts to rip it from us …
Because out of the overflow of this heart, our mouth speaks
and what you hear coming out of your mouth is really the story of
your heart.
Of what has been buried deep within it,
lowering your immunity
and attacking what Truth still resides there.

And so, we face the conundrum of our times when fiction is
masquerading as fact,
and our realities are playing out like a bad dream.
How must we live when we look and see all the oppression that is
taking place under the sun?
Perhaps we must now ask the same burning question that Pilate
asked.
What is Truth?
And we must be more prepared to accept the answer that he was
not.

And Year 9, while we live through such turbulent times,
I can only speak to you of the greatest protest in human history;
a protest against the most pernicious of lies spoken into us.

I can only speak to you of one led like a lamb to the slaughter,
innocent of any crime, unfairly treated, discriminated against and
subject to Roman brutality.

Of one who did not open His mouth as the accusations flew at Him
thick and fast,
full of bile and spit …

Of one stretched out on an instrument of torture designed to
asphyxiate Him …
Scripture fulfilled in the most anatomical of ways.

Of one whose heart melted like wax, as the pericardium, the sac
surrounding the heart, slowly filled with serum and began to crush
His chest with pain,
leaving Him to literally die of a broken heart.

For you, for me, for justice, for love.

And so, Year 9, I can only ask that before you speak
You put the blowtorch to your own heart, as I must do as well,
not to burn it in shame
but to cauterise it
to mitigate the bleeding
so it can heal …

But first there will be pain,
because every epoch will have its tyranny and its response.
And every epoch will ask us to walk the long road to Calvary with
Jesus.

To see in His witness the relevance and the remedy for our times.

To place ourselves in every stone of that road.

To examine who we would betray for 30 pieces of silver.

To think about whose ear we will hack off in our irrepressible rage.

To think of who and what we will deny for fear of reprisal or
ridicule.

To think of whose name we will shout out and use as a scapegoat.

I can only ask you, Year 9, to examine your heart as I must do
when I look at Christ crucified in the middle of three trees
with a man on His left and a man on His right.
But do not see Christ in the middle as symbolising neutrality,
indifference or impartiality
because there is nothing meek and mild about a cross—
I see it as the place where the past, present and future are one
element in time,
where histories, ideologies, philosophies and theologies intersect
and are reconciled,
where the relativity of Deception meets the Incarnate and Absolute
Truth and says
The Lie is Finished.

The pandemic is over.

And so, Year 9,
This Truth has a face.
And we must seek it above all else.
You are in His heart.
Pour yours out before Him like water.

Let Him cradle the brokenness of it in His gentle hands,
allowing what should not be there to slip through His fingers.

Let Him repair the damage inflicted upon it by a broken world.

And do not fear or resent what He must do to restore your heart
from within,
or underestimate how a recalibrated heart can be used by Him to
love humanity back into health with
God-breathed words overflowing from our lips:
a reservoir of hope.

LOCKDOWN

The first thing that I thought of when I was put into Covid
lockdown was my roots.
Not the familial, family heritage kind,
But the follicular variety.
I could only think about the appointment that I had scheduled with
my hairdresser that weekend …
Hamlet said that his times were "out of joint; O cursed spite"
And I have to empathise.

I should have got my hair done the week before lockdown was
decreed but thought I could stretch it out for another week.

It is one of the grave inequalities of life that when my husband visits
the barber for a trim it costs $15, but when I go for a trim $15 is just
the entrance fee before my stylist even picks up the scissors.
And when you have paid off one visit it is just about time to turn
around and do it all again …

But what happened to my hair in that extra week was nothing short of apocalyptic—it's as if it knew a crisis was coming and it now had me captive behind the barricades of my vanity.

My cancelled hair appointment coincided with the move to an online teaching platform.
Now my students would discover who I really was under Joico colour 7RC with the 8RG lift for better grey coverage over the hairline.

The pretence was over.

I was stripped back.

As one of my Year 7 students observed on the first day I went live online,
"Mrs Bradshaw, I thought you had red hair."
And then there was the indignity of hearing my voice echoing back at me on a Zoom platform …
I had become an episode of Kath and Kim with vowels strangled by my Australian accent
And accentuated by the poor microphone quality on my computer.
I even heard myself say
'Noice.'

Why does it always take a crisis to cut straight to the heart of our hidden lives?

Who would have thought that one of the gladiatorial quests of the 21st century would involve toilet rolls

And our arenas would be supermarket aisles
A wrestle to the death for the last pack of Quilton.
Hand sanitiser as precious as Incan gold
And we Conquistadors in search of it …

And so the retreat began
as fear chased us into our houses, into our caves.
And so I started making my Iso To Do List
for how better to wait out a pandemic than to turn time into
another enterprise—
Productivity, efficiency, economy.
Time not to be wasted but to achieve and to accomplish.
A time to sort
A time to cull
A time to clean the ceiling fans
A time to reorganise the cutlery drawer
A time to start a sourdough culture and make kombucha
A time to do online pilates …

But what does the worker gain from his toil?

I began to poke the bear of this question in a moment of
recalibration.

What if inactivity is the kind of activity God actually wants from us?

To just sit and be present
To receive the unseen ministrations of the Holy Spirit
To Be

To Be Still
To Know

A time to let my unquiet soul be rested
A time to walk through the Valley of the Shadow of our Times—
A time that is not so out of joint after all
Because we were born into it.

And so the real retreat begins
Into the miraculous space of the human soul captured by the spirit
of prayer—
A space to contemplate our world stripped back to its roots,
For us to ask,
Is this the greatest moment in our history?
To be woven into an intricate pattern of interdependence through
prayer,
A multi-generational, multicultural network with exhaustive
bandwidth and unlimited coverage,
A place of advocacy for the grieving, the despairing, the frightened,
the refugee, the incarcerated,
The lost.

And in this moment might we discover that our purpose is to be the
plumb line for the building and realignment of the whole world,
A reconfiguring of God's people.
For how is it that we have become more connected as the body of
Christ in isolation than when our doors were open?
A new song is being put into our mouths
And we must emerge from our isolation

Ready to sing it over a broken world reeling,
Confronted by the precarious nature of our systems,
The Babels we have built to fortify ourselves against the reality of
our mortality.

And I remember how Jesus wept for Lazarus.
Even His friend could not escape the invisible tyrant that is death.

And in His weeping, perhaps Jesus saw a vision of our empty streets
in 2020,
Of mass graves and not enough ventilators …
Of all the lives that death will stalk.

But in calling Lazarus out of the tomb
Jesus knew He must take His place in it
To endure an isolation, a separation unprecedented,
Agonising in its loneliness,
An act of complete solidarity with the human condition—
The elimination of death itself.

So may we in our caves of isolation hear the voice of one calling us
back to life,
Jesus the shepherd who lay across the gates of hell
So we would not pass through them.

Now is the time to usher in the King of Glory—
Our doors closed to others but never closed to Him.
Now is the time for us to live again in the most excellent way;
To put away the clanging gongs and cymbals
Because we live in love.

And even when my hair is grey
God will not forsake me,
But, Caleb-like, I will declare His power to the next generation,
His might to all who are to come.

We will move out of the caves of our isolation
To our mountain,
A resurrected people
For a resurrected church
On behalf of a resurrected Saviour.

BENTO MUSSOLINI
Benito Mussolini
lavorato e
bene della Patria e de
A noi!

LAMENTATION

Theodicy is the theological study of why there is pain and suffering in the world. There has been a lot written about the subject and most of it is unhelpful. We sometimes just need to lament. We need to sit with others while they lament. Sometimes it is what it is, and no words can adequately explain why it has happened or how we will ever recover from it. We must sit in the dust and ashes and be silent.

LAMENT
(For Talitha)

Since the dawn of time,
The beginning of Creation,
You, little girl, came into being.
The breath of the sovereign God blew life into your tiny cells
And deemed that you should live.

You were woven together in the depths of the earth and given Life,
Life—beyond what we could ask for and imagine—
But life just the same.

You grew not in accordance with
Human reasoning,

Scientific fact,
Biologically an abomination—

But divinely inspired.

Wrenched from that secret place,
They willed it that you should not live.

They despised the frame not hidden from the Lord of all Creation.
For His eyes saw what they did to you
And His ears heard your silent screaming in the darkness;
His heart knew of the anguish and confusion
Of a little soul invisible but perfectly formed—
Spirit poured out for man.

Heaven is mourning another sacrifice—
But not, this time, for righteousness.

What pain you felt I do not know
But I know you felt it
Because you lived
And all your days had been ordained before one of them came to be.

And however they disposed of your body,
Of this I am certain—
You are now being held in the palm of His hand
And He who gave you life will not forsake you
For all Eternity.

And what of these visionless men and their microscopes?
These men of science, these wise men, these scholars?

It would be better if they had thrown themselves into the fire
For they have harmed one of His little ones.

They have forgotten
That God has chosen the foolish things of the world to shame the wise,
The weak things to shame the strong,
The lowly things,
The despised things,
The things that are not—to nullify the things that are.

Let no man boast before Him.

Inspired by Psalm 139, 1 Corinthians 1:20–31, Matthew 18:7, Ephesians 3:20, Isaiah 49:16

JOB AT
GROUND ZERO

It's Tuesday night 8.30pm
A household ritual
Get kids into bed
Don't answer the phone
It is time to watch *The Bill*

It's the cliffhanging episode …
Detectives Don Beech and John Boulton engaged in a titanic
struggle on opposite sides of the law
The good cop getting nasty, the bad cop getting nastier
No justice is served tonight
As the wrong man pays for another man's crime
This is life in all its sordid detail
At a safe distance
We suspend our disbelief
Until the credits roll
Then we slip comfortably back into our ordinary routine …

Wash dishes, pack away toys, iron a shirt for the morning
The end of another day

September 11, 2001.

News flash teletext rolls across the screen
I am momentarily annoyed that reality should impinge upon my
evening off
But then we cross live to CNN
And watch in surreal disbelief
A grotesque inversion of reality television
The stuff of a B-grade Hollywood disaster film
Life now imitating art
Only in this version George Clooney doesn't make it there in time

And there are no credits rolling now
In the comfort of my living room
I am watching the 21st century unlock a whole new chamber of
horrors
And there is no safe distance from this …
No safe distance from a fallen imagination
Plundering unexplored territories of evil

Hear this, you elders
And give ear, all you inhabitants of the land!
Has anything like this happened in your days
Or even in the days of your father?

I know that it has
I know that every generation has its story

Of life lived in the grip of darkness …
Of mankind refusing to live under the shadow of God's wings

But to my generation?

To whom shall I speak and give warning that they might hear?

For in that morning's aftermath
I could not take enough air into my lungs—
Reverencing life in the simplest of tasks—
Folding my children's socks
Hanging tea towels on the Hills Hoist
Doing five loads of washing in the laundry of sleepy, suburban
Sydney
Seemed to me a privilege
Thinking of women in Afghanistan who would willingly take my
place
Trying to make sense of an incongruous world where children have
no home and no food
But Barbie can have a designer wardrobe.
Thinking of the innocent suffering for the injustice of others
The consequences echoing long after choices have been made

And now I understand why
Jesus wept
For all that has been
And all that is
And all that will come
Arms outstretched
He broke our Fall

Epiphany and the Shopping Trolley

By nailing it to his hands and to his feet
A grand reconciliation taking place in one agonising embrace

One man engaged in a titanic struggle between good and evil
The right man, the worthy one, dying for everything that is chipped
and cracked and wrong and twisted and warped in a world that has
broken faith with its Creator.

One man to release a greater power than any evil unleashed
One man to offer us a way forward, a way out, a way beyond
One man to repay us for the years the locusts had eaten
One man to give us immeasurably more
One man to empower us in the wake of all that we have seen
To help us contemplate the smaller sites of compassion
The smaller tasks of reconstruction in our own private universe
One man to walk into the carnage of Ground Zero and draw all
peoples unto himself
One mediator between God and man

So *to whom shall I speak and give warning that they might hear?*

Do not rejoice over me, my enemy
When I fall, I will arise
When I sit in darkness,
The Lord will be a light to me

For today, *Love has been perfected among us*
An inseparable love …
If only humanity could suspend its disbelief …

Scriptures taken from Job, Jeremiah, Joel, Micah, John 11, Romans 8, Ephesians 3.

THE ARRIVAL

My father grew up under the shadow of a Big Chin.
It was 1934 and Mussolini was doing his best to make the trains run
on time in Italy …
while over in Germany, Hitler was giving civilisation the Autobahn,
the Volkswagen, and the Holocaust.

Together, the countries that gave the world the music of Puccini,
Verdi, Bach and Beethoven were about to make the 20th century
goose step to the frightening rhythms of Fascism.

And my paternal grandmother, the long suffering and gentle
Angelina, was called upon to play her part in reviving the glory days
of the Roman Empire.

Marshalled single-file into the town square in Molfetta Vecchio, she,
along with all good Molfettese wives, was asked to part with the only
thing of real value she had ever owned.

Her gold wedding ring was thrown into a big melting pot:
a cauldron melting precious metal into capital for bombs.

As a personal thank you from Il Duce, each loyal Italian wife was
issued with a substitute ring
made of tin.

But my grandfather, Francesco, a wiry, strong fisherman, did not
like the idea of my grandmother being married to Mussolini.
And being a fisherman, he could read the weather
And did not like the tide that was turning.

He decided to slip the net.

Leaving the pregnant Angelina in Italy
He jumped ship
And anchored himself in Port Pirie, South Australia—
a place far beyond the reach of the long arm of the Black Shirts
a place that seemed as far away to my grandmother as a
constellation of stars.

It would be three years before he saw his wife again
And three years before the father would meet his son.

Francesco …
Skin seasoned with the salt of the Mediterranean Sea
he had a heart rusted by too much exposure to life.
His face was severe and foreign to my three-year-old father.
On first meeting the man they called papa,
the bewildered child started to cry.

And on that first day on Australian soil,
after a three-year separation from his family,

my grandfather imparted to his son a piece of fatherly advice:
No son of mine cries.
Giving his son a swift backhander,
He picked him up and kicked him like a soccer ball into the
concreted backyard.

My grandfather would not have understood irony.
But his granddaughter does.
Leaving a violent and oppressive regime on the brink of a war to
protect his young family,
My grandfather had transported within him a totalitarianism of the
heart.
And this made my father a casualty of war.
One of many
in a world torn and fractured by the sins of the fathers visited upon
their sons—
And their daughters.

The legacy of Adam—the first migrant, the first displaced person,
The first to have his paradise lost.

So in this Eden, the site of humanity's first ground zero,
Seeds were sown for more corporate destructions—
Cultivated first in the potting shed of the human heart and
the shaded interiors of individual thought.
And later reaped on the battlefields of France, the gas chambers of
Auschwitz, the blast of Hiroshima, the Killing Fields of Cambodia,
Yet harvested also in a suburban backyard when a frightened child
went flying across the concrete like a football …

We all feel the aftershocks of a single decision
We are all tethered to the moment when mankind tried to
supersede God;
And no United Nations Peacekeeping Force or NATO Summit can
ever make recompense
for this …

It needed the arrival of another Son

And this Son on a cross would nail past, present and future to His
hands
in an incredible exchange.

His life would turn our tin into gold.
His death would wage the greatest ever war against terror.
His resurrection would be the only way to bring the migrant soul
safely home …

I pray that my father will arrive safely home
Only this time he will recognise the Father without fear
Because he has seen His face already in the Son.

And I pray that this time his bewilderment will be met with
understanding
And his tears wiped away with the touch of tender mercies
And the memories of everything sordid and painful, destructive and
disappointing will be healed in the twinkling of an eye.

And after this arrival,
This life will seem

As far away

As distant

As remote

As the constellation my grandmother thought was Australia.

P. ZUFFEREY.

ROI

For refugee children everywhere

I know of a little boy.
He was six years old before he saw a tree.
Born in Syria,
surrounded by rubble and war,
his landscape was grey.
Concrete and wire.

Who'd have thought a tree to be such a luxury
in a world that began in a garden…

His parents took us at our word.
With promises of boundless plains to share,
they made their escape.

For who could begrudge a child a tree
when we have so many?

And there in the Blue Mountains
the wizened, brown eyes of innocence interrupted

beheld the spectacle of scattering.
Of electromagnetics and volatile terpenoids
creating the illusion of blue.
Everything tinged with blue.
Mountains, clouds, trees.
So many trees
stretching far into the distance
filling the void between Damascus and Echo Point.

The boy.
Scorched by fire.
Is a Eucalypt.

An imperishable seed,
hidden in his heart
starts to germinate.
Regeneration has begun.

A tree to bring healing to the nations.
Who'd have thought?

EPIPHANY

epiphany
/ɪˈpɪfəni/

noun
1. *The manifestation of Christ to the Gentiles as represented by the Magi (Matthew 2:1-12)*

2. *a moment of sudden and great revelation or realisation.*

EPIPHANY AND
THE HILLS HOIST

Ecclesiastes tells us that He has placed Eternity in our hearts
But as I venture into my laundry for the fifth time today, I realise
that it has been placed in the laundry basket as well.

Washing … a self-sustaining ecosystem all of its own.

David Attenborough could do a documentary on it.
In fact, as I sort through the whites, delicates and coloureds, I can
almost hear his voiceover …

The Bradshaw washing pile is a fascinating study in an organic lifeform that has managed to adapt itself to many hostile environments and yet still reproduce itself day in, day out.

For example, the humble Bonds boxer shorts and underpants have adapted beautifully and are quite prolific … for every pair put into the machine, five miraculously appear when the lid is opened.

The same cannot be said for the sock.

Of all the species here, the sock has been less able to adapt itself to the environmental pressure of the Fisher & Paykel.

Somewhere in this delicate cycle of survival it has not transitioned well from foot to the clothesline.

Casualties are high.

Like Noah, the human being may have sent them into this technological ark two by two, but quite often only one makes it through the spin cycle.

Scientists are yet to fully explain the reason for their disappearance.

Some phenomenologists claim there is a sock equivalent of the Bermuda Triangle inside every washing machine, while

Pentecostal theologians claim that there is an Elijah in every pair of socks And only one has the anointing to be raptured during the final rinse.

And then of course there have been the natural disasters …

The white tissue left in the pocket of the blue PE shorts has a devastating impact on the species known as the dark load.

And then there have been unsuccessful attempts at biodiversity …

The hand wash-only linen shirt faced extinction when it was accidentally crossbred in the regular wash with the green tea towels.

Both of these catastrophes have resulted in increased global warming within the Bradshaw household.

I realise that hearing David Attenborough in my laundry means I
should get out more.

So I carry my overloaded basket to the clothesline,
And to amuse myself I look over the fence at my neighbours'
immaculate clothesline,
Everything symmetrical and hung out with colour-coordinated
pegs,
A designated line for each item—
A class system, in fact.

For example, all items of intimate apparel such as the bras,
underpants and socks are hung on the far side of the line away from
the tea towels
And the bathmats never rub shoulders with the pillowcases.

It is at this moment that hanging out the washing becomes a
political statement.
There will be no such segregation in my backyard.
My Hills Hoist is the United Nations of the suburbs,
My washing basket is the great melting pot of humanity.
Here there is no slave, no freeman, no young, no old;
Here the humble pair of gardening shorts can be placed side-by-side
with the lofty business shirt who in turn flaps his egalitarian arms
against the washable ENJO cleaning gloves.

If only the world could coexist so harmoniously.

But before I get too excited about my symbol of world peace,
I am suddenly overcome with the futility of it all,

Because by morning, I will have to take them all off the line, sort them into piles and put them away in their separate places only to start the whole process again like some very bad progressive barn dance.

There is a time to wash and a time to rinse, a time to hang out and a time to bring in, a time to sort and a time to fold …
All is vanity.

I blame Adam and Eve.
This really is all their fault.
Their disobedience has had far-reaching consequences.
Before the Fall, nakedness was *haute couture* in the Garden of Eden
And nudity is a fashion statement in itself.
But sin brought about the fig leaf
And then climate change saw the introduction of the fur skin
And then in no time we had the front loader, Fabulon, Napisan grease reducing enzymes.

The Fall of Man is responsible for the Rise of the Laundry Basket!

And yet, through the gap in the sheets I see that everything is
filtered through the purple hue of the jacaranda trees,
December's warm evening air is scented with jasmine,
And the trees are lit by a daylight saving twilight.
My backyard looks like a box of Derwent pencils.
There are so many contrasting and varied shades of green—
Juniper, Bottle, Emerald, May, Olive and Moss.

And the hydrangeas …
Like elegant and immaculately groomed elderly ladies sipping tea,
They're clothed in Imperial Purple, Delft Blue and Violet Lake.

And then making a statement along the back fence
Is the Deep Vermillion of the Canna Lily.
Exotic and tall, she tilts her head in the direction of the Terracotta
sunset
And in her I see an image of a world beyond my own …
Of a landscape more sunburnt than this one …
Of a Maasai tribesman silhouetted against the heat and haze of an
African horizon.

I am filled with wonder at the
Derwent pencil God
Who has sketched my backyard
With the colours of His love,
The artist who has put all of Himself into His art.

How could anything seem futile in this place?
How could anything feel futile when He is at the centre of it?
An ordinary everyday task has become extraordinary in the light of
His presence.

And I begin to sense what it must have been like
To walk with Him as a friend
In the cool of the evening
In a bond of love.
In that first garden,
The first man and woman

Walked in the rhythm of conversation,
In the intimacy of relationship
With the Alpha and Omega
And I begin to see the enormity of what was lost when they broke
faith with their Creator.

I stand in the twilight with my empty washing basket,
Conscious that I am not alone here.
His presence fills every corner of my garden,
His Spirit is alive in me,
And as I stand here like a rainwater tank collecting the peace that it
brings,
A peace that tells my embattled soul to put down her weapons of
war
And rejoice,
Things have been changed forever.
Peace is possible.

Because in a stable
On a night less inviting than this one,
God made an entry point into our lives
And opened a door that could never be closed.
He paved the way for the reconstruction of that first garden,
Creating a new place for walking and talking,
A new relationship of faith, hope and love,
A place of victory not only over death
But over the weariness of a life we chose to live without Him.
The Word entering this world as tiny flesh,
All flailing arms, gulping to breathe the same air as us,
Fully human, fully divine

So that He could take us forward
To a place where we will one day eat from the Tree of Life in the
Paradise of God.

Tonight I have tasted a little of this fruit
And it is miraculous and it is wonderful.

God so loved
Not to get but to give.
Himself.

Christmas is in the air
But it is always in the air.
He has come to us and can never leave us.
He wants to walk with us in the cool of our evenings, in the despair
of our loneliness, in the joy of our success, in the solitude of our
thoughts, in the spaces of our emptiness, in the monotony of our
laundries.

He was flesh.

He knows.
He came so that we might find Him.
And tonight He says
The search is over.
Emmanuel

God with us
Is here.

O come let us adore Him.

About the Author and Illustrator

Catherine Bradshaw is responsible for the words and Pauline Zufferey is responsible for the images. In the photo, Catherine is the one with red hair and Italian nose while Pauline is the raven haired Cedar of Lebanon! Both are ENFPs if you know anything about Myers-Briggs Indicators. If you met them, it would all make perfect sense. Both are school teachers, despite their best efforts not to be. It is a calling that shouts very loudly at them every time they try to walk away from it. This book contains their combined wisdom of over 100 years of life experience, sixty years in education and over fifty years of parenting. For them, the mundane is miraculous because they are so very grateful to be here.

Catherine Bradshaw holds a BA Dip Ed in English and History and an MA (English Literature) from The University of Sydney. She has a Certificate IV in Christian Ministry & Theology from the C3 School of Ministry, Oxford Falls and a MA (Theology) from ACCS. She served as a Children's Pastor at C3 Ryde for fourteen years and has taught from preschool to tertiary level before becoming a School Chaplain. She is currently the Leader of Christian Development and chaplain at a school in Sydney's south west.

Pauline Zufferey has a Fine Arts Degree from COFA at The University of New South Wales majoring in Photography and Design. She has a BA in Art Education from COFA and a Grad Dip in Psychology from Monash University. Pauline also has a Masters of Psychotherapy and Counselling from Western Sydney University. She is an award winning artist having won the Nora Hyson Award twice as well as being a finalist in the Gosford Art Show. She is currently teaching art at a secondary school in Sydney's North West.

www.ingramcontent.com/pod-product-compliance
Lightning Source LLC
Chambersburg PA
CBHW060750210726
48292CB00014B/2693

found a yard to hide in. It was yours?" Keller looked up at him as he nodded.

"It is. Now, I have a friend on the force who I can call. Aidan will be glad to come here and take your statement." Kaelen didn't rise or reach for his phone. He was waiting on permission from Keller, which didn't seem to be coming.

Keller stared at him, wondering at his caring for a stranger. Her eyes moved past him and she screamed as the door was violently broken in and three men charged into the room. Kaelen didn't have a chance to respond, the shove from behind sending him to the floor where he was forced to lie still, a heavy foot on his lower back.

On her feet, Keller moved back until she could not move any further, her back to a wall. She stared in horror at the men, realizing that she was once more in her captors' hands. Her gaze fell to Kaelen, to find him watching her with a look that said he was ready to defend her. She frowned at him before looking at the leader of the men once more. A soft sigh rose from her. Keller was once more a captive. Only this time? Someone else was as well. This time, she was not on her own but that didn't bring any consolation to her. Her eyes lifted up as she prayed for protection and release from this captivity. God was there, she acknowledged, but for some reason, He was silent and allowing this. She had to accept that and wait for His leading.

Chapter 2

Kaelen was almost afraid to breathe, afraid that if he did anything, Keller would pay the price for it. He had been around the block enough times and seen his friends go through danger to recognize that this was one of those situations that could go bad and go bad quickly. All he could do was remain stretched out on the floor, his hands locked behind his neck, and his eyes on Keller. No, he thought, he could do more than that. He could pray. Kaelen did just that, finding peace in the situation and acknowledged that God was in control. He was there in the very centre of this and all he could do was trust.

Keller watched in fear as the man refused to let Kaelen rise from the floor. She watched the other two men from under her brows as they searched his home. Finally, one of them hauled Kaelen to his feet and reached into his pocket for his keys. That man disappeared and they heard the sound of his truck leaving. He was shoved into a chair, a gun pressed to his temple before it was pointed at Keller. Kaelen refused to move, not sure that if he did that Keller would be harmed. And he would not and could not allow that to happen.

An hour later, Kaelen was surprised to see two more men enter the house, one of them the man who had taken his keys. He watched the looks as they were exchanged.

Keller was hauled to her feet, protesting as that was done. Kaelen was dragged up as well and then shoved through the house towards the front door. He could hear Keller still protesting and all he wanted to do was to reach out for her and hold her and keep her safe. That was not him, he knew. Something about Keller caused Kaelen to want to protect her.

They were shoved into a large car with seatbelts snapped around them. He searched the area that now lay in darkness. He frowned as he saw the path that they were taking. Back towards the airport? He was not happy about that. Was he to be made to fly them out somewhere? He would resist that as much as he could.

His worst fear was realized as the car stopped near his helicopter. This could not be happening, he decided. There was no way that he would willingly fly out of that airport.

The two were pulled from the car and shoved towards the helicopter. Kaelen resisted, his shoulder shoved forward as he planted his feet and refused to move.

"Get in there, Cooper. You're flying us out of here and now." The man's rough and coarse voice sounded in his ear.

"Not a chance. I'm not flying you anywhere." Kaelen was adamant about that. That was, until the hair of the back of his head was grasped in a hard manner and he was pulled around to see Keller with a gun planted at her temple.

"You'll fly us out or she dies. It will be on you if that happens." The man was furious with Kaelen and his refusal.

Kaelen paled. He was not ready to do this. He looked up briefly, begging God to defuse this situation and release them. Kaelen drew in a deep breath. God was not letting him out of this. He had no choice but to continue. Kaelen finally nodded, watching as the gun was shoved harder into Keller's temple before it was removed. He could hear her faint whimper of fear and then saw the slight relief that crossed her face.

Walking towards his helicopter, he began to prepare to take off. He prayed that the mechanic on duty would stay away. He was certain that he would be harmed if he didn't.

Kaelen seated himself in the pilot's seat, the leader of the men seating himself beside him. He watched carefully as Keller was shoved into the centre seat behind him, one of the men on either side of her.

The helicopter lifted into the night sky. Kaelen set the course that he had been given, arguing with the man that he had to according to the rules. He had no choice. He was not going to lose his license just because the man didn't want him to do that.

Forced to fly away from Oak City, Kaelen kept an eye on the instruments and as well as he could on Keller. He could see the fear that she was trying hard to hide. All he could do was pray for her, not understanding why they were being forced to fly from his hometown. It was definitely not what he had planned for that night.

Keller wrapped her arms around herself. She shivered, not just from cold but from fear. She had not known that the man who had been so kind to her was a pilot. She didn't like that he was forced to fly them somewhere, just where that was she had no idea.

The man finally spoke, his angry voice directing Kaelen off of his course and to an area to his right. Kaelen stared at the man before he looked that way. He shook his head. It was not a large area and it would be difficult in the daylight to land. In the dark, it would almost impossible.

"You want me to land there?" Kaelen's voice was incredulous as he circled over the treetops, the light from his helicopter showing the landscape of the clearing. It would be a difficult and dangerous task to land there and equally dangerous and difficult to take off from.

"Land. You have enough space." The man spat the words at Kaelen.

Kaelen drew in a deep breath before he breathed a prayer for help. He carefully started his landing, not prepared for the blow that he took from the man sitting behind him. His vision darkened as he heard Keller's scream. He did not feel the hard jolt that happened as the helicopter crashed to the ground. The people inside were tossed around, their heads banging against whatever was near by. Keller was the only one not to lose consciousness. She had been protected by the men on either side of her but she was tossed around and hurt because of it.

Waiting for the men to rouse, Keller finally reached for her seatbelt and released herself. She shoved at the man beside her but could not rouse him. Instead, she then shoved at the door and crawled over the man to escape. She landed on her hands and knees, taking time to recover before she was on her feet and reaching for Kaelen's door. She shook him, finding him rousing somewhat.

Keller searched for anything that might help them to escape, finding a backpack with water and granola bars and containers of nuts. She smiled happily as she found a flashlight. Throwing it over her shoulders, Keller once more reached for Kaelen, helping him to remove his seatbelt and then steadying him as he slid from his seat.

Kaelen reached a shaking hand out to brace himself against the open door before his arm was around Keller's shoulders and her arm was around his waist. He simply nodded at her question if he was able to walk. She searched the area and then started a slow walk in the direction that they had come from, trying as best that she could remember.

Kaelen stumbled, his mind not functioning. All he knew was that he was walking in the dark, illuminated by the flashlight that bobbled in Keller's hand. He finally had to stop, dropping to the ground, his arm sliding from Keller's shoulders. Keller landed on the ground beside him, the flashlight dropping from her hand and rolling a few feet away.

Keller was dismayed. There was no way that she could get Kaelen on his feet again. How were they to do it? She thought back on the camping trips that she had been forced to take and then do all the work. She searched through the backpack, finding the emergency blankets that Kaelen had tucked in there. One was quickly shaken out and wrapped around him.

———

Keller looked around, not afraid at the moment, but unsettled at being out in the open as they were. She reached for the flashlight and gathered what wood she could find. She scarped the grass away near Kaelen until she had a large spot just down to dirt. Carefully piling the wood, Keller started a small fire, knowing that she would need to stay awake all night to monitor it and add more wood. Her hand went to Kaelen's head, raising it slightly. He stared at her through blurry eyes before he slumped to his side. Keller was dismayed. This made it even worse for her. She positioned the blanket better around him before she made him drink from a water bottle. This was all that she could do. Reaching for the second blanket, Keller wrapped it around herself before she positioned herself against Kaelen, praying that someone would find them.

Chapter 3

On the Tuesday of the next week, Caleb Cullen drew up to Kaelen's home and jumped from the truck. He opened the garage door and reached for the lawn mower. He had been more than willing to help Kaelen out when he was away on vacation. Mowing the lawn was something simple that he could do for his friend. He whistled as he worked away, enjoying being out in God's nature.

Moving around the house, Caleb worked away, not seeing the back door. Putting away the mower, he reached for the grass trimmer, working away. Reaching the back deck, he paused and reached for his bottle of water. Uncapping it and sipping, Caleb looked around. He frowned. Something was off. He approached the back door, pausing as he saw the damage it had obtained the previous week. He stepped back abruptly and reached for his phone.

"Aidan? Where are you?" Caleb had reached out to a friend who was a police investigator.

"Just heading home. What's up?" Aidan knew that Caleb would not have that tone in his voice unless something was wrong. Caleb was part of a security team that worked out of Oak City and had been through a dangerous adventure of his own as had Aidan.

"I'm at Kaelen's. I had promised to do his yard work while he was away. The thing of it is? His back door is smashed in. He would not have left it that way." Caleb spun in a circle, trying to find out anything that he could.

"I'm on my way. I'll send some officers and a crime scene team." Aidan drew in a deep breath. He had had a conversation on Sunday when Don's team, Aidan, and their spouses had met for lunch. They had questioned who they would who would be the next victim. They had not thought that Kaelen would be him.

Aidan parked on the street, his eyes studying Kaelen's home. From the front, it didn't look as if anything was wrong. However, he knew that Caleb would not have made that call if everything had been as it should be. He left his car to walk towards where Caleb was waiting, leaning against his truck.

Caleb shot Aidan an unreadable look. He sighed. This was not how his Tuesday was to be. He had his Bible study and prayer that evening. Only he would never make it. Caleb had reached out to his wife, Cullea, to let her know what was going on. She had been dismayed, he could tell, but promised to reach out to the rest of the team. Kaelen was a good friend to them all.

"Caleb? What can you tell me?" Aidan leaned back against the truck, just waiting for his friend to speak.

"Not a lot. I had mowed the lawn and was working on the trimming. The back deck was the last part. I had just finished, taken a drink of water, and then saw the back door. It's broken it, smashed in would be how I would word it. I didn't go in. I left that for you guys. But Kaelen's truck isn't here."

Aidan nodded, his mind going through various scenarios.

"He has a security feed?" Just maybe, Aidan thought, that would show something.

"He does but he said on Thursday night when we talked that it was acting up. He wanted us to go over it when he got back. Where is he?" Caleb was distraught at the thought of another friend facing danger even though he was a firm believer that God was in control and would protect Kaelen.

"I see. You don't happen to have a code for it do you?" Aidan was grasping at straws.

"I do. I'll let you have it." Caleb scrawled out his code in Aidan's note book before Aidan walked away. Two patrol officers had approached the house and followed Aidan inside. The female officer was back in short order, beckoning Caleb to follow her.

Caleb stepped into the house, not sure what he would find. Aidan beckoned him through to the kitchen. Caleb could see that the crime scene team was already at work.

"Caleb? Do you see anything out of order? I don't but you might." Aidan waited for Caleb to search the room from where he stood.

"Just the water bottle on the table. And the glass with water in it. And the chairs are not pushed in to the table. Kaelen would not leave this without tidying it away." Caleb didn't see anything else out of order, except the broken door. "Where is he?"

"I have no idea." A thought crossed his mind and he reached for his phone. A quick conversation with the airport and he was tucking away his phone. Kaelen's truck was not there although an unknown car was. And Kaelen's helicopter had taken off in the evening. He had filed a flight plan but he was overdue on that. "He missed arriving at his destination Friday night. That's not him."

Caleb paled. Something had to have happened to Kaelen. He was too careful and cautious with his flight plans and if he had had difficulty of any sort, he would have radioed for help. Pacing back outside, Caleb reached for his phone. He turned it over and over in his hands, not sure who he should be calling but he felt that he had to call someone. Don won. He dialed the head of the security team that he worked for.

Don pulled at his phone at the incessant vibrating and then rose from where he was seated in a room at the church. He didn't see his team watching him before they shared a look and then their attention went back to their pastor.

Don paced outside, his phone to his ear.

"Caleb? You're calling. Where are you? Cullea is here but just said that you were delayed at Kaelen's."

"I am. Kaelen's disappeared. We think that it was likely Friday night but we're not sure. Aidan is here along with a team." Caleb was frustrated but took his frustrations to his Lord.

"Kaelen's missing? Wasn't he supposed to head off on vacation Friday night?" Don paced, his hand reaching for his wife who had appeared beside him.

—

"He was. Aidan has looked into that enough to find out that Kaelen took off in his helicopter, filed a flight plan, and then didn't arrive. I would suspect that a search is underway now." Caleb turned to watch Aidan and his team scouring the yard and house.

Delanie's hand tightened on Don's. Something was amiss, she decided, and did what all she could do. She prayed for whoever was in that situation.

Don reached to wrap Delanie in a hug. He prayed for Kaelen, a friend who had become close to his team over the past months. He worried about him. The thought of him being in a crash disturbed him greatly. Don looked towards the church and saw his team and their ladies heading his way. Caleb's wife, Cullea, was with them.

"Don?" Paul spoke for the group.

"It's Kaelen. His home has been broken into. He's missing. Caleb said that Aidan thinks it was Friday night. And his helicopter is overdue."

"I didn't think that he was flying." Joshua spoke for the group. "He told me that he was planning on driving somewhere. Is his truck there?" His phone was out as he sent a quick text to Caleb. "Caleb says it's not. Where is he?"

Chapter 4

Aidan watched somewhat impatiently as the security personnel at the airport searched through the security feeds from the Friday before. He leaned closer to watch.

"There's Kaelen leaving. He doesn't seem to be worried about anything." Aidan sighed. "And then can we move forward in the tape?" Aidan continued to watch, seeing no activity other than the guards until it was dark. The headlights of a car approached the airport and then parked in the visitors' parking lot. "Do you know that car?"

"No, I don't. It's never been here before that I know of. I can check for you once we've run this." Adam looked up at Aidan. He had been shocked when Aidan had asked to see the security feeds, not believing that Kaelen would have come back like that.

"That would be good. Now, where are they heading?" Aidan continued to watch, frowning. "They're heading for Kaelen's helicopter. Wait. There's a female with them. And one of them is Kaelen."

"You're right. Kaelen's not acting like himself. He's tense. You can see from his body posture that he's worried about something."

"He is, that is for sure."

The men watched as Kaelen and the group headed for his helicopter. They also watched as he did his pre-flight check and then took off. The whole group had been in the aircraft.

"That doesn't tell us much, does it?" Aidan looked around. "We'll need a copy of that and one from when Kaelen left this morning. If you could search for that vehicle, it would help."

Aidan was on his feet, his business card left on the desk for the man to access his email. He was puzzled. Kaelen certainly had not left on his own. That much was obvious. But who was the female with him? Kaelen was not dating. He was like his friends. None of them dated until they met their now wives and were in danger.

Walking around the airport, Aidan was alert for anything but nothing appeared in his line of sight that would explain anything. Returning to his car, he was not surprised to find Don waiting for him.

"Don?" Aidan stopped beside his friend.

"Where is he, Aidan? Did he really take off?" Don was puzzled at that.

"He did, and he wasn't alone. There were three men with him. There was also a lady." Aidan waited for Don to react.

Don nodded as he listened to Aidan. Then, his head shot around and he stared at Aidan.

"What did you just say?" Don waited for Aidan to reply. "Did you say a lady?"

"I said a lady. Kaelen isn't dating. So who is she?"

"I wonder? Is Kaelen off on one of those adventures?" Don gave a quick grin that Aidan responded to.

"I would suspect so. The team was not hopeful about finding any evidence."

"How bad was it?" Don was afraid to even ask.

"The door was shattered. I have someone coming in to block it for the night but by now it's been open since Friday at least. There wasn't much evidence. Whoever did this was very careful." Aidan pushed away from the truck. "Head off, Don. I'm off to the office." Aidan watched Don drive away before his eyes raised to the sky. "Lord, You are in control. You know where he is. Keep him safe. And the lady? If she's a victim as well, keep her safe."

Aidan shoved away from his computer at last. He yawned and stretched, his eyes closing against the comfort of his work office. He glanced at his watch and sighed. It was early morning and he had to be back there by seven. He turned to the cupboard in his office and pulled out a blanket and pillow. Aidan would simply sleep on the couch in his office that night. He was too tired to make the drive home. He sent a quick message off to his wife and then slept.

Don paced his kitchen early that morning. He was very worried about Kaelen and whoever the lady was. He hadn't heard of anyone else being missing but that wasn't unusual. He looked around, left a note for Delanie, and then headed for a favourite diner in the downtown area.

———

Ben looked up as Don entered, surprise on his face. He grabbed for mugs and filled them with coffee before he headed for the booth Don had found.

"Don?" You're puzzled and troubled. What can I do to help?" Ben slid onto the seat across from him.

"Don? Have you heard anything about Kaelen?" Don was puzzled by his friend's disappearance.

"Kaelen? No, I haven't. Should I have?" Ben watched Don closely. He knew all of the team well, particularly Paul who he had taken under his wing when he found him on the streets.

"He's disappeared. We think it was sometime on Friday. We have no idea where he's gone." Don was troubled by this.

"He has? That's not good." Ben frowned. "I haven't heard anything but I will certainly keep in touch with the street. I'll get word to you or Aidan. He's the investigator?"

"He is." Don was on his feet, walking away and leaving Ben staring after him.

Aidan frowned at his computer. He wasn't finding out anything at all. There was nothing about Aidan being found in another jurisdiction. Where was he? That was the question that he could not answer. He was on his feet and heading for Toryn Knight, their police chief.

"Toryn? Got a moment?" Aidan hesitated in his chief's doorway.

"Aidan? Sure. Come on in." Toryn watched as Aidan entered. He frowned. Something was bothering his detective. "What's going on?"

"It's Kaelen. He disappeared. As far as we can tell, it was on Friday night. His helicopter disappeared at the same time. I tracked him to the airport. The thing of it is that there were three other men and a female with him."

"There were? That is unusual. Have you photos?"

"No, just the security stream. And it isn't close enough to make out any features. I recognized Aidan as did the security guard." Aidan stared at Toryn, not sure where to go from there.

Chapter 5

Aidan was frustrated, to say the least. He had no idea where Kaelen was and no one else did either. The security feed didn't help as the features of the men were not clear enough to determine them. They had a vague idea of their height and weight but that didn't help much. It was also hard to describe the female on the tape. Aidan had played the clip many times but had not clear idea of what she looked like. And he had no idea of any female being missing from town.

Turning as he heard Lyle heading his way, Aidan frowned at his supervisor. He reached for the photo that Lyle kept thrusting at him.

"What's this?" Aidan frowned at the photo of a beautiful lady, about his age he decided.

"This lady? Keller Monaghan? She's been missing since about Tuesday or Wednesday of last week. She works as a studio singer and didn't show for what she had been booked for. That has sent her employer looking for her." Lyle tapped at the photo. "Her address is on the back of the photo as is her phone number."

Aidan nodded as he studied her before he frowned once more.

"She looks somewhat like the female who was on the security feed." Aidan turned abruptly back to his office to where the feed was still up on his screen. Lyle followed him, a hand resting on the back of the desk chair, squinting at the screen.

"I think you're correct, Aidan. It certainly appears to be her." Lyle stood up and walked away before he stopped in the doorway.

"Head over and talk to the people at the studios. Keep me updated on what you find." Lyle walked away, leaving Aidan staring after him.

Aidan walked away from the studio, more disturbed than before he walked into it. The studio head had not been able to provide much information. He stated that Keller kept to herself but was reliable in being there when she was scheduled. Aidan had spoken with the other staff who had shaken their heads and stated that Keller kept to herself but was pleasant and friendly.

He was no further ahead and that frustrated him. Kaelen was due to return tomorrow from his vacation, but it certainly didn't seem as if he would be. Aidan stood for a moment, staring around the parking lot. There were not answers there. And that was not what he had wanted. He turned for his car, intent of heading somewhere. He just didn't know where he was heading.

Toryn walked through the detachment that afternoon, just speaking with the officers who were there. He stopped at Aidan's door and then entered to sit in front of his desk.

Aidan looked up at last, blinking in surprise as he saw Toryn watching him. Toryn grinned at him before he spoke.

"What have you discovered?"

"Not what I want. I found out who the lady is, I think, that was with Kaelen. Her name is Keller Monaghan and she works for the music studio here in town." Aidan sat back. He had been by her home with no answer and no sign of a vehicle in her driveway.

"You have?" Toryn leaned forward. "What do you know about her?"

"Not a lot. I'm going back to redo interviews and then I'll go back to her home, just in the hope that she has returned home." Aidan stared down at his desk top and the folders cluttering it. He did not work in clutter and that clutter on his desk disturbed him.

"Take whoever you need." Toryn was on his feet, heading for a meeting that he really didn't want to be at. He was deeply concerned about Kaelen, who was a close friend to him as well.

Aidan rose at last, heading for his car. He drove aimlessly through town before he headed for Kaelen. He was praying that Kaelen would be there but he really didn't expect him to be. He walked the perimeter of the yard, not finding anything out of the ordinary. Aidan felt uneasy. Standing near the back of the yard, he studied the plantings. Lost in thought, he didn't hear the footsteps approaching him. A sound caught his ear and he started to turn. He didn't make it in time. A hard fist connected with his jaw and sent him to the ground. The man looked around, not sure if he had been seen before he wrapped arms around Aidan's limp body and then dumped him behind the plantings, almost in the same spot where Kaelen found Keller. He dusted off his hands and then jumped the fence into the neighbouring yard and disappeared.

———

Night passed and it was early morning when Lyle realized that Aidan was not where he should be. He searched the detachment and didn't find him. Sending out officers to search, he stood beside his car before he was driving rapidly towards Kaelen's home. He parked and walked towards Aidan's car.

A call for help was quickly answered. Lyle and the responding officers began their search. A sudden yell cut through the early morning air and sent the officers running towards the back of the yard. The officer was helping Aidan to his feet.

Aidan was unsteady on his feet, hands helping to hold him upright. His hand felt at his jaw, finding the large knot and knowing that it was bruised. He was also cold, being out overnight.

Lyle's hand drew him away from the yard and to his car, shoving him inside. He drove away rapidly, heading for the hospital. He would question Aidan himself.

Aidan shifted on the stretcher, the ice pack cold on his face. He hadn't seen anyone, that he was adamant on. His eyes closed and he slept, feeling warmer despite the ice pack on his face.

Toryn paused outside of his doorway, a frown on his face. He found Lyle beside him.

"Where did you find him?"

"At Kaelen's. He was hidden behind the shrubs at the back of the his yard." Lyle rubbed a finger on his temple, watching the activity around him. "And

—

that makes me wonder if they had hidden someone there before."

Toryn shook his head. He had no idea what Lyle was thinking. He paused once more for a moment before he walked away. He had been in touch with their friend, Don, and his security team. The six men were out looking for Kaelen but not one of them had found any clue as to where he was. Finding that a young lady was missing as well disturbed Toryn. They needed to be found and found that day.

Chapter 6

On the Monday morning, Keller had roused. She felt disoriented and out of sorts. Sitting up, she brushed her hair away from her face, not realizing that she was leaning back on Kaelen. She studied the area, frowning. Keller had no idea where she was other than that she was out in the open somewhere and that she was cold and very sleepy. She rose to her feet, bending over to pick up the water bottles that lay on the ground in front of her She staggered slightly before she caught her balance.

Walking towards the sound of a stream, Keller stared at the fast-moving water and then at the bottles. She shrugged. Stooping, she filled them and then hesitated. Something was off, she looked around before she trudged back towards where she had awakened. Her feet dragged somewhat, tripping her on the debris that littered the path that she had followed. Keller paused, her head hanging down, fatigue weighing her body down. She heard the sounds of nature in her ears and prayed for help. She didn't know where she was or why she was there but something drastic had certainly happened to her.

Her footsteps slowing, Keller stared at the form lying in front of her. She felt fear for a moment before she pushed herself to walk forward. She nudged the body with her foot, eliciting a groan from the man. On her knees, her hands reached to roll him to his back. His arm flopped lifelessly across his chest before his head turned towards him. He did not rouse.

Keller sat back on her legs, frowning at the man. She had no idea who he was or why he was there with her. She felt safe with him even though he was unconscious.

Looking up once more, Keller prayed for her companion. She sighed. She just could not stay away. Crowding close to Kaelen, Keller drew the emergency blanket over them both and pillowed her head on a bent arm. She slept, not realizing that help was nearby.

Late that morning, footsteps sounded close to them before they stopped. The man stood, shock on his face, at seeing Keller and Kaelen sleeping near the trees. He frowned. This was not normally a place where anyone camped. He cautiously approached, a hand rubbing at the coarse grey beard that covered his lower face. He reached for his cap and tugged his off, showing the grey hair that was slightly longer than normal.

On his knees, his hand reached to assess the couple. His head dropped for a moment as he realized that they were both alive. He frowned as he stared at Keller, thinking that he knew her or that she reminded him of someone, someone who he had loved and lost so many years ago.

Back on his feet, the man stared around before he was almost running for his truck that was parked nearby. He doubted that he would be able to manage to carry Kaelen back to his truck. He parked as close to the couple as he could before he stood staring down at them. A memory was still niggling at his mind before he stooped to gather Keller into his arms and then to his truck. She was fastened in the centre seat of the old truck's bench seat before he turned. He quickly hauled Kaelen to his feet before he positioned him over his shoulder and once more headed for his truck. He stood for an instance to gain his breath after fastening Kaelen into his seat.

Turning, he quickly gathered the blankets and backpack. He stared at the site where Keller had started a fire before he shrugged and headed for his truck once more. The objects that he carried were tucked behind his seat before he headed for the road and then his home. It was a small but neatly kept home, just the right size for him. He hesitated for a moment before he once more had Kaelen over his shoulder and headed for the second bedroom. Kaelen was quickly deposited on the bed and the man heading for Keller.

Keller was taken to the man's own bedroom, where she was placed carefully on the bed and then covered. Fairley Monaghan stared down at the lady, seeing familiar features that tugged at his memories once more. He shook his head. There was no way that he knew her.

Roaming between the two rooms over the day, Fairley kept a close watch on the two. He knew that he needed to take them in the hospital. He just didn't want to. He kept to himself, with few friends and few acquaintances, preferring it that way. Life had been hard on him and he had no desire to be part of anyone's world again. He prayed for the couple before he had a sudden thought.

Heading for Kaelen, he pulled out Kaelen's wallet and carefully opened it. He didn't want to appear to be prying but he needed to know who was under his roof. He stared at the name before he shook his head. He didn't know the man. The wallet was carefully place on the night stand beside the bed.

Fairley hesitated at the second doorway. He looked up, once more praying for the lady who slept there. She had roused to some degree but never enough that he could question her. Somehow, he knew that once he had her name, things would change. He had that deep conviction. He looked up once more, seeking permission from his Heavenly Father to move forward.

Stepping into the room, the man stared down at Keller, once more thinking that there was something familiar about her. His hand hesitated as he reached for the pack that had been around her waist and that he had carefully removed. Fairley felt a nudge at his hand and rested that hand on the head of the old German Shepherd dog that had been his companion for so many years.

Opening the pack and reaching for the identification that he saw, Fairley once more hesitated and prayed. He just knew that this was going to change his life. All he could do was beg God to be present in the moment and he had no doubt that God was there.

Staring down at the identification, Fairley's hand shook. He almost dropped the license before he set it on the dresser. He stared at it for a moment before tears began to flow down his cheeks. His dog nudged at him once more before the dog's paw rested against his chest and he licked at the tears on his master's face.

Composing himself to some degree, Fairley turned to the bed, staring down at Keller. Dropping to his knees beside the bed, his hand reached out tentatively more than once before it was laid on Keller's head. She moved slightly, her face turning towards him without her awakening.

His sobs shook his body. He stared at the young lady, seeing this time the familiar features that mimicked his beloved wife. This was his daughter, Keller, who had been torn so brutally from him all those years ago. He had searched for years, almost losing hope that he would see her again. His wife had died unexpectedly when Keller was six months old. Fairley had struggled to support his daughter only to return home when Keller was a year old to find her gone. He had searched relentlessly, never finding her. Now, here she was, hurt and battered.

On his feet, Fairley stalked from the house, his emotions almost too much for him. He dropped to his knees in front of his favourite outdoor chair and buried his face in his arms. Sobs shook him before he quieted before his Heavenly Father. He just waited for peace, knowing that it would come no matter how long it took.

—

Chapter 7

Keller gradually roused, snuggling down under the blanket. She felt it, a frown on her face. This is not where she expected to be. It wasn't her own bedroom. Her body shot upright as she stared around, fear uppermost in her mind. Shoving back the blankets, Keller struggled to her feet and then ran from the room. She needed to find Kaelen. She just didn't know if he would be there or somewhere else.

Her running feet stopped as she found Kaelen. She was at his bedside and on her knees, a hand on his as she begged him to awaken. Her pleas seemed to be falling on deaf ears for the first bit before his body began to move. His hand slid from under hers before his strong clasp held hers. His eyes opened as he gradually focused on the room.

Kaelen could hear a lady's voice begging God to let him wake up. She needed him awake. His head turned slightly and he stared at her before his memory returned. He sighed to himself. He remembered the crash but not much after that.

"Keller?" Kaelen had to clear his throat. "Are you okay? And where are we?"

"I'm okay. But what about you? How are you?" Keller watched as he moved, knowing that he was hurting. "You crashed, you know."

"I know. What about the men who were there?" Kaelen watched her as she shrugged.

—

"I have no idea. I got us away and then tried to keep us alive and warm. It was really hard, you know." The three men had been the least of her thoughts, and to be frank, she really didn't care if they had lived or died. As far as she was concerned, they could have died. She didn't have it in her heart at that moment to forgive them.

"I see. Help me up, please." Kaelen rested back against her arm for a moment as he sat on the side of the bed, his head spinning. He squinted as he looked around at the comfortable room.

"Where are we?" He squinted at Keller as she didn't respond.

Keller shrugged. She had not explored the house when she put her feet on the wooden floor. She was too worried about finding Kaelen.

Kaelen suddenly reached to hug her. He could feel the shudders of fear that shook her body and prayed for his new friend. He realized that they had shared an adventure that he could not remember and that troubled him greatly.

Taking her hand, Kaelen walked slowly from the bedroom. coming to an abrupt halt as he saw the dog waiting in front of him. He didn't move, letting the dog approach them, sniff them, and then greet them. Keller was looking around, trying to determine just where they were and was unable to. Kaelen walked towards the back door, opening it and pulling Keller with him. The dog slipped by them to find his master still bowed over his chair. A nudge from the dog had a gnarled and workworn hand rubbing at the dog's head before Fairley was on his feet.

He studied the couple in front of him but most of his attention was on Keller. He could see the image of his beloved wife, Kennedy, in her and that caused more sorrow to move through his heart. He walked slowly towards them, his steps that of a tired and heartsick old man.

"Hi. I'm sorry. We didn't mean to disturb you. We're just not sure who you are and where we are." Keller spoke for the two of them, a frown on her face as she studied the older man in front of him. She trusted him without even thinking about it and that puzzled her. She did not give her trust that easily, not after what her life had been like.

Fairley's mouth opened and closed. He was at a loss for words for a moment. Keller's voice had the melodic tones to her that her mother had had. Fairley wiped at his eyes for a moment, gathering his thoughts and emotions.

"It's okay. I found you this morning in a clearing near here. I wasn't planning on going there but God sent me. My name ..." Fairley's voice died away for a moment.

Keller frowned at him once more and then shared a look with Kaelen. Kaelen was not sure what was happening but something was.

"My name's Kaelen Cooper and this is Keller Monaghan." Kaelen's voice died away at the look on Fairley's face. "Did I say something wrong?"

"No, not at all." Fairley stepped closer to Keller, his hand on the dog's head. "My name's Fairley Monaghan." He stopped as he saw the look on Keller's face and then the dawning comprehension.

"Fairley Monaghan?" Keller stared at him, trying to comprehend his name. "Did you say Fairley Monaghan?" At his nod, Keller felt Kaelen's arm around her to support her. It was not what she had expected but she needed that contact with him. His concern was for the lady next to him until he saw the look on the older man's face. "Are you my father?"

Kaelen was shocked at her words. He knew from what she had told him that she had been raised in foster care. If this was her father, where had he been been?

"I think so. You look like your momma, Keller, as beautiful as she was." Fairley waited for Keller to move, knowing that he had to let her take that step.

"Where have you been?" Keller was angry and she felt that it was well deserved. "Do you know what my life was like? Do you understand the physical and emotional abuse that I had to endure? I can never get that life back that I should have lived." Keller was in tears as she spoke, her eyes glued to Fairley's face. "Where were you?"

"I'm sorry, Keller. I am so sorry. Your momma died when you were six months old. A brain aneurysm that we didn't know about. Then, I came home from work when you were one year old and you were gone. I couldn't find the woman who was looking after you. I searched so hard for you. I called everyone and every organization that I could think of. No one would admit to seeing you. I still was looking every day. I hired private investigators who couldn't find you. All they found were dead ends. Can you forgive me?" Fairley's face was covered with his tears.

Keller didn't move towards him. In fact, it felt as if her feet were nailed or glued to the ground. She felt Kaelen's arm tighten around her and was grateful for his support. She was in shock at what the man who claimed to be her father had said. That couldn't be right, she decided. It just couldn't be.

Kaelen watched both Fairley and Keller, not sure what was happening or if he had heard correctly. He wanted to support his new friend, Keller, but he really was torn.

Kaelen studied the man in tears in front of her. She could see some resemblance to herself but didn't know if that was just wishful thinking. She prayed, begging God for answers and not knowing if she would get them.

"Why? Who did this? Who hated you that much?" Keller's cries were unanswered. Fairley had no answer to give her. He didn't have one that he could give himself.

Chapter 8

Kaelen drew Keller to a seat, sitting on the ground beside her. His arm was around her as he studied first her and then the man who claimed to be his father. Kaelen didn't know about that but he knew that he would reach out to his friends to find out if that was the case. It just seemed too out there to be true but he knew that it could well be. He didn't have enough facts to make that decision. Someone who was an investigator would need to.

"Fairley? May I call you that?" Kaelen waited patiently for the man to compose himself and then nod. "Can you tell us what happened? I'm sure that you have been trying to determine who would do this. Perhaps, we can help. I think that Keller would need to know."

Fairley kept his eyes on the ground. He thought through Kaelen's words. His eyes were raised to the young lady sitting across from him. His daughter. How long had he wanted that and never thought he would ever see her this side of heaven?

"I don't know, son. I really don't know." Fairley looked toward Kaelen. "You're Kaelen?"

"I am. I suspect that you looked at our identification. I don't mind. What I need to know is how you found us."

"God. He sent me to that clearing. I wasn't planning on going that way this morning. God sent me that way. You were unconscious as was Keller. I brought you here." Fairley drew in a shaking breath. "I don't know how long you were there. How did you get out there?"

"We were taken captive Friday night. I found Keller hiding in the back of my yard. I was forced to take up my helicopter. We flew for a bit and then the men wanted me to land in a clearing. It wasn't as large as it should have been for a proper landing. I crashed. I have no idea how I got to that clearing." Kaelen frowned at Keller.

"I was able to get you out. I didn't lose consciousness. I was able to get you to wake up enough to walk away from there. I found the pack that you had in there. I don't know what happened to the men." Keller was disturbed by that. "Shouldn't we go and look for them?"

"I did that. I found the helicopter." Fairley had left during the date, searching for anything that would help explain what the couple was doing out there. "There were no men there. I don't know what happened to them. We will need to report this to the authorities." Fairley had waited until he could speak with the couple. "Where do you two live?"

"I live in Oak City." Kaelen saw Keller nodding that she did so. "I can reach out to a friend who is a police detective."

Fairley nodded. He was well aware of who Kaelen was speaking about. Aidan was well known in the community.

"I'll reach out to him. For now, let's get some light food into you two and then you'll sleep once more. Your bodies need to recover." Fairley was on his feet and heading for his house, his dog pacing at his side.

Kaelen watched him walk away before he turned to Keller.

"Keller? What are your thoughts?" Kaelen waited patiently for her to speak.

Keller studied him before she studied the ground at her feet. She shrugged, not knowing what to say.

"I don't know what to say, Kaelen. To think that this is my father? I want to believe him but I need proof. It's been so many years. How do we do that?" Keller leaned against him without realizing that she had done so.

"We'll do that. It's been a shock for both of you. He had time to come to terms with the knowledge that you are back in his life. You haven't. You need to pray through this, trusting that God is here and is leading you. We'll figure it out." Kaelen tightened an arm around her, his chin resting on the top of her hair. "Come on, sweetheart. Let's find that meal that Fairley promised us and then I need to sleep."

Keller approached Fairley early that evening. She had been studying the photos that he had around the house, seeing her mother in so many. And she was there as a baby, if indeed Fairley was correct. She didn't doubt him. She just needed to have it proven and to have answers provided that would explain why her life had been like it had been.

"Fairley? I'm sorry. I can't call you father as yet." Keller was saddened by that. "Where is God? Where was He?"

"Right here, Keller. Right here in the midst of where we are. He has allowed this for His reasons. We may never understand why here on earth. But this I know. God is walking with us along this pathway. He was there every day with both of us. He saw the tears that we have both shed. He was there when you underwent the abuse that you did. I wish it had been different. My prayer was daily that I might find you. I never did." Fairley wiped at the tears on his face.

"I get that. I just don't have to like that we were torn apart." Keller walked away, heading for the bedroom and her rest. She was exhausted in so many ways and really didn't know if she would sleep that night.

Fairley paced his home. He knew that he needed to sleep but he also needed to stay awake and pray. There were so many unknowns in this situation but he was at a loss to explain what was going on. He reached for his phone, sending off a text to a friend, simply asking that he contact Aidan about the helicopter. That needed to be done. He was just not ready to let anyone know where Keller and Kaelen were. Yet, they needed to go home. Fairley was afraid that Keller would walk away from him and not want to be part of his life ever again.

The old dog, Shep by name, eyed his master, knowing that he was upset. Shep walked towards the bedrooms, standing to watch Kaelen as he slept before he moved to the other bedroom. He gave a leap and was on the bed to cuddle down beside Keller, his chin on her neck as he eyed the door. His house was in an upset and he could not fix it.

Fairley stood and watched Shep before he gave a small smile and walked away to the bed that he had made for himself on the couch. He slept, his sleep restless however. He could hear Shep's nails as he paced the house over the night. This was not unusual but Shep had not done it for a while. Fairley smiled to himself for a moment before he slept again, knowing that he needed that rest.

Chapter 9

The next morning, Keller was on her feet in the early morning. She reached for the coffee that was already dripped, pouring herself a mug and then hitting the outdoors. She didn't feel safe inside but had no reason to understand why. Keller stood for a moment, assessing the area around her. It was comfortable and welcoming. She felt at home.

A nudge at her hand had her looking down at Shep. Keller dropped to her knees, her mug set to one side as she hugged the dog. Shep stood still for a moment before his tongue was out and swiping across her face. She giggled slightly at that.

Fairley watched her, a sad smile on his face. He had found his daughter, he knew, but he also knew that she had had a rough life, the type of life that had damaged her in ways that he would have prayed not to have had happened. He mourned that before he turned that mourning over to God. It was how he had learned to live, to give all his worries and cares to his Heavenly Father, his Abba Father.

He walked slowly forward to drop to a sitting position beside Keller. Fairley did not look at her. Instead, he stared ahead and thought through what needed to be done. His friend had responded that he had reached out to Aidan but that Aidan would get back to him. He didn't say why and the friend did not answer.

Keller hugged Shep closer, finding comfort from the contact with him. Her mouth opened and closed many times before she snapped it shut.

Fairley turned an eye to her before he smiled. He knew that Keller had many questions as did he. He heard Kaelen moving behind him and then sitting beside Keller.

"Morning, Fairley. What are the plans for the day?" Kaelen sipped at his coffee, his eyes on the sky and the few clouds that were scudding across it.

"The plans for the day? I would think that we need to get you two home. Someone will have been looking for you." Fairley was not aware of Kaelen's family or if he even had one. This was not a topic that they had covered the day before.

"Yeah, I guess that we need to do that. I need to make arrangements to recover my copter and see how much damage has been done." Kaelen drew in a deep breath. "It's a crime scene now, isn't it?"

"It would be considered that, Kaelen. I'm sorry that happened. But I am not sorry in another way because Keller is back with me." Fairley gave a sad smile at his daughter.

"There is that." Keller was on her feet, heading back into the house. She stood with her back against the closed door, her head dropped forward. Her emotions were in a muddle as she termed it. Not only being kidnapped and kept captive but to be dropped at Kaelen's, having him find there, and then taken captive again had taken a toll on her emotions. To have been in a crash as well had strained her emotions and physical strength beyond what she thought that she could handle. Now, to have found her father? She had no emotions left to try and work through. Only God could lead her and she was confident that He would.

Kaelen had turned his head to watch Keller as she walked away, a frown on his face. He was deeply troubled by what happened. He needed to get back to his home and then find Aidan. He knew that Aidan would work with him to find out what had happened.

Fairley watched Kaelen in turn, nodding as he saw the look in the younger man's eyes. He was developing feelings for Keller, Fairley was sure of that. He just wanted some time with his daughter and didn't know how much that he would get. He was also very worried about her and the trouble that she was involved in.

Aidan had walked back through Kaelen's property that morning. He was disturbed. There had been just no word from Kaelen himself, just the text from a friend. Aidan walked back towards his car and then drove out of town, heading towards the area where he was told that he would find the helicopter. Fighting his way through the underbrush, Aidan came to a halt. The caller had been correct. There was the helicopter. Aidan walked closer to it, not seeing anyone around it. He searched the area and then turned to search the trees. He had no idea where anyone was. None of the five were there. Aidan could only pray that Kaelen and the lady had made it out safely. He just didn't have anything to prove it. A call went out to the county force who promised to be there.

Standing back and watching the activity, Aidan shook his head. He had no idea how Kaelen had managed to set the bird as he called it down. He had no idea how they would get it out but he would leave that to the ones properly equipped to do that. His head turned as the county detective walked his way.

"Kevin? What do you have?" Aidan waited patiently for Kevin to speak.

"How did he land?" Kevin was in awe somewhat at how Kaelen had managed to land.

"I don't know. He's good, Kevin. What can you tell me?" Aidan's notebook and pen were out.

"I don't have much information, Aidan. There is not a lot of evidence that we can see. We have no idea how injured any of them were." Kevin looked around, trying to come up with something that would explain the absence of the five people.

"Can you check? Kaelen always has a backpack with supplies in there. Is it still there?" Aidan waited somewhat impatiently as Keven stared at him and then almost ran for the helicopter.

Kevin ran back towards Aidan, a thought crossing his mind. The backpack was gone, but who had taken it? He could only pray that it was Kaelen and the lady.

"There's no backpack, Aidan. We just don't know which one took it." Kevin stared at Aidan as Aidan stared back at him.

"I can only pray that it was Kaelen and Keller. How do we find them?" Aidan spun in a circle, staring around before he pointed. "That path? Where does it lead?"

Kevin was nodding, already with his phone out and bringing up a topographic map of the area. Aidan watched the map before he pointed.

"That clearing over there? It's not that far. Can we take a look at it?" Aidan was hopeful that he would find his friend there.

"We can." Kevin headed that way, noting that someone had managed to get through there. "Someone went through here. It looks like a man and a woman."

"Kaelen and Keller." Aidan broke through the last of the brush and stood in the clearing. His keen eyes searched the area before he was pointing and then running that way. "Here. Someone made a fire. But how long were they here for?"

Kevin nodded, his eyes searching the ground before he saw the tire tracks.

"Someone drove in here with what I suspect is a truck. You can see the heavy footprints where it looks as if someone or two someones were carried to it."

Aidan searched around as well, tracking the path that the truck had taken.

"I pray that someone found them and they're safe." Aidan stood up and stood, hands on his hips. "How do we now find them?"

"We search home to home. Someone might know something." Kevin sighed. This was going to be a big task, he decided, before he headed back towards the other clearing. Aidan hesitated for a moment before he too walked that way. He would search until he found his friend and then work to determine who was responsible and then arrest them. It was who he was and what he did. Aidan looked up at the sky, studying the clouds before his head dropped as he prayed. Only God could intervene in this situation and reunite Kaelen with his friends. Aidan's thoughts turned to Kaelen's family. He had none. He had been raised by a family friend who had taken on his care when he was a toddler when his parents were killed in a tornado.

Chapter 10

Keller paced the backyard of the house, her arms wrapped around herself. She was at a loss, she decided, as to what to do. Fairley had promised to take them to town, knowing that they needed to be seen by a physician. She was just reluctant to do that. Keller was afraid that the men would find her again and this time, she would not escape them. She was also afraid for Kaelen, sure that he would be taken captive again and she didn't want that, not if she was responsible for it.

Kaelen watched her closely, seeing how close to the edge of breaking down that she was. He had had a long conversation with Fairley, not about Keller, but about where they were, who his neighbours were, and how they needed to find their own homes once more. Fairley had nodded, knowing that Kaelen was correct. They did need to go home. He just didn't want to let Keller out of his sight.

Hearing a sound from the front yard and then a loud yell from Fairley, Kaelen jumped and then ran for Keller, catching her hand and pulling her towards the surrounding trees. He found the pile of branches and then shoved Keller to the ground. His body covered hers, his arms wrapping around their heads. Keller was shoving at the ground as she tried to rise, protesting that he wouldn't let her.

"Keller. Enough! Stay on the ground. Something was going on at the front of the house that I didn't like. Your father was dealing with it, I think.

We need to stay down." He finally managed to get through to Keller and she was still. He didn't know how long that they stayed that way before he sat up and then helped Keller to sit up. Kaelen didn't move for a few moments, not sure if it was safe to do so. He didn't hear any sounds but that didn't mean that men were not waiting for them.

On his feet, Kaelen reached for Keller's hand, pulling her upright and then walking slowly towards the house. He didn't see anything that seemed amiss, but he was well aware that something could be. His hand touched the back door before he opened it and walked in. Shep was waiting for them, anxiety in his manner. Kaelen dropped Keller's hand and walked through the house, searching for Fairley. His feet hit the front porch as he searched for Fairley.

Fairley was sitting in a chair, his head in his hands. Kaelen was crouching beside him, a hand on his arm.

"Fairley? What happened?" Kaelen was impatient as he waited for Fairley to speak.

"Those men? They were connected with the ones who abducted you two. They are looking for you. I wasn't threatened. They were just going home to home. Somehow, they know that you two escaped. They want Keller again. I don't know why." Fairley was distraught. He looked past Kaelen. "Where's Keller?"

"In the house. I heard the voices and hid us." Kaelen gave a grim smile as he thought of where they had hidden.

—

55

"Good. We need to get you two back to town. You need to reach out to your friends who can help." Fairley was on his feet, heading into the house to find Keller standing and waiting for him. She walked into his hug, finding the father's hug that she had been missing.

"Fairley?" Keller stood back, not sure what to say.

"We're heading into town, Keller. We'll get you both assessed, and then Kaelen will find his friends. Then, we can start to think through what has happened to you and why."

"Thank you." Keller felt Kaelen's arm around her and leaned against him. She wasn't sure why she did, but he made her feel safe. It was as if God had provided someone on earth to do that, to stand in His stead in a physical way.

Reaching the edge of town, Fairley parked his truck in an almost-empty parking lot, his fingers tapping at the steering wheel. None of them spoke, waiting for each other to speak.

Kaelen shifted on the seat, his eyes on Keller. This was where they would part, probably never to see one another again other than for an official interrogation or court if it ever came to that.

"Where to, Kaelen?" Fairley spoke at last, eyeing the younger man.

"The hospital, I think, Fairley. We need to be assessed just because it was an accident and a criminal act at that." Kaelen sighed, a headache beginning once

---

more. "And then I need to reach out to my friends." He was reluctant to do that. He didn't want anyone hovering over or about him and he knew that was exactly what would happen. He also didn't want to lose contact with Keller.

"We can go there. I'll wait with you." Fairley headed that way, knowing that he also did not want to lose contact with either of the young couple.

Assessed at the hospital and told that their injuries were minor considering what they had been through, Keller walked out of the hospital, her hand tight in Kaelen. Fairley walked on her other side, heading for his truck.

"Where to now, Kaelen?"

"Can we find a store and get some clean clothes for Keller? I don't think that she should go home until we speak with the authorities. She can clean up at my place." Kaelen shared a look with Keller who looked surprised before she nodded.

Keller didn't want to leave Kaelen. He made her feel safe, cherished, and loved, something that she didn't think that she had felt in her life, her life that was after she had disappeared from her father's care. She also knew that she needed to speak with someone in the police, who that was she wasn't quite sure. She felt that Kaelen would know who that would be but she refused to ask him.

Kaelen unlocked the door to his home, his hand out for Keller's. It felt as if it had been weeks since he had been there even though it had only been a few days. He stepped inside, drawing Keller with him and with Fairley following him. The house felt stuffy as he did so, being closed up for that number of days. Dropping Keller's hand, he motioned for her to wait there as he walked through the house and then returned to her.

"Everything seems okay, Keller, Fairley. I know that Aidan has likely been through. It's what Wednesday now?" Kaelen had lost track of time.

"No, it's Thursday." Fairley grinned at him for a moment. "We've lost some days there, young man."

"It is, isn't it? Okay. Keller, let's get you to one of the bedrooms. They all have their own attached ensuite." He paused in front of the one that was painted in a soft cream with peach accents. "This one, I think. The colours are you. I think that it was waiting just for you." He dropped the bags on the bed and then hugged her before he walked away and closed the door behind him. Kaelen hesitated for a moment before he headed for the kitchen.

Fairley turned to face him, the coffee pot in his hand as he reached for the tap. He frowned at the younger man, seeing the strain and fatigue on Kaelen's face.

"Go and get cleaned up as well, Kaelen. I'll be fine. I'll make some coffee for us and find something for us to eat." Fairley frowned even harder at the younger man.

Kaelen nodded, swaying on his feet. The headache had worsened as he had been told that it would.

—

"Thank you, Fairley. You've been a Godsend the last few days. I have some soup frozen in the freezer of the fridge. That will do, unless you find something else. There should be a loaf of bread in there as well." Kaelen walked away at that point, heading for his own bedroom and a shower, shave, and clean clothes.

Chapter 11

Kaelen padded back through his house, his bare feet hitting softly on the wooden floor. He could hear the faint conversation from the kitchen before he headed into his office. He had set his phone to charge and needed to check it. He had not taken the time to check any messages. And he did have messages and texts as well as missed calls. Kaelen sighed. It would take him time to respond to them. His friends were quite worried about him, he could tell.

His fingers flew over the keyboard as he sent a quick text off to Aidan, letting him know that he was at home and needed to see him. Was he available? He was not surprised at a quick response from Aidan, stating that he was and then asking if he was okay. Kaelen responded briefly that he was as best as he could be and that he would explain when he saw him.

Aidan stared down at his phone. Even though he had replied to Kaelen's text, he was not sure that Kaelen was the one who had sent the text message. Aidan was on a crime scene and could not leave. He sighed, turning away for a moment, deep in thought. He reached out to Caleb, simply asking if he was free and could head to Kaelen. Caleb responded quickly, asking why. Aidan responded that Kaelen was home and that he needed someone with him until he himself could get there.

Caleb turned from his office in the security building and headed for Don, the head of their security team.

"Don? Kaelen's supposedly home. He sent a text to Aidan. Aidan asked if I could head that way." Caleb was torn. He wanted to speed that way but he was too savvy to do it on his own.

Don looked up from his paperwork and then was on his feet.

"Who's all here?" Don was referring to his team.

"We all are." Caleb could hear the conversation from the others. "You want us all."

"I do." Don stood in the hallway and raised his voice slightly. "Come on, guys. I know it's almost quitting time but Aidan has heard from Kaelen. We need to head that way."

The other four had appeared, nodding before they all ran for their vehicles and headed Kaelen's way. Caleb and Don headed for the front door as the other four spread out around the property, searching for anything that was out of the ordinary. Joshua frowned at the old truck sitting in the driveway beside Kaelen's truck, not recognizing it. He inspected it, taken with the good condition of the classic truck.

Kaelen heard the quiet tap at the front door and set his spoon back on the table. He excused himself, on his feet to head that way. He paused to stare back at Keller, finding her watching him with a solemn look on her face.

Opening the door, Kaelen was not surprised to find Don and Caleb facing him nor to see the other men walking through his yard. Aidan would have done that, he knew, just to ensure that there was no danger to Kaelen present there.

Don's keen eyes studied his friend. He could see the changes that had come as a result of what Kaelen had gone through. He could also see that Kaelen was fighting a headache. It was obvious in his eyes and with the frown that was on his face.

"Kaelen?" Caleb spoke. Of the six men who were all friends with Kaelen, Caleb was the closest.

"Caleb. Don. Thanks for coming." Kaelen stepped outside, closing the door behind him. "You'll need to know what happened."

"Not until you talk with Aidan. He's on his way, just tied up at a crime scene." Don stared past Kaelen as the front door opened and Keller and Fairley stood there. "Care to introduce us to your friends?"

Kaelen turned and then reached for Keller, pulling her forward to stand beside him and kept his arm around her. Fairley stepped forward to stand beside his daughter.

"This is Keller Monaghan. She's the lady who appeared here on Friday night and then was abducted the second time with me. I'll explain after I talk with Aidan." He turned his head to study Fairley, finding Fairley studying his friends. "And this is Fairley Monaghan. He found us and took us in, caring for us as we needed it. He is also Keller's father. There's a long and sad story there, fellows. We need to do what you do best, finding out the why's and who's."

Don nodded. He knew there was a lot that Kaelen would not and could not say at present. Caleb nodded as well. He had seen Keller at church, he realized.

"You're part of the ladies's Bible study." His words surprised Keller

"I am. Why would you ask?" Keller did not back down from him.

"My wife, Cullea? She's mentioned you at times. She wanted to become your friend but you were never around much after the meetings ended."

"She did. Yes, I recognize her name." Keller frowned at him. "She's there with other friends."

Caleb grinned at her, knowing who she was referring to.

"She is. The rest of our security team? Their wives. Don's sister. The detective who is on his way here? His wife. The police chief? His wife. They all have expressed concern at some point about you, worried about you without knowing why. They have prayed for you. It's what they do. But they have all expressed interest in becoming a friend with you. They just didn't know how to approach you."

"They do? Well, I don't know what to say." Keller's hand tightened on Kaelen's. "I guess it's okay. I don't do people very well." She felt Fairley's hand on her shoulder. "Fairley?"

"It's good to have friends, Keller. It's what your mother would have wanted." Fairley had trouble controlling his emotions. Keller had been honest with him that morning, telling him exactly what she had faced. Anger had laced her words at times as well as sorrow and mourning. She had not had the childhood that she deserved. Both of them had just joined their hands and prayed, asking for forgiveness and peace. Keller was not yet ready to take a hug from her father.

"You don't?" Don was not surprised. He was reading her and reading her correctly, that people made her very nervous. "It's okay. If you need to talk to just one or two, that's fine. My sister, Daci, might be a good one to speak with. She runs the local women's shelter." His hand went up as her mouth opened. "I don't know what you've been through, Keller, but Daci listens well and will not share what you tell her. She's had the experience of working with many ladies and their children over the years. I doubt that there is much that she has not heard at some point or other."

Chapter 12

Caleb walked away from the front door an hour later. He found his team members waiting for him and quickly told them what he knew. They stared at him, at one another, and then at the house. None of them were comfortable leaving but they didn't have much choice. They all had commitments with their wives that they needed to be at.

Don walked away as well, heading for Aidan who had just now arrived. He was shaking his head at what little he had been told. Kaelen had asked that he remain, if that was okay. Don had nodded, stating that he would ask Delanie to come for support for Keller, if she wanted that. Keller had looked surprised and then grateful for that.

Aidan paused in his walk forward. To find Don there had not surprised him. It was who Don was, particularly with his friends.

"Don? Talk to me. What's going on?" Aidan was not surprised that Don hesitated to speak.

"Delanie's here. Keller needed a lady to be here for her." Don bit at his lip, not quite sure what to say.

"Keller? As in Keller Monaghan?"

"That's correct. She's here. There is something weird going on. A man is here who says that he is her father. Keller told me that she had been raised in horrible foster care. There's a story there, Aidan." Don turned to face the house, seeing Kaelen waiting for them on the front porch.

"Her father? His name?" Aidan waited for Don to speak, his eyes on Kaelen.

"Fairley Monaghan. I know him from somewhere. I just can't place him. He's not from our church."

"Fairley Monaghan? I tried to connect with him earlier today but he wasn't home. We found the helicopter and the county is investigating that." Aidan walked forward, Don pacing at his side. He approached Kaelen, assessing him much as Don had done earlier. "Has he said much?"

"No. He won't until he talks with you." Don walked past Kaelen, a hand resting on his shoulder for a moment.

"Aidan? Can we talk?" Kaelen was hesitant, not sure what to say or how much that Aidan knew already.

"Sure. Let's talk out here, Kaelen. Then, I understand that Keller Monaghan is here."

"She is. She's the reason I disappeared. I found her in my yard on Friday night, brought her into the house, and gave her some water. We were talking when some men broke in and took us away. I was forced to fly them out in my helicopter. They wanted me to land in a clearing but it wasn't as large as I should have had for landing. We crashed. I don't remember much about that or for a few days afterwards. I woke up at Fairley's home and then he managed to get us home."

Aidan was making notes and asking the questions that he needed to. He was puzzled by it all.

—

This was not making much sense, he knew, but at some point it would. He would talk with Kaelen again and again. He looked around as he heard a soft noise, rising to his feet. Keller had appeared, desperate to find Kaelen. He was her lifeline right now, even though she didn't understand why. She had no idea that there was an attraction happening between the two.

"Hi. You must be Keller. I'm Aidan, the investigator on this case. We need to talk." Aidan watched as she scooted past him and found Kaelen. He stifled a smile as Kaelen's arm came around her.

"I am. I do need to talk. I just don't understand any of it. Can you help?" Keller could see her father standing just out of sight in the doorway before he nodded and turned back to where Don and Delanie were waiting for him.

"I will do my best." Aidan waited until Kaelen and Keller were sitting before he sat himself. "Talk to me, Keller, if I may call you that. Tell me what has happened." Aidan gave her a swift smile. He was not prepared for the torrent of words that erupted from her. His heart filled with sorrow as she talked, knowing that she had had a very rough life. He just didn't see what the abduction had to do with her past life. He would be looking into that, Aidan decided.

Keller drooped back against Kaelen, turning to frown up at him as she realized that he had his arm around her. He didn't speak, just gave a small smile, a smile that said she was special and that he didn't want to let her go through this on her own.

—

"Can you help me?" Keller's tone was almost plaintive as she looked at Aidan, hope on her face.

"I will do my best. I will come back and talk with you over and over. It's what we do. Now, what I would suggest is that both of you keep a journal. Write down anything and everything that you think may or may not be related to this. Keller, you have had a hard and difficult life. We'll look into your foster family to see if they are connected to this." His hand went up as she started to protest. "It's what we do. We'll do the same for Kaelen. Kaelen, you and I have talked over the years about your life. I'll need names of anyone who you can think of."

Kaelen nodded. He had expected to have to do that. And he would do that gladly. He just didn't see how this was all related to him but he knew that it could well be.

Keller continued to frown. She had no idea who all to place on that list but she would gladly list anyone and everyone who might be behind it.

"My father?" Keller frowned harder at Aidan as he paused in his writing before looking up at her.

"Your father? I don't understand." Aidan had missed the fact that the Fairley mentioned was her father.

"Fairley Monaghan. He's my father. I was taken from him when I was one. I told you that." Keller was angry for a moment that Aidan didn't understand that. Her eyes were flashing with that anger before she looked past Aidan and saw Fairley. "Dad?" She didn't understand that she had called Fairley "Dad".

―

Fairley moved towards her, a hand out to take hers. He turned to face Aidan, finding that man studying him. He smiled slightly, knowing full well that he had a story to tell, more of a story than he had told the young couple.

"Aidan, is it?" At Aidan's nod, he sighed. "I do have a story to tell, Aidan. I'm not sure what to say."

"Just start talking, Fairley. I'll make my notes and then we'll talk over and over. It's what we do."

Fairley nodded. He was well aware of that. He turned his head to find Keller watching him, concern in her eyes. He didn't want her to hear what he had to say but she needed to. Kaelen was watching him too, a smile of encouragement on his face. Don and Delanie had crept out to the porch as well. Aidan sighed. This was not what he wanted but Fairley was not a victim of the current crime or even the culprit.

—

Chapter 13

That evening, Kaelen reached for his computer mouse, preparatory to answering some of his messages. He didn't realize that so many people were concerned about his disappearance. His hand paused as his head dropped and he prayed for Keller. He was deeply worried about her, even though he could not be there beside her all the time.

Keller had insisted on returning to her own home. Aidan had taken her, shaking his head at Kaelen. As much as Kaelen wanted to be there with her, he couldn't. Aidan would need to treat her home as a crime scene, that much he knew and understood. He sighed. Having spent the last few days with Keller, even if he could not remember some of them, he didn't want to be apart from her. Kaelen wanted to be close to her and protect her.

The soft chiming of his phone had him reaching for it. He gave a smile, seeing Gideon's name on the caller ID. Gideon was their pastor and had just recently gone through one of those adventures with his now wife, Garnet.

"Kaelen? Don called and let me know that you are home." Gideon settled back into his black leather desk chair.

"I am. I'm just not sure what is going on though." Kaelen drew in a deep breath before the words were tumbling out of his mouth, explaining what had happened and where he had been.

—

"I see. You're on one of those adventures, aren't you?" Gideon gave a soft laugh before he sobered. "What can I do for you, Kaelen?"

"What can you do?" Kaelen rubbed at his temple with his hand. His headache was growing worse and he needed to take something. Only, he didn't want to. He was determined to stay awake and alert and ready to run to Keller's aid if she called. Kaelen just didn't know if she would. "I'm not sure, Gideon. I know that you are praying for me and for the situation. I have to meet with the insurance agent tomorrow and I'm not looking forward to that."

"How be I come with you?" Gideon had often done just that, meeting with one of his congregation and authorities of some kind.

"That would be great. I think that Keller will be there as well." Kaelen grew silent, not knowing if she would be willing to do that or not.

"Keller? Keller Monaghan? How is she involved in this?" Gideon had not been aware that Kaelen even knew Keller.

"Keller? She was kidnapped last week, ended up at my place, and then we were both taken from here. She was the one who dragged me from the downed copter and to safety. We just don't know where the men who kidnapped us are." Kaelen bit at his lip, knowing that he needed to continue but not sure how to do that. "Gideon? How well do you know Keller?"

"How well do I know her?" Gideon had to think about that. "I don't know her that well at all. She slips in as the service starts and slips out as it ends. She does the same with the ladies' Bible study." He wasn't sure what else to say. "You're saying that she's part of all this?"

"She is. She has quite the story that I'll ask her to share with you and Garnet. The thing is? We were found by a man out in the forest where we were stranded. It turns out to be her father."

"Her father?" Gideon sat forward, frowning at that. "Who is he? Do we know them?"

"His name is Fairley Monaghan. He lives just outside of town. He found us and took us in for a couple of days. I'm not sure if he went home or stayed with Keller. He's been hurting for so many years as has she. I wish that I could tell you the whole story."

"Find a time to get us all together in the next couple of days. We'll meet, find out what we can do for them, and then spend time in prayer. If Keller wishes, Garnet would be willing to meet with us." Gideon looked up to see Garnet standing in the soft light of the hallway and reached out a hand for her. "Kaelen, let me pray with you right now. You're in the middle of a storm and need that. Just remember that while the storm rages around you, God is in the midst of it. He will provide the peace and protection that you need."

"I know. You know how I lost my parents in that tornado. This feels so much like that." Kaelen wiped at his face. He was struggling with his faith right now and had been for a few months. He needed that lifeline that God was holding out for him. Kaelen just needed to reach for that hand that was there and he would be safe despite what he was involved in.

"That is it, Kaelen. We can meet as a group of friends if you like. You know our stories. Keller needs to hear them." Gideon looked around, not sure what to say. He felt Garnet's arm around his shoulder as she perched on his knee. "Don said that he and Delanie had been there as had the rest of the team."

"They were. Speaking with Delanie seemed to help." Kaelen yawned and then apologized. "I need to sleep, Gideon. I'll speak with Keller in the morning and then call you."

"Do that. Any time will work. I'll make it work." Gideon dropped his phone to his desktop, looking at Garnet as he did so. "Garnet?"

"Kaelen? Is he really involved in something?" Garnet spoke at last.

"He is. Keller Monaghan is involved as well." Gideon hugged Garnet, grateful that God had provided just who he needed as a helpmeet.

"Keller? I know her slightly. Do you want me to reach out to her?" This was not the first time this couple had had this type of conversation.

"We'll meet with them tomorrow, I think, and go on from there." Gideon reached to kiss his wife before he bowed his head and prayed for Kaelen, Keller, and Fairley.

Kaelen sought his rest, pulling the covers up to his ears. He felt a sense of loss for some reason. He was missing his parents greatly, even though he had been so small when he had lost them. He would reach out to his foster parents tomorrow. Kaelen had received a text from them and had simply replied that he was okay at present and would call them. His foster father had just responded with an "we love you, son" and "we're praying for you".

Keller paced her apartment. She no longer found safe there and that frustrated her. She too finally found her rest, albeit that sleep was not restful. Keller smiled slightly as she thought of the text that Kaelen had sent her, just stating that he was praying for her and could they meet on the next day?

Chapter 14

The next morning found Kaelen on his feet while it was still dark. He was searching inside his house, not sure what he was searching for. He sighed and turned back to his office and reached for his phone. Scrolling through the messages that were waiting for him, Kaelen paused at one and then was on his feet and headed for the front door.

Pulling open the front door, Kaelen stared at Fairley before his hand was reaching out and pulling the older man into the house. He stared at him, seeing that Fairley had taken time to trim his hair and beard.

"Fairley? What are you doing here so early?" Kaelen paced towards the kitchen, flicking on the light, and squinting at the clock. "Did you even go home last night?"

"I did, Kaelen. I did. Now, I'm here." Fairley rested a hand on Kaelen's shoulder. "Let me do that for you, son." He shoved Kaelen into a chair and reached for food to prepare a meal for them.

Kaelen just sat, watching Fairley as he moved around his kitchen, searching for whatever it was that he needed. He felt as if he had another father. That was strange, given that he had known Fairley for only a few days.

"Thank you, Fairley." Kaelen was on his feet again, heading for the back door this time as he heard a soft tap. He opened it, not surprised to see Keller standing there. He swept her into a hug and then drawing her into the kitchen, shutting the door behind her and locking it. "Keller? What are you doing here so early? And how did you get here?"

"A taxi. I needed to see you, Kaelen. I needed to make sure that you were safe." She looked up at him, not seeing Fairley who had turned to watch the couple.

"A taxi? Keller? How safe was that?" Kaelen was growing worried about her.

"It was okay. I know him. He's driven me before." Keller struggled to escape Kaelen's arm and then approached Fairley. "You're here?"

"Of course, I am. I would be nowhere else, Keller. You need me. We will work to rebuild our relationship. It won't be what it should be but it will be what God has provided for us." Fairley's hands closed and opened before he reached to hug his daughter for the first time in way too many years. Keller clung to him, sobs shaking both of their bodies.

Kaelen stood and watched before he had to walk away. He just had to. He reached for his phone that he had left on the office desk and scrolled through his messages. Kaelen sent a quick text off to Aidan, responding to his text that Keller and Fairley were with him. Gideon and Garnet wanted to be there. And yes, he was meeting with the insurance investigator early that morning. Did he need to be there?

Aidan studied the message that Kaelen had sent and then responded with a positive response. He stretched before he reached for his clothes and dressed. It was early, he knew, but it would be a long day. Sitting on the side of his bed, Aidan's head bowed as he prayed and then spent time in silence before his Heavenly Father. His hand reached for his Bible as he read through the passages that spoke of protection and peace.

Three hours later, Kaelen stepped back to let the insurance investigator into his home. He pointed towards the office.

"In there, I think, George. Keller and her father are here and so is Aidan." Kaelen moved that way.

"That's good. It saves me from tracking them down." George, the investigator, was a middle-aged man who knew Aidan. He frowned as he studied Keller and Fairley before he turned to Kaelen. "What can you tell me, Kaelen? This is not you to crash your copter."

"No, it's not." Kaelen sat at his desk, his words almost running over one another.

George sat quickly, making his notes and his questions, knowing that he would go back over what Kaelen was telling him. He had been out to the crash site and watched as the helicopter was maneuvered into the air and then dropped onto a large flat-bed truck. He was puzzled at why this had happened.

An hour later, George stuffed his paperwork into his briefcase and rose. Kaelen walked with him to the door, stepping outside.

"What are your thoughts, George?" Kaelen dug his hands into his jeans' pockets.

"I'm not sure what to think, Kaelen. It is very obvious that you were abducted as was Keller. It is not your fault that you crashed. I have the camera footage from the helicopter and can clearly hear you protesting that you couldn't land there. It cuts out once the crash happens."

"Can I see the footage? I would like to know if I could identify any of the men."

"It's part of the official investigation now, Kaelen. I can't let you see it. Talk with Aidan. He may be able to make those arrangements. Take care, Kaelen. Someone is after either you or Keller. I don't want to see a friend and brother in Christ hurt." George walked away, leaving Kaelen to study the neighbourhood. He was frustrated, to say the least. He turned back into the house, not seeing the men standing near the edge of his property and watching him.

Keller was waiting for him, desperate for his hug and reassurance that he was there for her. She walked into his arms, feeling them tighten around her. She was afraid but had no idea why.

"Keller? Has your apartment been searched?" Kaelen rested his chin on the top of her head.

"Aidan did last night when he dropped me off. I didn't realize that investigators did that."

"Aidan would. He considers you a friend. It's what we do for friends." He turned her back towards the office. "What is going on in there?"

"They're talking about things that I don't understand. Gideon and Garnet showed up through the back door when you were outside with George." Keller had studied them, not sure why they were there.

—

78

"They are? Good. You need to hear their story."
Kaelen stopped for a moment. "You need to hear the
stories of Don and his men, as well as Toryn and his
wife, Slaney. He's our police chief. And there's Aidan
and his wife. We'll meet on the weekend, if you're up
to it. And your father is welcome as well. He needs to
know the history of our friends."

"Our friends?" Keller stared up at Kaelen, not
sure that she had heard him correctly. She didn't have
friends in Oak City.

"Our friends. You are part of our group now,
Keller, and we won't let you leave it." Kaelen hugged
her tighter before he released her and then led her back
into the office. He waved at Gideon before he seated
Keller and then sat beside her. He watched as Gideon
simply bowed his head and began to pray. This was
who Gideon was, and Kaelen accepted that.

—

Chapter 15

A week later, Kaelen walked dejectedly from the airport hangar. He was still waiting for word on his helicopter, but it was taking time, time that he didn't want to give to this. He stood for a moment, his eyes on the sky, hearing the sounds of nature in his ears. Kaelen wanted to be up there, among the clouds. That is where he felt close to God and would spend time in prayer and meditation.

Kaelen walked quickly towards his truck. He didn't know what to do. His life was in flying and he could not do that at the present time. Looking around, Kaelen shuddered unexpectedly. He felt afraid and that was unusual for him. He didn't see the truck that pulled out to follow him as he headed back into town.

Waiting for a red light to turn to green, Kaelen's fingers tapped at the steering wheel before he turned right and headed for Don's security office. He needed to talk to a friend and find out what steps he should be taking. He was torn, though. He really wanted to find Keller but knew that she would be at work. Or at least, he thought that she would be.

Paul watched as Kaelen dropped down out of his truck and shut the door. He frowned. He wasn't aware that Kaelen was due here but he wasn't surprised. They didn't have a team in for training that week and had done their own training, just to keep themselves up to date on the latest techniques.

"Kaelen?" Paul's voice echoed across the lawn.

Kaelen spun, not sure who had called him. His eyes closed for a moment when he spied Paul striding rapidly towards him across the lawn.

"Paul? Aren't you supposed to be training or something like that?" Kaelen grinned at his friend.

"Not today. You're here for a reason. Come on in. The others are just tidying away what we used today." Paul held the building door for Kaelen to enter and then followed him, the door swinging closed behind him.

Don looked around, not surprised that Kaelen was there. It was what he had expected.

"Kaelen? You're looking a little lost." Don pointed towards the conference room. "What can we do for you? And we have started our own research into you, Keller, and Fairley." Don rubbed at the back of his neck. "It's hard to understand what happened with Keller and Fairley."

"It is. And I'm mixed up in it somehow. I just don't get it. Do you?" Kaelen turned a puzzled look towards Don, seeing the other men gathering around them.

"No, I can't say that any of us understand it. How did Keller turn up at your place?" Joshua was trying to understand that.

"I really don't know. She was there and we talked. I was still trying to understand it when we were taken captive." Kaelen dropped his head into his hands. "How long will it take to understand?"

"As long as it takes." Thomas gave a quick grin at Kaelen as he glared at him. "Sorry, Kaelen. We want this over for you yesterday but that's not how it works."

"I know. I know." Kaelen blew out a deep breath, his eyes squinting at the white boards in the room. "We don't have much information to work with."

"No, we don't. That's why we need to meet as a group and find out exactly what you three know. Fairley has to be part of it. It's part of the healing that he and Keller will need to do." Mark spoke up. The team had been discussing what they knew and realized it really wasn't a lot.

"He will be. Keller does need that." Kaelen slumped in his chair, totally discouraged and at the moment doubting his faith in God.

"It's okay to doubt, Kaelen." Matthew nodded. "We all did. It's part of being human to do that. We know in our hearts that God is in control and that He only wants the best for us. It's had to trust in times such as we faced and such as you and Keller are facing now. It will take a lot of discussion, digging into the past, and digging into your present to come to the right conclusion and find out who is behind it all."

Kaelen had turned to watch him, listening to what he was not saying. He was right. It was easy to doubt even as they each acknowledged that God was there and in control. He was their Protector and Help.

"When do you want to meet?" Kaelen would ensure that Keller and Fairley would be there.

"How about Saturday? We're all available during the day, including Toryn and Slaney. Can we do that? Make it an all day event?" Caleb looked around, catching the nods of each of the men. "Saturday it is. Who else do we need here?"

"Emma." Paul's voice was soft. "We need Emma and Abe. She'll help."

"She will." Kaelen rose, still not confident that they would come up with anything that would help.

Mark walked out with Kaelen, not sure what to say to his friend. He knew how he had felt when he had gone through what he did with McKala.

"We're praying for you, Kaelen. I don't know that we will get very far ahead on Saturday, but you know us. We'll do our best."

"I know that you will." Kaelen paused, staring down at the keys in his hands. "Where do we find the keys that we need? I don't want this to go on for a long time with Keller. I am so afraid for her."

"I know that you are. She's been through a lot the last few days. Finding her father as well has to mess with her mind." Mark dug his hands into his pockets.

"It is. We're talking, Mark, if that's what you're asking. She's also seeking someone to talk with. Garnet is helping with that." Kaelen drew in a deep breath, looking around for answers, answers that weren't really readily available.

"That's good. We've all been there, seeking counselling." Mark nodded towards his truck. "Head off, Kaelen. I will follow you home." Mark was as good as his word. His hand was raised as Kaelen parked in his driveway.

Kaelen sat for a moment, his eyes on his home. It didn't feel like home or feel safe any more, and he understood that was appropriate for the circumstances. He walked through his house and then looked through his security system video. All was safe for now, but he understood that could and would likely change.

Chapter 16

Saturday found Kaelen knocking at Keller's door. He could hear muttering coming from her as her voice grew louder and she approached the door. He smiled, needing that bit of relief and fun at the moment. He stared at Keller as she stood in her doorway, taking in her beauty. He reached to hug her and then stood back with his hands on upper arms.

"Keller? Do you know how beautiful you are?" Kaelen hadn't meant to say that but once the words were out, he realized that was how he really viewed the lady standing in front of him. He was also certain that he didn't want her to walk away from him ever.

"Kaelen! What are you saying? Don't we need to get on the road? And, thank you. I have not been told that very much. In fact, it was always that I was ugly." Tears briefly clouded her vision.

"You are very beautiful. I am glad to call you my friend." Kaelen stepped back as she shut the door and locked it. His hand went out to grasp her hand, finding her frowning at him. He grinned and shrugged.

Keller muttered to herself, not loud enough that Kaelen could hear her correctly, but he thought he heard something about him not asking her permission but she sighed and muttered that it was just okay with her.

Kaelen parked amid the number of vehicles at Don's. He was not surprised to see the number of vehicles there. This is what his friends did.

Keller stared around, shocked she had to admit. She turned a questioning gaze towards Kaelen.

"These are all your friends?"

"They are. Aidan is here as is Toryn, our police chief. He's around our age." Kaelen was around at her door, a hand out to help her down to the ground, a hand that he did not drop. He walked them towards Don's home, not the office building. That was where they had agreed to initially meet.

"I see." Keller was growing increasingly uncomfortable. This was pushing her past her anxiety level. She just knew that she would never remember all the names.

Kaelen was watching her closing, praying for comfort for her. He looked up as Daci appeared in front of him, frowning as she slapped a festive name tag to his shirt and then gently attached one to Keller's sweater. He frowned at it and then at her.

"We're wearing name tags. That way? Keller doesn't have to struggle to remember who all we are. We know each other, the group growing by ones. This is different for Keller. She's meeting us all at once." Daci linked an arm with Keller and drew her away from Kaelen, somewhat reluctantly she noted with a smile.

Kaelen stared after the ladies before he nodded. Daci was doing what she did best, making it easy to meet strangers. He felt a hand on his shoulder, something that he seemed to be feeling on a daily basis. Toryn stood beside him, not watching him, but watching the group of friends gathered in Don's backyard.

"Kaelen? How are you ?" Toryn had a good idea about how Kaelen was feeling.

"It's hard, you know, Toryn. The uncertainty and the danger. The testing of our faith. How did you ever get through it?" Kaelen had asked each of his friends that and was pondering what they had said to him.

"It's tough, Kaelen. It's really tough. What I went through with Slaney? It's different than what you are going through." Toryn nodded towards Keller. "How's Keller taking it all?"

Kaelen shrugged, not sure what to say. They had been talking every night for ages and going back over what they had faced and then comparing their lives. They were growing closer, closer to a time when Kaelen would ask her out on a date.

"It's hard trusting at this time. God is there with us. Sometimes, it's nice just to have someone human to work with." Kaelen didn't think that he was expressing his thoughts all that well. "Keller asked me last night if we shouldn't be receiving letters, photos, phone calls, other threats."

"You should be. You likely will at some point. For now, I would suspect that they are staying very close to you two. Aidan feels the same. He wants Don to go over some security measures with you two." Toryn walked away, heading for Abe Finlay, someone who had a security team as well but had seen all of his team, himself included, face danger with their ladies.

—

87

Kaelen walked through the crowd, finding Fairley standing by himself for the moment. He approached the man, seeing that he looked more relaxed and peaceful.

"Fairley?" Kaelen's voice was quiet.

"Kaelen? You're okay? I saw Keller arrive with Daci." He looked at the name tag on his own shirt. "These name tags are a wonderful idea. It makes it easier."

Kaelen nodded, taking a look at his own tag. He began to laugh. Daci had been at work and taken the name tags to a new level. She had included each one's occupation on it, making it a lot easier for Keller. And he suspected that there was a file with each one's photos, name, and occupation as well waiting for Keller to take home with her.

Fairley laughed with Kaelen when the younger man had explained why he was laughing. He watched his daughter closely, seeing that Keller was gradually relaxing over time. He hated that she was in danger and that he could not prevent it from drawing closer to her.

"Fairley? What are your thoughts?" Aidan had approached the two men. He had asked Fairley that question before without the man answering.

"What are my thoughts? Do you really want to know them?" Fairley had sobered. He pulled out an envelope, studied it, and then handed it over to the investigator. "These are my thoughts. Read them over when you have some quiet time to do it. I have given Don a copy as well and Kaelen? Here's your copy."

Fairley walked away, leaving the two younger men staring at the envelopes and then at one another.

"Did he just do that?" Aidan turned to stare after him.

"He did. He's correct to do that. It gives us time to go over what he's thinking, see where it matches ours, and then prepare our questions to ask him." Kaelen tucked the envelope into a pocket. "For now, I need to find Keller and make sure that she's okay."

Aidan watched him and then turned as he heard a throat clear beside him. Abe stood there.

"Aidan? We need to talk. Frankie asked that we do. He came across some information that puzzled both of us until I realized that it applied to Keller and Kaelen." Abe was disturbed by the information. He was not wanting to speak to Aidan but he knew that he had no choice.

Chapter 17

Aidan sighed. He knew that this was a day when they planned on working on Kaelen's and Keller's adventure but he had prayed that they would. He looked around and then pointed towards a more quiet area. Abe followed him as he walked that way.

"Abe? What's up?" Aidan waited for Abe to speak.

"Emma's been looking into all of them. She has some information for you but is continuing to research and investigate. She will forward it to you as she comes across what she feels is related to the three." Abe was disturbed. "There is quite a history there, Aidan. Fairley may not even be aware of what had been going on in the past."

Aidan nodded. He had already received preliminary information from her. He had quickly looked through it and then set it aside to read again next week.

"I'm off until Monday. I'll read through it more thoroughly then. Emma's on the line of something once more, isn't she?"

Abe nodded, a grin crossing his face. Aidan understood Emma and how her mind worked, to some degree. Not even Abe could fully understand Emma's mind and how it worked. She was able to find information that no one else could.

Keller looked around a couple of hours later. She was exhausted from meeting so many people, but it was a good exhaustion. She felt welcomed and loved by her new friends. Watching Fairley, she could see that he had been welcomed by the group. At the moment, he was standing with Toryn, Don, and Abe, deep in discussion. She prayed for healing for him and for their relationship. They would need a lot of work and counselling to get to even a point where they could be a family. God was working that way, she acknowledged. They just had to get through whatever it was that they were trying to get through.

Slaney sat beside Keller, startling her for a moment. She was deeply concerned about her friend but also glad that Keller was now a part of their group. She had watched the interaction between Kaelen and Keller and seeing the interest between the couple. Slaney knew that there was interest on both sides but she wasn't sure that they would take it any further. Only God knew that. She would just pray for them and for whatever happened to them to be part of God's will for them.

"Slaney? What are your thoughts?" Keller turned to Slaney in almost a desperate manner. "What are we missing?"

"Keller? You mean missing from what you know?" Slaney watched Keller closely as she nodded. "Okay. So, to go back, you disappeared from your home and your father could not find you. Have they found the woman who was looking after you? That would be something that I would be looking into. Next, your father searched for years for you, not finding you even though you both live in or near the same town. God has kept you apart for some reason that only He knows. We have to accept that."

"That's what I don't get. We've likely crossed paths at some point, but I would never have recognized him. I don't remember him as I was too young and couldn't remember him. Dad might have seen me but not recognized me other than thinking that I might look somewhat familiar. That's what we've decided." Keller was sober as she spoke.

"That is likely true. We see in people what we sometimes want to see. We can see people who we are looking for and not realize that they are the ones." Slaney reached to hug Keller. "We'll work on it. All of us are committed to that. It's what we do for each other." She sat back, her eyes on the other ladies as they mingled, sounds of laughter coming from them at times. "This is how we are the feet and hands of Christ on earth."

"That's a good way to look at it." Keller sat back, her eyes on the group without really seeing them. "This is good, you know. A community of believers gathering around those who are hurting. The way the early church would act. Thank you, Slaney. That thought will help. I just don't want any harm to come to you."

Slaney smiled, knowing that was how she had felt.

"The men can take it. For most of them, it's what they do and who they are. They would want to stand in front of you and prevent you from being harmed. Gideon would be there, praying it through. Your father? He would be too. He's found you again and doesn't want to see you harmed or worse, dead. However, he is realistic enough to know that neither he nor anyone else can prevent that unless we find out who it is quickly. And I don't see that happening."

Keller nodded soberly, finding Kaelen crouching down beside her, an arm around her. She leaned into him, feeling comfort from contact with him.

"I don't think that will happen very quickly." She turned to study Kaelen, seeing the concern on his face. "Kaelen, what have you discovered so far?"

"What have I discovered? That I have a great group of friends and that there's a lady here who is hurting and I want to stop that. I just can't. Not yet." Kaelen shared a look with Slaney, who watched them with interest on her face. "I should be speaking to you in private, Keller, but Slaney won't say a word. I want to date you. You are the very image of the lady that my foster mother wove into my bedtime stories. No pressure. Pray about it and then let me know. Either way, I'm not leaving your side while you are in danger." Kaelen dropped a kiss on her cheek and then rose and walked away, answering a call from Gideon.

Keller sat in shock, her hand on her cheek. She heard a soft laugh from Slaney and turned that way, seeing the smile on the other lady's face.

"Slaney?" Keller's voice was low and hesitant. She was not sure at all what had just happened, except that Kaelen had spoken the words that she had wished to hear. Those words were ones that she had buried in the deepest recesses of her heart, the harsh words from her foster mothers resounding in her ears that she was no good and that no man would ever look at her.

"He's in love, Keller. He has never looked at a lady before. None of the men did before they met their wives." She nodded at the men. "And I think that you are just awakening to the fact that you are a beautiful, compassionate, caring lady who needs a knight in her life. Kaelen may or may not be God's choice for you. Pray it over. We'll pray together, my friend, for this. Your past life has driven your wants, wishes, hopes, and dreams deep inside you. You need to release that to God, Keller. He is well aware of what you faced, what you want and dream for, and He wants only the best for you."

"He does, doesn't he?" Keller stared at Slaney for a moment. "Thank you." She was on her feet, wending her way through the group until she found Kaelen. She hugged him and then walked away, leaving him staring after her with a softened look on his face and surprise on the faces of the men that he had been speaking with.

Chapter 18

A week later, Keller wandered through the downtown area of Oak City. She liked to do that, finding the small shops and stores more to her liking than the big stores in the malls or set in plazas on their own. She stared up at the name of one and then entered it. Keller could not resist a book store. She loved reading but her foster parents had ensured that she had little time to do that.

The owner looked up and smiled. Keller was a frequent customer even though she didn't always buy something.

"We have new Christian suspense novels at the back, Keller. I think you'll enjoy them."

Keller gave a small wave and wandered through the store, ending up at the display. She reached for one of the books and was lost in the synopsis on the back and then reading the first few pages. This was a new author to her, someone named Burnie Cummings. She would buy this one and then look for more from him. He had her hooked from the first few pages and she was eager to read the rest of the book.

A small sound caught at her ear and had Keller jumping in fear. She quickly walked back to the front of the store, a hesitant smile on her face.

"Keller? You've picked up Burnie's new book. You'll enjoy it." Eileen, the store owner, smiled wide at her. "He lives near here, you know."

"He does? Maybe someday I'll get to meet him."
Keller didn't see the couple who had entered the store
behind her. "I'll be back for more, I suspect, Eileen."
She looked up as Eileen didn't respond at first.
"Eileen?"

"I think that someday is today, Keller. Burnie
and his wife, Muir, are standing right behind you.
Burnie? Muir? You're here today but not really that
far from home. This is Keller. I think you have just
found a new fan."

Keller turned, feeling uncomfortable for a
moment. Muir took one lookout her and then hugged
her.

"You're running from something, aren't you?"
Muir's voice was low but just loud enough that Burnie
heard her.

"I guess that I am." Keller was taken aback as
Burnie hugged her as well. She watched him walk
away to speak with Eileen.

"We went through that." Muir looked around
before she drew Keller from the store and to the nearby
diner. She waved at Ben as she entered. "Here. We'll
have coffee. Burnie really doesn't need my help. He'll
find us."

Keller stared at her before she shrugged.
Whatever, she decided. She decided that she was not
going to live her life in fear or be beaten down any
more. Life was meant to be lived, and with both
Kaelen and her father in her life, she was ready to do
that. She suspected that at some point, Kaelen would

ask her to share that life with him. She was praying through this, with Slaney praying right along with her.

"Okay, Keller. May I call you that?" At Keller's nod, Muir grinned. "I need to take you home and introduce you to the other ladies. There are fourteen of us in that home and two others who live outside our building. We all had adventures, you know."

Keller stared at her before she snapped her mouth closed. She mentally counted the numbers.

"There are that many of you? How?"

"Burnie and I live in the building that the Barnabas Foundation owns. He is employed by them as are the others. And each one of us had a life and death adventure. We are a close-knit group but open up to welcome someone new in. Now, where is your fellow?" Muir looked around, not seeing anyone approaching them.

"Kaelen? I'm not sure that he's around today. He didn't say." Keller looked sad for a moment. "I'm not sure that he's my fellow. I'm broken, Muir. I was taken from my father at age one and spent time in foster care. We've just reconnected but it's a struggle at times. We met him during the start of whatever it is we're going through."

"That's so sad, Keller." Muir looked up as Burnie sat beside her. "Burnie? Everything's set?"

"It is, Muir. Now, Keller is it? What would you like to eat? We would like to share a meal with you and then pray with you. I'm sure that Muir has already told you a bit of our story."

"Actually, I haven't gotten quite that far, Burnie. Keller's story sounds like a plot line that you would create." Muir grinned at Keller, who was just sitting and staring at them, not sure what she had walked into.

"Well, then, let's give a synopsis as we say. Keller, I rescued Muir from a very bad situation where she was basically held hostage. She had managed to get her Granny away a few months before that. Long story short? The man who held her was trying to take over her small village which her father had helped to start. We helped to bring him to justice."

"That we did. But you forget one of the important details. There was a man named Michel who helped get Granny away and then appeared over time during our adventures. I am convinced as is Granny that he was an angel."

Keller nodded. It was not uncommon, she decided, to hear that. At times, she had felt that someone had stepped in to intervene for her. She just hadn't seen that person. Keller had taken opportunity each time that happened to breathe out a thank you to her Heavenly Father.

"We need to get together with you and Kaelen. Yes, we know Kaelen. Andy, a friend of ours, is the pilot for the Barnabas Foundation. He knows Kaelen just because of their love of aircrafts and flying. He'll want to know that you two are facing something." Burnie was lost to the two ladies at that point.

Keller stared at him, not sure what had exactly just happened. She turned to find Muir trying hard to smother her laughter.

—

"It's okay, Keller. He's off on another plot line, I think. That's what happened. He'll hear a bit of conversation, someone will say something to him, he'll see something, or find something, and then he'll be off, trying to figure out how to use it in a plot line." Muir continued to laugh.

"Is that what it's like being married to an author?" Keller sensed someone near her and looked up to see Kaelen waiting to sit beside her. She slid over as he sat, with a kiss dropped to her cheek before he was greeting Muir and Burnie.

Chapter 19

Keller walked away later that afternoon with Kaelen. Ben had not rushed them from the diner despite it being busy. He just kept refilling their coffee mugs.

Kaelen stared down at his lady. He saw a change in her that hadn't been there yesterday. He wanted to ask her what had changed but didn't want to push her.

"Kaelen? We need to talk. Only, we're out here in the open." Keller looked around, feeling someone following them. "Someone is following us."

"They are. Did you drive this morning?" Kaelen watched as she shook her head, frustrated at that. She was in danger and was walking. Then he sighed to himself. It was how she normally got around and that was not going to change. "Okay. Here. Into my truck. We'll find somewhere to talk."

"Can we talk in your backyard? This is where it all started. I feel that's where we'll find some answers. Don't ask me why I think that. It is something that God is impressing on me."

Kaelen studied her and then drove towards his home. He knew those feelings and the consequences of ignoring them. It had only taken one time of his ignoring God's nudge to realize that he had to listen and obey. There was no other objection to any further nudges. Kaelen was feeling those nudges now but wasn't sure what he was to do. All he could pray for guidance.

Keller watched the passing scenery. She wanted to run as far and as fast as she could from Oak City but she knew that was not an option. Besides, if she ran, she would be leaving both Kaelen and her father behind her. She was sure though that they would follow her without any question and just support her in whatever decision she made.

Walking through his house, Kaelen reached for two bottles of water from the fridge and then reached for Keller's hand as he headed for the backyard. He settled her into a wicker rocker on the back deck and then settled himself into a matching one. He didn't speak, just waited for Keller to speak.

Keller sat for a while, her eyes closing as she just waited patiently for just what, she wasn't sure. She could smell the scents from the flowers and whatever it was that was around. She heard the sounds of nature around her and smiled to herself. This is what she wanted, she decided. Keller decided that she wanted a house where she could be free to come in and out and do whatever it was in the yard that needed to be done.

Kaelen finally spoke. He had watched the relaxation that had appeared on Keller's face and didn't really want to disturb her.

"Were you expecting to meet Muir and Burnie this morning?" He grinned as her head turned on the back of the chair and her eyes opened before she shook her head and smiled.

"I absolutely was not. I had headed into the store and Eileen sent me to where she had set up new suspense novels. They walked in just as I paid for it.

Muir took me off to Ben's as Burnie was speaking with Eileen. They have quite the story."

"They all do from there. We'll travel that way one day and you can meet them all." Kaelen was content for the moment even though he felt the niggle of danger. "What were you thinking of, Keller?"

Keller shrugged. She wasn't sure what she was thinking. That was unusual for her. Her thoughts were usual concise and very well organized.

"Kaelen? Where do we go with the investigation?"

"I don't know. I really don't know." Kaelen was not sure where they were heading with the investigation. He had spoken with Aidan the day before. There really was not enough information for them to go anywhere with it.

"That's what I think. I wish this was over. I worry about you and Dad, that one of you will be hurt." Keller prayed daily for their safety.

"I do too, Keller, for many reasons." Kaelen bit at his lip. He was uncertain and unsettled, totally not him. He studied the sky, seeing the brilliant blue and then squinted from the brightness of the sun. "Have you talked with Aidan today?"

"No, I haven't. He said that they were away for the weekend. He needs time off. He has so many cases on the burner as he put it. Why are there so many?" Keller didn't really expect an answer to that.

Kaelen had gotten the same response from Aidan. He knew that Aidan was doing his best to keep up with them all but it was a difficult time for him. Theirs was only one of many.

"I don't know, Keller. We've been saying that for so long." Kaelen sensed that Keller had stiffened and looked her way. He found that she was deep in thought. "Keller? What are you thinking?"

"What am I thinking? That maybe I should change my job. I work as a studio singer as you know. I'm getting restless. I have my training in music." She looked up at him as she heard a soft sound from him. "Kaelen?"

"Have you ever thought about teaching voice? I know that there is a need here for that. We don't have many voice teachers." He grinned at her. "It's just a thought." He sobered. "Okay, about what you asked. Why would you think that?"

Keller shrugged. She had no idea why she had thought that one person might be behind so many of the crimes. She had had those sorts of thoughts before and they had been correct.

"It just would make sense if one person was behind them. Having too many crimes to investigate would ensure that he was never found or caught or prosecuted, wouldn't it?"

Kaelen was nodding by the time that she had finished speaking.

"I think that you're correct, Keller. We need to work on that, don't we? Maybe while we're working on that, we can solve our own adventure."

"That would be nice. I heard from Emma early this morning. She's working on our case but had an urgent investigation come in. I told her that was okay. She has one of her remote workers still on our investigation. She said that Evan would reach out to us and that I should ask him about his adventure." She frowned at him as he laughed. "Has everyone you know gone through something?"

"It's entirely possible. I think it's like a stone thrown into a pond and the ripples just keep spreading."

Chapter 20

Aidan walked towards Keller on the Monday morning. He had tracked her down at the studio and had waited patiently for her to leave the sound-proof room and head towards the break room. He did not want to be there but he had to be.

"Keller?"

Aidan's soft call had her spinning, fear on her face. She frowned at him for a moment before she sighed and turned to head into the break room. Aidan followed her.

"I don't like that you're here. What do you want?" Keller knew that she was not being very nice in how she was speaking but she had not slept well the night before and was exhausted.

"It's okay, Keller. Get whatever it is you were after. I just have some questions about your foster parents." Aidan pulled back a chair for her to sit at the table and then sat himself. He waited patiently for her to look at him. Only, she never did. "Keller?"

"I'm sorry, Aidan. Today is not a good day." Keller yawned and then her head was down on her folded arms and she slept.

Aidan stared at her in disbelief. Had she really just done that? He shook his head and then rose, knowing that he would need to speak with her later. He just didn't want to walk away from her.

Keller was awake thirty minutes later, looking for Aidan. She shrugged as she realized that he had left. He would find her again at some point, she knew.

Walking up to her apartment late that afternoon, Keller's feet dragged. She had no desire to enter an empty apartment to spend a lonely evening on her own before she retired. Her feet slowed as she approached her door. A parcel rested against the door. Only thing was? Keller had not ordered anything. She very seldom ordered on line and when she did, it was delivered to a local store for her to pick up. She didn't give out her address to very many people or businesses.

Keller leaned over to read the label. It was addressed to her with her correct name and address. She stepped back, not wanting to touch it. There was no return address and that frightened her. Reaching for her phone, Keller searched for Aidan's phone number and simply sent him a text message. She walked back down the stairs and to the picnic area at the side of the building. She sat and waited patiently for Aidan or whoever it was that he would send to find her.

Aidan pulled out his phone to look at the text message. It seemed that his phone had been chiming every few moments all day. He stared down at the message before he spun, searching for someone who he could send to Keller. Aidan almost ran for an officer, speaking quickly and send Ed towards Keller.

Ed stared at him for a moment before he was running for his vehicle. Aidan didn't react like this for nothing, he knew. He knew what had happened to Kaelen and his lady, as they all were now calling her, and worried about him.

Ed walked back down the stairs and towards the crime scene tech who was waiting for him.

"There's a parcel all right. It's addressed to her but with no return address. Do what you can here and then head back to the lab." Ed headed for the manager's office, working with the manager to retrieve any security feed that he could.

Keller watched the activity, distraught that it was because of her and then worried for the other tenants. She didn't want any harm to come to anyone else. She felt an arm around her and knew that Kaelen had found her. They had planned on sharing a meal that night. This was not how Keller had planned for it to happen.

Kaelen studied her and then the activity around them. Keller was not speaking and he didn't want to break her train of thought. He simply hugged her tighter to him.

"Keller?" Kaelen finally broke the silence. "What happened?"

"I had a parcel at my door. I didn't order anything." She sighed even as she leaned against him, her eyes following Aidan as he walked towards the apartment building. "We're making him an awful lot of work."

"He's okay with that. It's part of his job. He's intense when he's investigating." Kaelen prayed for his lady and then for Aidan and the other officers who were involved in the investigation. "Your thought from the other day?"

"What?" Keller mentally shook her head and realized that Kaelen had her in his arms. She frowned at that before she shrugged. "What thought was that? I've had too many to remember."

Kaelen grinned at her words, realizing that she really hadn't heard herself or what she said.

"Your thought that someone was behind all the crimes or some of them." Kaelen watched as Aidan ran for his car and then took off. Something had happened. He prayed for his friend and whatever it was that he was facing.

"That? Oh, that. I guess that I was just thinking aloud, trying to understand what this was all about. It's a long shot, you know." Keller turned as she heard other footsteps and saw that Fairley was approaching them. "What's going on? Who phoned Dad?"

"I don't know that anyone did. He likely showed up just because he was worried about you. Were we to have dinner with him tonight?" Kaelen really could not remember.

"Not that I know of." She stared at her father as he sat across the picnic table from her. "Dad? What are you doing?"

"God." His answer was really quite simple. "God told me to come here. I didn't know why, Keller. I have no idea what's going on. It was enough that you needed me and for once, I could come."

"I know, Dad. I do need you. And you can't help all those times that I did and you couldn't. You didn't know. You prayed for me. That was what God asked of you. Because of your prayers, He protected me. I couldn't ask for more than that." Keller was on her feet, moving towards Ed as he approached her. "What did you find?"

"Not a lot yet. I would like your keys, please, Keller. I need to go through your apartment. It's just protocol and a precaution." Ed took her keys and walked away, not seeing that she still stood with her hand raised in the position from which he had taken her keys.

Keller blinked back tears. She did not need this. Her life was complicated enough as it was right now without this. She felt an arm around her and heard Fairley praying for her. She blinked harder but could not control the tears.

Chapter 21

Kaelen watched Keller carefully the next night before he turned his attention to Fairley. Father and daughter were hurting and the only One who could heal them was the Great Physician. He was praying for that but knew also that healing would be in God's timing.

Keller turned to Kaelen, her mouth opening and then closing for a moment. She frowned at him before she spoke.

"Kaelen? What about your helicopter? Have they fixed it or replaced it?"

Kaelen looked up at that. He had spoken with the insurance investigator that day. He would need to replace it, he was told. While he was waiting for that, he would have to rent one to work. He had been assured that the costs would be covered.

"I have to get a new one. I'm not happy about that." Kaelen frowned at the thought. He had a lot of good memories with the one that had been damaged.

"Oh. I guess that's good. I was worried about you flying one that had been damaged." Keller turned away, her frown still in place.

Fairley's attention went from Keller to Kaelen and then back to Keller. He smiled to himself. Yes, he decided, they were dancing around one another. He suspected that they would soon be dating. He was glad for that. Kaelen was a good man, a strong Christian, but it still hurt that he had not been the one to raise his daughter to be ready for such a man. She still struggled at times with her faith and her acceptance of herself. Fairley would like to have a long, hard talk with the people who had had her in their care.

Keller turned back to Kaelen, a question in her eyes. She had been puzzled by the package. Aidan had been in touch that morning. He needed to see her and asked that both Kaelen and Fairley be there. He had not indicated why or what was in the package. That had angered her. Even though she knew that she had made the right move in calling Aidan, she still felt that she should have opened the package no matter how great her fear was.

"Keller?" Fairley's voice reached through the fog that Keller seemed to be in.

Keller turned towards Fairly and then walked to him. She was frowning at him, not quite sure what he wanted.

"Dad?" She signed as he hesitated to speak. "What is it?"

"That package from last night? What was in it? You've never said." Fairley watched as Keller seemed to freeze before his hand was on her arm, giving her a gentle shake. "Keller?"

Keller stared at her father, fear rising from deep within her.

"That package? All it held as a single piece of paper." Keller still felt the intense fear that had overcome her when Aidan had approached her late the night before. She had not been prepared for what was on that piece of paper.

"A single piece of paper?" Kaelen had approached her as well, stopping short of her as her hand went up to halt his steps.

"Yes. A single piece of paper." Keller shook for a moment. "A single piece of paper that said "You're dead". Who does that?"

Kaelen and Fairley stared at her, horror on their faces. Fairley moved in on her to hug her before she moved into Kaelen's arms. They were horrified at that. Now, Kaelen decided, he would need to find a way to protect her and keep her alive.

"Keller? What else happened?" Kaelen didn't think that was all that she had faced.

Keller's anger grew as she pondered the words that Aidan had spoken to her. She had no idea who was responsible. She wanted that person. She wanted that person to tell her why. Keller also wanted that person to tell her why Kaelen had been targeted. Aidan had been frank with her that day, simply stating that it was not random that she was dropped off near his home and that she found refuge there. Whoever was behind her troubles had orchestrated that, he had no doubt about that.

"What else happened?" Keller's words were spit out at Kaelen, taking him by surprise. He had not seen her anger before but realized that she was justified in it. "Isn't it enough that someone wants me dead?"

"Keller?" Fairley's voice reached through to his daughter in the midst of the deep fog of anger. She spun to glare at him. "We will do everything that we can to keep you safe. Just how safe are you at your apartment?"

Keller sighed. Her father had gone right to the centre of what she was afraid of. She was afraid that whoever it was would come after her and someone innocent would get hurt. She spun away from the two men and stalked outside, not surprised to find Shep waiting for her. Keller reached to hug the dog, his fur soaking up the tears that she could not contain, not any longer.

Kaelen stared after her, a hand to his cheek. He wasn't sure what had just happened or what he should be doing. He had never been in such a situation before. Kaelen's head dropped as he prayed for his lady, begging God to intervene and keep her safe.

Fairley had watched with amusement as Kaelen struggled to comprehend what happened. It had not surprised him. Keller had reacted as her mother would have done. Sadness wafted through his heart for a moment before he prayed for his daughter and her knight.

"Kaelen? You're going to see emotions such as this." Fairley watched with compassion as Kaelen hesitated and then nodded.

"I get that, Fairley. I really do. I just don't have to like it." Kaelen jammed his hands into his pockets, a new habit for him. "How do we do this?"

"How do we do this? Protect her? Keep Keller safe?" At Kaelen's nod, Fairley drew in a deep breath. "It's not going to be easy. She will fight us every step of the way. Keller is finding her freedom, coming out from under the burden of the life that she had been forced to live as a child. We've talked, Keller and I have. She didn't have a pretty life. In contrast, even though you were raised in foster care, you were with only one family who raised you as if you were their very own. Keller didn't have that. She was maltreated physically and emotionally throughout her childhood and teen years. She was not free to be herself as she would have had I still had her with me. We need to pray for Keller and for you. God is the only one who can solve this and keep you both safe." Fairley had to walk away at that point, turning from the kitchen and heading for the front door. Kaelen needed time to absorb what he had said.

Chapter 22

Keller paced the grounds around her apartment. She was restless and unsettled and didn't know how to proceed with anything that she wanted to do. She could feel the chains and bonds that had held her bound for so long starting to loosen and fall away. Keller could feel the freedom that she had longed for becoming closer to her. She thanked God for that, but still was afraid to move forward. Her past life drove that fear into her.

Hearing a noise, Keller turned, a sense of fear moving across her face before she relaxed. Kaelen was walking towards her with Caleb. She had no idea what was going on but she was glad to see her fellow as she had begun to think of him. Keller moved into his hug without stopping to think about it. He made her feel cherished, something that she had never remembered feeling. God was working in her heart, releasing her to live life.

"Keller? What are you up to? Do you have time for a coffee?" Caleb grinned at her. "Cullea is waiting in my truck."

"Coffee? Did you say coffee? And a lady to talk to?" Keller broke away from Kaelen and almost ran towards the parking lot, leaving Kaelen staring after her in disbelief.

Caleb could not control his laughter. Kaelen glared at him before he shook his head and laughed as well.

"She's got you there, my friend." Caleb pointed to where they could see Cullea greeting Keller. "She needs the companionship of the ladies."

"She does. She talks to me but she needs to have that contact. With you all going through things, she can hear your stories and take from them what she needs to."

Caleb walked beside Kaelen as they walked towards the ladies. Kaelen reached for his lady, wrapping an arm around her, watching as Caleb did that to his wife.

"So, what are we doing? I think we need more than just coffee. How be we meet at Ben's?" Kaelen win't sure what the others were thinking.

"Food? You're offering food now?" Keller shoved at him, pushing him towards his truck. She could hear the laughter behind her as she did so. She smirked at Kaelen, who stared down at her for a moment before he lifted her into the truck.

"You're on a roll tonight, sweetheart. I like that." Kaelen shut the truck door on her look of surprise and then joy. He sensed that Keller had reached a point where she was not afraid to let the feelings that were being loosed free.

Ben watched the two couples and smiled. He had watched Kaelen stand off to one side as his friends had found their ladies and saw the sadness that would flicker across his face. Now, he had a lady in his life and he was glad for his young friend. Ben's attention turned to Keller. He didn't know her well but had her sing when she wasn't aware that he was around to hear

———

her. He felt that her voice was almost heavenly, if that was possible. He approached the booth where they were sitting, hearing the laughter and light conversation. Ben was glad to hear that.

"Ben? What's the special for tonight?" Keller leaned forward to look around Kaelen.

"For you? Fish and chips, I think." Ben grinned at her.

"That is exactly what I want." Keller sat back, a slight smirk on her face.

"And we will too." Caleb spoke for the other three. "It will be a change for you, Ben, us not taking what we usually do."

Ben shrugged. He usually would just bring their usual meal but tonight was not one of those nights.

Keller leaned against Kaelen as they sat and talked with Caleb and Cullea. That couple shared a look and a smile. Kaelen shifted on his seat to wrap an arm around Keller.

"Where would you go from here, Caleb?" Keller frowned at him as her thoughts darkened.

"Where would I go? That's a good question, Keller. I wouldn't run, no matter how much I felt like it. And we did feel like that many times. It won't work. They would either follow you or wait for you to return."

Cullea was nodding. Caleb and she had discussed running away many times and she knew that the others had as well.

"Caleb's correct, Keller. It doesn't work. Not unless you could completely disappear, change your appearance, your name, and everything about you. That doesn't really work." Cullea watched with compassion as Keller thought through Cullea's words.

"I get that. It still seems like a good idea." Keller looked around, feeling someone watching them. "Someone is watching us."

"I am sure that they are. They always do." Caleb looked around, seeing only people who he recognized from town in the diner. He then turned his attention to the window and searched out that way.

"Someone's out there, aren't they?" Keller was growing angry and then sighed to herself. Anger would not help the situation in any way. She felt Kaelen's arm tighten slightly around her. "So, what do we do now?"

"We continue to work through it. We have not forgotten you, Keller. We are working on your adventure as we can." Caleb was adamant about that. "And we will help to solve it."

"And you will help. That much I know." Keller sat back, exhausted. "This is tiring, you know."

"It is very exhausting." Cullea knew those feelings all too well. "You are mentally and emotionally drained. Your faith is being tested as it never has been before. I understand what you are saying, Keller. The physical effects are there as well. How did I get through it? For myself, it was reaching out to God, crying for His presence, realizing that He knew before time what I would face and had prepared for it. It was remembering that I was prayed for in the Garden by my Lord and Saviour. It was reaching out to touch the hem of that garment. He provides all healing, not just physical. It is a daily battle at times to keep going but you do." Cullea nodded at Kaelen. "He's going through similar emotions and whatever as you are. He wants to protect you but can't be with you all the time. We are praying for you both, you know that.

"And we can't thank you enough for that. Those prayers are sometimes what is keeping me going." Keller blinked, her emotions almost too much. "I am so glad that you are in my life. I never had friends. Refused to and was refused in turn. My early life did that. I escaped before I was eighteen to go to school. They tried their best to get me back but I ran. A family reached out to me. They had watched me for years and wanted to intervene but were spurned from that." Keller thought of the family who had taken her in. That family was the one who owned the music studio and had provided her with the college education that she had so desired.

Chapter 23

That night, Kaelen was unable to sleep. He had those nights when sleep fled and he was unable to find any rest. Those were the nights that he spent in prayer and meditation and then just being silent and still before his Father.

Morning found him rising from his knees where he had been for the night. He stretched and then wandered through his home. He was at a loss, he knew; just why that was, he didn't know. Kaelen reached for his phone, scrolling through his messages. There were a number that he needed to answer, but the first one that he would answer was from Keller. He then paused as he realized that he had a text from his insurance investigator. He would return that call soon.

Kaelen set his phone to one side on his desk, before burying his head in his hands. He had not expected to receive the call from the insurance company to advise him that a brand new, top of the line helicopter was waiting for him. And when questioned they had said that it was not them who had provided it. Someone who wished to remain anonymous had reached out to them. How that person had managed to find his insurance company, Kaelen didn't know. He was just grateful that he had another copter to fly. He was eager to see it and would head that way shortly.

Keller watched as Kaelen almost danced across the lawn towards her and swept her into a tight hug. She hugged him back, not sure what was up but knowing that her knight was ecstatic.

"Keller? Do you have to go in and use your singing voice today?" Kaelen leaned back to grin down at her. He refused to let go of her.

"No, actually, I'm done for the day. It was really simple today." She frowned at him. "What is going on with you?"

"I need to take you somewhere. I have something to show both of us." Kaelen shoved her into the truck and sped away from where he had found her, a wide grin on his face as he kept shaking his head at her questions.

"Kaelen? Where are we going?" Keller paled a bit as he drove up to the airport. "We're not getting kidnapped again, are we?"

"I pray not." Kaelen was out of his truck, running around to lift her down despite her protests. "I have a new helicopter waiting for me. Someone purchased it for me."

"They did? Who?" Keller glared at him as he just grinned at her. "Okay. So, this copter as you call it. Where is it?" She looked around. "I don't see it."

"This way." Kaelen reached for her hand and pulled her with him despite her protests. He slid to a stop, his mouth dropping open. His eyes were huge as he stared at the slick, green and white helicopter that sat there. He could not move for a moment. The only thing that he could do was praise God that someone had done that for him. He didn't know who but he would like the opportunity to thank that person.

"Wow!" Keller had no words other than that.

"It's beautiful." Kaelen walked towards it, his steps slow. Keller kept pace with him just because he didn't let go of her hand.

"It's gorgeous, that's what it is." Keller tugged her hand loose and watched at Kaelen spent a long time examining the outside before he reached for the door and then lifted himself up behind the controls. She watched as his head moved as he examined everything, knowing that this was a gift from God for him. Keller was well aware of how he missed his other copter.

Turning as she heard footsteps, Keller frowned at Aidan and then the man who was the owner of the airport.

"Aidan? Who did this?" Keller didn't know if he would say or not. She was content not to know.

Aidan shrugged. He had his suspicions who had but he had no confirmation of it. The airport owner did but would not say. It was not his place to do that.

Kaelen dropped down to the ground again, the door closing softly behind him. He walked towards the trio and wrapped Keller in his arms. His smile almost split his face in two, it was so wide.

"Kaelen? Is it what you were expecting?" David, the airport owner, grinned at him. He knew Kaelen's wishes for a new bird as he called it and this certainly surpassed that.

"It's a top of the line model, David. I was not expecting this. I'm almost afraid to fly it." Kaelen turned a bit to look behind him. "I'll need to reach out to the manufacturer."

"Just be here tomorrow at 10 a.m. Someone from there will be here tomorrow." David waved as he walked away, a grin on his face. Kaelen needed this, David knew. He deserved it as well.

Aidan studied the helicopter and then Kaelen. Then, he caught the look on Keller's face. He frowned. He didn't know what the look meant but he really wanted to find out.

"Keller?"

Aidan's soft question had Keller turning to him. She had an inscrutable look on her face.

"Aidan? You wanted something?"

Their conversation or what there was of it had been missed by Kaelen up to that point. He turned, a frown on his face, to watch the two facing off against each other. He looked between the two, a slight smile on his face. He wondered who would win the battle of the gazes. His bet was on Keller.

"What is it, Aidan? If you're not speaking, I have places to go and people to see." When he didn't respond, she walked away, heading for his truck. She completely forgot that he had driven them to the airport that morning.

Kaelen stared after her, his mouth opening and closing without a sound coming from him. He heard Aidan begin to laugh and spun to stare at him.

"Did Keller just do that?"

"She did. And you drove here this morning. You'll need to give her a ride home. When you've finished admiring your new ride." Aidan continued to grin at his friend.

Kaelen shook his head, still in disbelief that Keller had done that. He would have to have a talk with her, he decided.

"Yeah, I'm ready to go." Kaelen took one more walk around his new helicopter, thanking God that someone had thought of him before he headed for his truck.

———

Chapter 24

The next morning, Kaelen lifted off in his new helicopter. He was so happy, he decided, being able to fly again. He had already been up with the manufacturing representative, who had simply shaken his head when Kaelen asked who had gifted him the helicopter.

Keller sat next to him, not sure that she should be there. She had known that someone had followed them that morning. She had seen the shadowy figure watching them closely. Keller didn't have the heart to Kaelen that. She had sent a text off to Aidan who had not responded.

"You don't like this much, do you?" Keller grinned as she teased Kaelen.

"I do. This is so wonderful. I just wish that I knew who had done this." Kaelen searched around him, his smile still on his face.

"The Barnabas Foundation." Keller was certain about that. She shrugged as he stared at her. "It's possible that they did. It's what they do."

"I have heard that." Kaelen was lost in thought for a moment. "Keller? What are your thoughts about what it going on?"

"My thoughts? I have no idea. I am at a loss." Keller shook her head. "We were followed this morning. I sent off a text to Aidan but haven't heard from him."

"We were? I wondered if there was someone out there." Kaelen headed back for the airport, needing to head for a meeting. "Aidan's in court this morning."

"He is? That explains why he didn't answer." Keller jumped down to the ground and then stood waiting for Kaelen to finish what he had to do post-flight. She was surprised when the mechanic appeared and helped Kaelen move the helicopter into a hanger. She shrugged, not really concerned or interested in what was happening.

Kaelen walked back towards Keller, his eyes searching around them. He could feel that someone was out there, someone out there watching them, and someone out there wanting to bring harm to them. All he could do was pray for them. Kaelen reached for Keller's hand, drawing her closer to him and then heading for his truck. Tucking her inside, he watched for a moment, seeing the discomfort and fear that she was showing him. He knew that was not her, that she didn't show her emotions like that. Hiding her emotions had been beaten into her when she was young. Kaelen could only thank God that she felt comfortable enough to share those very emotions with him.

"Kaelen? Where are we going?" Keller had to speak up. She could see that they were not heading back into their town.

"I'm heading for a small town called Elmton. We need to get away for the day. I can do what I need to at the office tonight." He grinned at her for a moment before he sobered. "That is, if you're okay with this."

"I am. Thank you. But are we safe enough?" Keller was twisting slightly in her seat, watching outside for anyone who meant them harm.

"We can't hide, Keller. We need to live our lives. I want to date you. And I don't date. I never have. You're the special lady I was waiting for." Kaelen reached a hand to touch her face before his attention was back to the traffic around them. He frowned as he saw a car keeping pace with his truck and then nodded. He had company but that company was of the right sort.

Late that evening, Keller moved through her home. She was happy and content. The day had been a blessing for them both, she knew, an enjoyable day that was only the first of many to follow. She found her favourite chair and curled up in it. Her thoughts turned to prayer and Keller begged God to protect Kaelen and herself and that whatever this was that they were involved in would be solved and solved quickly.

Kaelen looked up from his desk work at last. He frowned at the clock and sighed. It was early morning and he needed to be up early. He had a flight to take that morning to a conference. He sighed and then headed for his bed.

Two days later, Kaelen walked back into his house, dropping his bag in his bedroom and then heading for the kitchen. A pot of coffee was set to drip and he turned then to open the backyard and stepped out onto the deck. His eyes closed as he drew in a deep breath of fresh air and then opened them. Kaelen nodded. Caleb had been around, he thought, tidying up the yard for him. He was grateful for that. He had good friends and tried to be that in return.

Retrieving his mug of coffee, Kaelen headed back outside. He had been indoors for the last couple of days and needed that time outside with his Heavenly Father. That was a given, he knew. His head bowed as he waited silently for the peace that always came and this time was no different.

Keller turned from her living room window. She was afraid and could not tell why. She was alone and hated that. She wanted to be with Kaelen but didn't know if he was even home as of yet. The chiming of her phone startled her and caused her to spin, a hand covering her mouth to stifle her scream. Keller crept towards her phone on the coffee table and sat, staring at it. A quick movement with a finger woke it up and then she reached to pull up her text messages. Keller was almost afraid to do that. There had been far too many text messages that were threatening in nature. Her face softened as she read the text from Kaelen. He simply said that he loved her and would she go out for dinner with him tomorrow? Her fingers flew over the keyboard as she responded, telling him that she loved him too and yes, she would be happy to go out for a meal with him.

The men watching both houses were frustrated. They needed to take those two into their custody again and it wasn't happening. There had just not been an opportunity to do so. Someone was standing in their way and frustrating them in their evil task. Night dropped down on them as they headed away from the houses.

Daylight found Kaelen on his feet and heading through his house, his steps measured and determined. Something seemed off to him in there. He then headed outside, searching around the house and then heading through the yard. He stopped near the bushes where he had found Keller and sighed. There was something there and he disliked that immensely. His phone was out as he placed a call to Aidan, leaving a voice mail for Aidan to call him. He had found one of those unwanted packages.

Chapter 25

Dropping to his hands and knees, Kaelen tried had to remember to breathe. Only, that task was very difficult. He wanted to reach for his ribs, to cradle them to help ease his breathing difficulties. That couldn't happen. Someone was holding him in the position that he was. Kaelen could not move. His body collapsed at last, to land him in a sprawled heap. Kaelen didn't move from the concrete floor of the hangar. He didn't hear the door slam shut behind his assailants.

His whistle ringing through the air, David headed for the airport business office. He saw Kaelen's truck in the lot and shrugged. He must have had an early flight. Setting his travel coffee mug on the desk before he headed for the work room. He looked over the lists of scheduled flights and frowned. Kaelen didn't have a flight that had been scheduled. Sudden fear had David running for the stairs and then heading for the hangars. He ran through them, heading for the one that Kaelen used. The keys shook in his hand as he tried to insert them into the lock, not succeeding at first. He reached for the light switches and flipped them to the on position, their light shining through the hangar. The light didn't illuminate the far reaches of the building and that frustrated David.

David walked rapidly around the building and then approached the helicopter. He frowned down at the floor before he stopped and touched a rusty spot on the floor. He raised himself back up, staring at his finger before he gave a yell and then was running back for his office. That was blood on the floor, and that blood could only have come from Kaelen. Where was his friend, he pondered, even as he reached for the office phone and made the call that would bring the authorities to help.

Leaning against a patrol vehicle, David's hands jammed into his trousers' pockets. He watched the activity around the hangar before he turned his head slightly to find Aidan standing nearby.

"Aidan? What can you tell me? I have to put out some sort of message." David was frustrated at the situation as well as being very worried.

"I know, David. Kaelen isn't there. We have found a trail that he left as he walked out of the hangar. Unfortunately, it's disappeared. We're bringing in a K-9 unit to search." Aidan was deeply worried about his friend. He had received word from the street that Kaelen was to disappear that day. He had prayed for Kaelen as he had risen and started his day. Aidan had expected that phone call that Kaelen was missing but not that he had been hurt.

Keller walked slowly towards Aidan, who had turned as he heard a vehicle. Her eyes were on the hangar before she stopped and then dropped to her knees, her face buried in her hands. Aidan ran towards her, lifting her to her feet and then turning her back to her car.

"Aidan? Kaelen? Where is he?" Keller kept trying to turn back towards the hangar.

"He's missing, Keller. We have evidence that he was here early this morning. He's not here now." Aidan tried to watch her and monitor the activity at the hangar.

"They've taken him? He was to call me an hour ago and didn't. That's not like him." Keller tried to control her emotions. To lose Kaelen like this? It just brought back all the memories of loss that she had dealt with all her life.

"We don't know, Keller. There is nothing on the video feed to show that. It looks as if he just walked away." Aidan beckoned a female officer over to stand with her as he turned back to the investigation.

Keller drew in a quivering breath before she looked around. Kaelen wasn't here, of that she was sure. Feeling her phone vibrate in her pocket, she reached for it, frowning at the message that was shown. She frowned harder as she tried to figure out the cryptic message before she was behind the wheel of her car and driving away. The female officer stared in disbelief before she heard Aidan beside her.

"What happened?" Aidan stared at the small amount of dust that lingered in the air.

"I don't know, Aidan. She got a text message or something and then drove off. I'm sorry. I didn't expect her to do that." The officer was disturbed that she had let this happen.

"It's okay, Bev. You couldn't stop her. I'll track her down later and find out what is going on. For now, how be you head back to your patrol?" Aidan stood and stared at the entrance to the airport property. He was puzzled by what had happened. He had no idea where Kaelen was. The arrival of the K-9 officer and her Malinois drew his attention before he walked that way.

"Aidan? I heard that it was Kaelen?" Joyce was a friend from church.

"It is. We think that he was attacked in the hangar but he disappeared from there. He's injured to some degree. We just don't know how much." Aidan walked back towards the hangar, the dog handler keeping pace with him.

"I see. Okay. Sage and I will see what we can find out for you." Joyce walked away, her dog already in work mode.

Aidan watched them before he turned away. He had done what he could for now at this crime scene and needed to be on another. He sighed. There was just too much crime, he decided. He had no idea why but all he knew was that all the investigators were overwhelmed with work.

Keller pulled into a nearby parking lot, pulling out her phone. She re-read the text message, frowning once more as she did. It was cryptic, she knew. It said it came from Kaelen's phone but it didn't sound like him. She waited as she was asked to, watching around her for any danger.

A tap at the passenger's window had her jumping and giving a small scream. She stared at the man who was bent over and staring in at her. She lowered the window somewhat and waited, fear showing on her face.

"Keller? You don't know me very well, I get that." Andrew Phelps was from their church and in a Bible study group for young adults.

"What do you want? I got a message from Kaelen's phone." She scowled at him. "Was that you?"

"It was. I found Kaelen wandering down the road. He's been hurt, Keller, and is asking for you. He is refusing to go to the hospital. I have assessed him and he needs to be there. Maybe you can persuade him." Andrew was a paramedic by trade. He waited as Keller thought his words and then unlocked the door.

"Where is he?" Keller refused to drive away, her attention totally on Andrew as she waited for him to speak.

"At my cabin. You know that I live just outside of town. At least, I pray that he still is. He kept wanting to leave." Andrew settled back on the seat, the seatbelt fastened around him.

Keller drove the circuitous route that Andrew demanded her to follow. She didn't like it. She wanted to find Kaelen and felt that Andrew was preventing that. Keller finally pulled to the side of a street and shifted in her seat to stare intently at Andrew. He stared back just as intently.

"Just where are we going, Andrew?" Keller's words were spit at him.

Andrew gave a grim smile. He had been watching around as they traveled and finally felt that they had ditched the car that was tailing them.

"We had someone following us, Keller. That's why we've been driving like this." Andrew's body was moving as he looked around the car. "We're okay to leave. Do you know where I live?"

"No, I don't. I've never been there. How would I know that?" Keller spit her words out at him, angry that she was being followed and also angry that Andrew would not let her see Kaelen.

"Okay, Keller. Draw in the claws. We can head that way now." Andrew hesitated. "Will you let me drive?"

Keller stared at him in shock for a moment before she nodded. She slipped from behind the wheel and headed for the passenger's seat. Safely buckled in once more, Keller watched as Andrew drove off, heading in a direction that she had not expected.

"Andrew?   Just where do you think you are heading?"

"Towards my home, Keller. We'll be there is five minutes. Just pray that Kaelen has stayed put. He was threatening to walk away and find you. He's hurt, Keller, and hurt bad. He needs to be at the hospital but he won't go. He's worrying about you. And that makes it dangerous for him. He'll go looking for you." Andrew spared her a comforting smile. "He's in love with you, Keller. I don't know if you are aware of that."

Keller sat back. She was not aware that Kaelen's interest in her was that apparent. They had talked, those two, and acknowledged that they did indeed love one another. They were taking it slow, just because of what Keller had been through. She was grateful for that. They were praying through their relationship, wanting to only move forward as God willed. He had to be the centre of it all. They both agreed on that.

"I know he does. We've talked, Andrew." She looked bleak, worry uppermost in her mind. "How badly is he hurt?"

"He's been beaten, Keller. He's having trouble breathing. He could have a pneumothorax, you know, a punctured lung."

"And it could just be bruising." Keller bit at her lip. "Who is doing this? And how do we find them?"

"We'll look into it, Keller. I have a cousin who can help. He's a private investigator. In fact, I would not be surprised if he hasn't already done so. Mac is like that."

"Mac? As in Mac Phelps? I've spoken with him about other things. I was trying to find my family. Now, Dad is back in my life. Mac said that he would look into how I was taken from Dad."

"I had heard that your dad was back in your life." Andrew slowed the car and turned into a laneway that didn't seem to be there. He grinned at Keller's comment that she would never had found it. "I like this. It is difficult sometimes when we have heavy snow. It's my sanctuary."

"I can see that." Keller watched with interest as the lane led to a comfortable looking small home centred in a large clearing. "This is nice, Andrew."

"Thank you." Andrew's hand on her arm kept Keller in her seat. "Let me pray for you, Keller. This is not over for you or Kaelen. It will only get worse. You need the comfort of our prayers." Andrew was as good as his word. Once he was finished, he was out of the car and around to open the door for her. He pointed towards the door and rushed her that way. Andrew didn't think that he had been followed but he was not taking any chances on that.

Keller stepped inside the house, standing still for a moment as she studied Andrew's home. She liked it. It was a haven after all. She turned to Andrew, finding him watching her closely. He had shut and locked the door behind them.

"Andrew? Where's Kaelen?" Keller was desperate to find him. She could feel the vibrating of her phone in her pocket. She thought it was likely

Aidan and didn't really want to speak with him at the moment.

"This way." Andrew kicked off his shoes, watching as Keller did the same. "I'm not sure that he's awake, Keller. He was beaten by the looks of it. When I asked him, he didn't know or didn't want to say. He'll need to heal."

"Beaten?" Keller had trouble controlling her emotions. She stood in the doorway of the bedroom, her eyes on Andrew for a moment before they dropped to the bed. She was across the room and on her knees. Her hand reached for the on that lay on Kaelen's chest.

Kaelen jumped as he felt someone touch him. That person didn't mean him harm, he decided, and then slept once more. He needed that, he decided. He just didn't have any idea why he hurt or where he was.

Keller stayed on her knees for what seemed hours. Andrew approached at last, drawing her to her feet and then out to the living room. He smiled sadly at her reluctance to leave Kaelen.

"You need to eat, Keller, whether you want to or not. Kaelen would want you to." Andrew set a tray on the low table near a chair. "I have to head in to work. My phone number is on the tray. Call me if you need anything."

Andrew walked away to head for his shift, not wanting to but knowing that he had to. He stared back at his home for a moment before he drove away. He trusted God to take care of these two.

Keller rose at last, the tray in her hands, and headed for the kitchen. She washed the dishes and then stood for a moment, uncertain as to what she should be doing. Her eyes raised to the ceiling as she prayed before she was walking towards the bedroom. Keller stood watching Kaelen, who had managed to turn onto a side.

Keller was on the floor, her head cradled on her arm as her other hand reached for Kaelen's. His tightened on her as he roused slightly. Keller slept, her fatigue not letting her do anything else. Worry had been keeping her away and that had led to the bone-deep fatigue that dogged her every day.

Chapter 27

Keller roused late that afternoon. Her eyes were on Kaelen, who still slept. She frowned. He didn't seem to be in pain but that was likely not the case. On her feet, she raised Kaelen's head enough so that he could sip at the glass of water. A soft thank-you came from him.

Walking through the house, Keller made her way to the kitchen. She squinted at the clock and nodded. It would soon be suppertime and she was hungry for a change. She didn't think that Andrew would mind if she helped herself to food.

A bowl of soup was placed on a tray along with a bottle of juice. Keller hesitated for a moment before she sighed. She headed for Kaelen, rousing him enough to sit up against a pile of pillows that she stuffed behind him.

Kaelen stared at her through blurry eyes. He frowned. He should know this lady but he wasn't sure who she was. He nodded as she helped him to eat some of the soup and then drink from the juice bottle before she was removing the pillows and then helping him to rise from the bed and to the washroom.

Keller walked away, knowing that Kaelen was hurting. Her phone had kept vibrating, much to her frustration. She pulled out the phone and frowned at it. She really didn't want to look at any of her messages. Keller was hiding and she knew that wasn't likely a smart move on her part.

Working through her messages, Keller paused at the last one from Aidan. He simply asked if she was safe and would she contact him at some point? He needed to talk with her. If she was in hiding, he was okay with that. More than likely, he noted, she was smart to do that.

Sighing, Keller's fingers moved across the keyboard. She let Aidan know that she was in fact hiding and that Kaelen was with her. No, she would not tell him where they were. That she was adamant about. She tucked her phone away, not answering his responding text.

Aidan stared across the room, not taking in the certificates hanging on his office wall. He was frustrated, to say the least. He had not been able to find Kaelen. Joyce and Sage had tracked him to the road but then lost his scent. That had not helped the investigation at all. Now, to have Keller tell him that she was with Kaelen and that they were hiding? That worried him even though he was glad that they were hiding. Aidan paused for a moment before he nodded. Someone was helping them. He would try contacting Keller later. He just wasn't sure that she would respond.

Andrew stepped quietly into his home that evening, a frown on his face. There were lights on but not too many. He nodded. Kaelen was taking it carefully, he could see, despite the fact that his home was hidden. He dropped his bag in his bedroom and then walked through the house, looking for Keller. Andrew paused in the bedroom doorway, a smile crossing his face. Keller had moved in a chair from the living room. She was curled up, covered with a blanket and with a pillow tucked under her face, and was sound asleep. His eyes turned to Kaelen, finding that man starting to rouse.

Kaelen's eyes cracked open, not sure where he was. He hurt all over and his head was aching in the worst way that he thought he had ever experienced. He frowned as he saw Andrew.

"Andrew? Where am I?" His voice was hoarse from disuse.

"At my place." Andrew walked closer to the bed. "Feel like getting cleaned up?"

"That would be nice." Kaelen shifted on the bed, sitting for a moment on the side of it. He started as he saw the bed and then Keller. "Keller?"

"Keller. She won't leave your side." Andrew helped Kaelen to his feet, holding him upright until he felt steadier. "I'll lend you some clean clothes, Kaelen. Then we need to talk."

Andrew waited for Kaelen to finish. He studied the other man as he opened the bathroom door and shuffled out.

"Here, Kaelen. Sit in the living room. I'll find something for you." Andrew was as good as his word, setting a tray down near the other man. "Eat, Kaelen. Then we need to talk. And talk before Keller comes out."

Kaelen nodded, knowing that Andrew was correct. He didn't know the other man that well but well enough to trust him. He finally shoved the tray aside, keeping his mug of coffee in his hand.

"Talk to me, Andrew. What happened?"

"What happened? You were beaten, I think, in your hangar. Somehow, you managed to reach the road. I happened to be driving by and found you. When I got you into my truck, you were adamant that you would not go to the hospital and asked that I help you. You were very worried about Keller but couldn't tell me why. I found her at last. Jimmy drove me to town without asking why. He doesn't know that you are here. Keller was reluctant to come here but she did. She's been looking after you for the day." Andrew paused, not sure how to continue. "You need to be see by a physician, Kaelen."

Kaelen was shaking his head. He tilted his head at one point and then held out a hand for Keller. She was beside him and tucked under that arm before Andrew even realized that she had appeared.

"Not happening, Andrew. I'll be fine. I've been hurt worse playing sports." Kaelen's eyes closed for a moment as he sought the peace that only comes from his Heavenly Father. "What now?"

"What now? We need to get you two home at some point. And you do need to speak with Aidan." Andrew was adamant about that.

Kaelen nodded. He was well aware that he had to. He just didn't want to. His head bent as he studied the lady who he was holding. Kaelen didn't know where they were heading as a couple. All he knew was that he had finally acknowledged that he loved her, even on such short acquaintance. He didn't know how Keller felt about marrying him and that was the only thing that he wanted.

Keller watched the two men. She felt safe for the moment but knew that would change as soon as they walked away from Andrew. She could feel Kaelen's arm tight around her and felt secure and cherished by his actions.

"Kaelen? What do you remember?" Keller spoke at last, wanting to understand what had happened that morning.

Kaelen shrugged. He had no memories about what happened. He could only remember the evening before. He stated as much, his eyes on Andrew as he said that.

Andrew nodded. It was about what he had expected. He looked at Keller, finding her with her phone out and studying a message.

"Keller?"

Andrew's voice started Keller for a moment. She sighed. Aidan was becoming more vocal in wanting to speak with her. Did she even understand that she was in danger, he asked? And with Kaelen missing, he was deeply worried about her.

Chapter 28

Aidan dropped down into his desk chair, his phone hitting the desk top, before he sighed. It had been a long, tiring day with little accomplished. He was worried about Kaelen, not knowing where he was. Keller had finally responded that she was safe and so was Kaelen. They were with a friend. Yes, she admitted, Kaelen was hurt but he refused to come to the hospital. When it was safe, Keller stated, they would find him.

He didn't like that, Aidan decided. He just didn't know where to find them. That bothered him. The rumblings on the street were getting wilder, he knew, with information reaching him that both Keller and Kaelen were targets for murder. He couldn't protect them if he didn't know where they were. All Aidan could do at the moment was pray for them.

Toryn paused as he passed Aidan's office, watching the young detective closely. He entered the office and dropped into a chair across from Aidan, finding Aidan watching him.

"Aidan? What word do you have?" Toryn waited patiently for Aidan to gather his thoughts. He knew that Aidan had been out and about all that day on crime scenes.

"Not a lot. Keller is with Kaelen. She's just not saying where they are." Aidan sat back in his chair, a hand rubbing at his face.

"She is? And no, she won't. She's very protective of him, I can see. It comes from what she went through in foster care. Does Fairley know where she is?"

"No, I asked him. He hasn't heard from her today but that's not unusual, he said. She doesn't always contact him every day. She's still working through that relationship and what happened to her." Aidan blew out a breath. "I wish I could understand why."

"We all do, Aidan. God is in control of all of it. We'll find the information we need as we need it. Unfortunately, it doesn't make it any easier to walk forward. We can only pray for them. Make sure you take some time off. You're burning out." Toryn walked away, intent on finding Lyle and having him make Aidan take a few days off. The young detective needed it.

Aidan paced through his home late that night. He had looked at Lyle as his supervisor had sent him home and told him that he was not to work for the next week. He needed that break. Aidan had protested but Lyle had been adamant. Aidan was burning out, Lyle said, and had not had a vacation in a bit. He needed to do that to stay fresh and alert.

Reaching for his phone as it chimed, Aidan sighed. It was Keller. She wanted to talk but not in person. Could they do that? Aidan could only agree to that. He turned as he felt a hand on his back and wrapped his wife in his arms. Artis had found him, coming in from a late meeting.

"Aidan? You're troubled." Artis simply kept hugging her husband, trying to help relieve his worry.

"I am. Keller wants to talk but not in person. I'm not sure how to do this. Lyle made me take the next week off." Aidan was troubled by that.

"Then, that's what you do. We need this, Aidan. Let's find that cabin in the woods for a few days. If you don't get away, you'll want to work." Artis reached for her phone, sending off a quick message to a friend who had that cabin. The response came back quickly. The cabin was theirs for however long they wanted it for. The keys would be dropped off in the morning for them. They just needed to collect their clothes and food.

"How is Keller?" Artis had left and then returned with mugs of coffee and a plate of treats.

"I have no idea. She's not at home. Whenever she is, she's with Kaelen. And Kaelen is hurt. I just don't know how badly." Aidan was distraught at that. He turned to Artis, finding her handing him his Bible. "You're right. We do need this."

Keller set her phone aside. Kaelen had been sent back to bed, despite his protests. Andrew had retired as well, having an early shift in the morning. That left Keller on her own with her thoughts. They were black, she decided, and that would not do at all. Reaching for her phone again, she sent a message to her father, who quickly replied that he loved her and what could he do for her. Keller was hesitant to respond and then sent him details of what had happened that day.

———

Fairley set aside his phone at last. The text messages with Keller had ceased at last. He could only pray for his daughter. She had refused to say where she was, other than she was with a friend and Kaelen was there as well. He knew that Kaelen had gone missing. Aidan had reached out to him. He sighed. This is not what he wanted for his daughter.

Keller finally curled up on the couch, pulling a blanket over her. Andrew had told her to use the other bedroom. She had nodded but felt too afraid to do so. She wanted to be where she could watch for Kaelen. Keller was too afraid to let him out of her sight. He might just disappear again or worse, die. She didn't know if she could continue to live if that happened.

Andrew was up early the next morning. He checked on Kaelen, finding him in a deep sleep. He nodded. Kaelen needed that. His steps paused as he saw that Keller was still curled up on the couch. He gave a sad smile.

Keller was on her feet not that long after Andrew had driven away. She was terrified, she decided. She paced the house, moving from window to window, studying the area. Hearing footsteps behind her, Keller spun to find Kaelen standing nearby. He looked somewhat more alert that morning. She moved towards him and found herself wrapped in his arms.

"Keller? What are you thinking?" Kaelen spoke at last.

"I think that we need to leave here, Kaelen. I am sure that whoever is after you will start searching for us. Where can we go?" Keller was reluctant to move away from Kaelen, finding his arms were comforting for her.

"Then, that's what we do. Any thoughts on where to go?" Kaelen waited patiently for Keller to speak.

"I have no idea, Kaelen. We can't keep running on our own. It's not right." Keller moved away from him, not seeing the look of distress that flickered across his face.

Kaelen watched her for a moment before he approached her. His hands raised and his fists opened and closed before his hands rested gently on her shoulders.

"Keller, I have a suggestion. We'll need to pray it over. Marry me. That way, we can stay together and more around as we need to. It's not how I should propose to you. I love you. I want you in my life forever." Kaelen felt Keller stiffen and removed his hands, ready to walk away.

Keller turned to him, a hand out to stop him.

"Do you mean that, Kaelen? Do you really love me?" At his nod, Keller had to blink back her tears. "Do you know how much I prayed for some man to tell me that? That is part of what has kept me going. I love you too. And yes, I will do that." She began to weep and found Kaelen had gathered her close. "I need my Dad."

"And we will find him. Do we have transportation?" He wasn't sure that they had a vehicle with them.

"We do. Andrew drove me out in my car." Keller reached for his hand and ran for her car, heading off towards her father, knowing that Kaelen was watching for anyone who meant them harm.

———

Chapter 29

Fairley watched his daughter as she moved around his kitchen, preparing a meal for herself and Kaelen. Something had changed with them, he could tell. He just didn't know what. He turned to find Kaelen standing beside him, swaying slightly as the pain was rising once more.

"Kaelen. Sit. If you don't, we'll be picking you up off the floor. And I have no desire to do that." Fairley shoved Kaelen into a chair, wincing along with Kaelen as the pain hit harder for a moment. "Here. Take these. It's only over the counter but it will help." He handed him the medication. He then turned to walk towards Keller. "Keller?"

Keller's hand stopped in the task that she was involved in. She blinked for a moment before she nodded. She did need to speak with him.

"Dad? We do need to talk. Kaelen and I have come to a decision." She looked towards Kaelen, finding him on his feet and then wrapping her in his arms.

"What Keller is trying to say and not saying is that we love each other. We have decided that we want to marry and marry now." Kaelen waited patiently as Keller wiped at the tears on her face and for Fairley to speak.

Fairley stared at them before he nodded. He had expected this but not so quickly. He reached to hug his daughter, holding on to her and grieving that her mother was not there to see her as a beautiful young lady who was starting off on a new adventure or to meet the young man who loved her daughter that much.

"When?" Fairley moved the younger couple to the table and then set their meal in front of them. He reached to refill his coffee mug and sat as well, his hand out to grasp his daughter's hand.

"Now, Dad. I don't want a big wedding. Just you and maybe a few friends." Keller sighed. "And how do we decide what friends? Kaelen has so many."

"I do, but I would suggest Don's team and their spouses. Aidan and Artis if they're around. Toryn and Slaney. They're your friends as well, sweetheart." Kaelen didn't look up at that, missing the look on Keller's face. She was devastated at not having friends of her own from her early life.

"It's okay, Kaelen. They are friends." Keller was on her feet, hunting for a pad of paper and pen and back in her seat. "We need to make some plans."

"We do. First, we eat. Then we'll pray." Kaelen reached for a piece of toast and bit into it, his eyes daring Keller to do anything different.

Keller saw the challenge that he was subtly sending her way. She took him up on that and reached for her own fork. Fairley watched them, a look of amusement in his eyes as he bit back his smile.

Fairley cleared away the remnants of the meal and then sat once more, bowing his head to pray for his daughter and her knight. They were not done with their adventure, not as yet. He feared that by them taking this step it would bring more danger to them.

"What are your plans, then?" Fairley watched as Keller's pen tapped at the pad of paper. "Keller?"

"Dad, how do we do this? I have never been to a wedding before." Keller blinked before she reached for her phone. She frowned at it. "Aidan's away for a week, he tells me. Kaelen, what did he tell you?"

Kaelen reached for his phone and pulled up the same message.

"The same as you. It sounds as if he was kicked out of the office for a week. He needs that." Kaelen paused, deep in thought. "Okay. You need to find a dress, Keller. And I will look after any flowers we need. Ben will cater for us. He's likely already planning that." Kaelen sent off a quick text to Ben, receiving confirmation that he indeed was planning that. He just needed a date. "When?"

"Give yourselves a few days to enjoy being engaged, as difficult as it is at the moment. I would suggest a week or ten days at the most." Fairley was watching the young couple and saw the little bit of relief that they showed. "You need to grow accustomed to the thought of living with one another for the rest of your lives."

Keller was nodding before she reached to hug her father. Her emotions were in a turmoil. She walked away, trying to decide who she could ask to help her. She didn't want to do this on her own. Her phone vibrated as someone sent a text message. Keller pulled out her phone, staring in disbelief at the message that Cullea had sent. She walked away to find privacy to call Cullea back.

"Cullea? It's Keller. I just got your message. What did you mean?" Keller curled up in a chair in the living room. She could see Kaelen from where she sat.

"Keller? Are you two safe? I just had a feeling that you were planning something. Kaelen proposed?" Cullea made a face at Caleb as he shook a finger at her.

"He did. This morning. He was hurt yesterday, Cullea. I don't know if you were aware of that. He was beaten in his hangar." She heard Cullea's confirmation of that. "He wants to marry me and marry me soon. I'm so torn."

Cullea simply prayed for her friend, Caleb praying as well. He was on his feet, heading for the office to call Don.

"Don? Kaelen's safe. He's with Keller. I suspect that they're at Fairley's place now."

"They are? That's good. Okay. Aidan is away for the next few days. We'll need to step in. How do we do this?"

"I'll head Fairley's way. The thing of it is? Kaelen proposed. They're planning on getting married. Cullea's on the phone with Keller right now." Caleb heard the deep sigh that sounded through the phone.

"He just had to do that, didn't he?" Don was pacing, Delanie watching him closely, waiting for him to explain his frustration. "Okay. Cullea and who else?"

"I would suggest Delanie. All the ladies will want to be involved, but we need a couple just to be the contacts for Keller. She's likely feeling overwhelmed. Without her mom, she'll be at a loss." Caleb was thinking through the possibilities.

"I think that you're right. You're heading for Fairley?" Don had no doubt that Caleb and Cullea would do that. "I don't want too many of us heading that way. He'll be watched." Don paused for a moment, to pray for his friends.

"I thought that as well. I'll drop by later to update you." Caleb walked back through the house, to find his wife in tears. He simply hugged her and then moved her out to his truck. He headed for Fairley, watching for anyone following them.

Chapter 30

Toryn walked towards Fairley's home. He had parked near the laneway before he had stepped down from his truck. Slaney was beside him, her hand in his. Fairley's request had been that he and Slaney come to see him. That had struck him as odd. Slaney had just shrugged.

Fairley was waiting for them, the cabin door closed behind him. He nodded at Toryn's questioning look.

"They're here, Toryn. You'll need to talk with them, I know. Slaney? They're engaged. Cullea and Caleb are here but I'm sure your input would be very welcome. My daughter doesn't have her own mom to help. I would appreciate it if some of you ladies would step in. Cullea said that Delanie is on board to help. The thing is that they want to marry within a week to ten days."

Toryn's steps slowed before he nodded and he walked past Fairley to enter the cabin. Slaney stayed with Fairley, her soft questions taking his attention away from the couple inside. Toryn stopped for a moment before his feet carried him forward. He pulled out a chair and sat, seeing that the couple knew that he was there but not taking their eyes from one another. He gave a grim smile.

"Okay, you two. Talk to me. Tell me what happened." Toryn's voice was stern as he spoke to them.

Keller and Kaelen did just that. Toryn asked the questions that he needed to. He shook his head. This was not what he had wanted to hear but what they had expected to hear. Kaelen could not identify the men. He had been struck from behind and from what he could remember, the men were wearing masks. Toryn didn't ask who had taken Keller to Kaelen. All he could get from her was that it was a friend.

On his feet, he drew Kaelen with him towards where Caleb was waiting outside. Cullea and Slaney moved in on Keller, hugging her and then praying with her before they began their plans. Keller didn't know exactly what she wanted other than something very simple. They could that, they informed her. And they would take her dress shopping on the morrow if she liked. Keller had stared at them before she shook her head, tears in her eyes. She had not expected that but she should have realized.

"Toryn?" Caleb's voice broke into the police chief's thoughts. "What are you thinking?"

"That this is far from over and that we are no further ahead in knowing who it is." Toryn was frustrated. Aidan was not here and needed to be. He would talk with Lyle the next day.

"I know. We need to keep them safe. We just don't know who to protect them from." Caleb watched Kaelen, seeing the fatigue and pain on his face. "Kaelen, you need to be sitting down. Or else I'll bundle you into my truck and take you to the hospital."

Kaelen nodded. He knew that he needed to see a physician and had reached out to his family physician and would see him on the next day. Keller was adamant about going with him. He had smiled at her and then hugged her, a kiss to her temple delivered at the same time.

"I see my GP tomorrow, Caleb. I won't go to the hospital unless I have to. That's where they'll look for me." Kaelen sank into one of the chairs on the front porch. "What are your thoughts?"

"I don't know, Kaelen. Caleb said that Don is on his way." Toryn perched on the porch rail, staring at Kaelen. "We're not getting any sense as to why. And we should be."

"We should be. I don't know why." Kaelen sighed. "I wonder if I saw something one day that I was out on a flight and didn't realize it. That's the only thing that makes sense."

"It is. We thought about that, Kaelen." Caleb and his team had been brainstorming and had come to that conclusion. "Unfortunately, we would have no idea what or where."

"No, we don't." Kaelen drew in a deep breath. "I wonder if it was that clearing where I crashed."

Caleb was nodding. That was the conclusion the team had come to.

"That's what we think, Kaelen. Do you have any photos from there that you can think of?" Caleb was grasping at straws at that point.

"I might have. I would have to go through the files on my backup." Kaelen sighed. He was exhausted and only wanted to crawl into bed at that point.

Caleb and Toryn shared a look before they reached to draw Kaelen to his feet and then into the cabin. Fairley pointed to a bedroom and followed the three men. Kaelen gratefully crawled under a blanket and slept, pain evident on his face.

Keller had stood and watched her fellow as he had stumbled to the bedroom, a hand on her throat. Slaney's arm was around her to support her before she walked away, her emotions taking too much from her for the moment.

Fairley walked to his daughter and held her as she sobbed. Her emotions had reached the breaking point and she could do nothing but weep. The others in the cabin watched with compassion before they moved to other tasks. Fairley finally swept his daughter into his arms and carried her to his bedroom. He tucked her into bed, a kiss on her head just as he had done when she was a baby. He walked away, in tears himself. The couple didn't need this, he decided. A look of determination took the place of his tears as he sought to find Caleb and Don who had now appeared.

"Fellows? What do we know? And how do we end this? Keller has had enough. And so has Kaelen." Fairley was distraught but also determined to solve this for his daughter.

"We don't know a lot, Fairley. We have reached out to friends but they're not finding much either, which is very unusual for them." Don was frustrated as well. "We're working this as we can. Kaelen has been too much of a friend to us." He studied the older man. "Just how are you coping? Do we need to find someone for you to talk with?"

Fairley shook his head. He appreciated the concern from the younger men. He had been meeting with Gideon on a weekly basis for months now and that was helping. He could not explain how it was helping but God knew that it was. God was working in his life, drawing him closer to Him.

Chapter 31

A week later, no one was any closer to solving Kaelen's assault. He was healing but the emotional and mental trauma still weighed on him. He had prayed for the burden to be removed. That had not happened. He had then prayed for peace in the situation.

He turned that afternoon to Keller. They were meeting with Gideon in an hour just to finish off their plans. They were determined not to let anyone stop them but that possibility was always in the back of their minds.

Keller was hesitant to move forward with their plans to some degree. She was deeply afraid that she was bringing danger to him but he had simply shaken his head. It could be the other way around, they knew.

The next day would be their wedding. Fairley had questioned them about it but they had shrugged. Richard, another friend who had a security team, had assured them that they would keep it as safe as they could. Even though Richard and his team were guests, they would be on watch for them. Don and his would be inside as guests. Kaelen knew that team and could not express his thanks enough.

The next afternoon, Keller studied herself in the floor-length mirror at Don's home. He had opened up his home for them to have their wedding, simply stating that was what he and Delanie wanted to do for them. She had hugged him before she had had to walk away.

She didn't recognize herself. The ladies had found a beautiful inexpensive dress for her. Slaney had insisted that she would look after Keller's hair and what little makeup that she wanted. Keller reached for the bouquet of yellow roses, a soft smile on her face. Kaelen had discovered that those were her favourite roses. She saw the few daisies that were mixed in the bouquet. He was so thoughtful, she decided.

Kaelen walked through the backyard of his home late that evening. He knew that Keller was inside the house, sorting through what she had brought. They would clear out her place later. Today had been about them. He stopped and stared up at the sky. Little did the couple know that the step that they had taken would lead to more threats and danger for them.

Keller was on her feet early the next morning. She was due at work and needed to be there. She couldn't refuse when the owner of the studio had taken a chance on her all those years ago.

Kaelen himself was headed for the airport. He had been back there but not to fly. He had a flight that morning, just a short one. It would be enough to help get him back into the groove of flying.

David walked towards Kaelen as Kaelen was hesitating in the hangar doorway. He knew that Kaelen was due to fly that day but he also could sense that Kaelen was hesitant to do so.

"Kaelen? How long is your flight today?"

"Not that long. Just to a nearby town where I wait and then fly back." Kaelen rubbed at his cheek. "I've taken this client there before. What I went through here changes it all. I am afraid, David, and that's not me."

"No, it's not. But it is understandable. I'll be around all day if you need to talk." David walked away, seeing Mark and Joshua heading for Kaelen. Don was looking after his friend.

"Kaelen?" Mark's call brought Kaelen's head around.

Kaelen frowned at them before he sighed. He was being taken care of by Don. That meant one of the two flew with him and his passenger that day. To tell the truth, Kaelen was grateful for that.

"I take it one of you is flying with me." Kaelen grinned. "Which one?"

Joshua held up his hand, an answering grin on his face.

"I am. Don has found out who you're flying today and cleared it with him. That man was ready to call off the flight and just do a video meeting even though he really needs to be there in person." Joshua turned as he heard footsteps and stepped back as Kaelen greeted his passenger. The man was high in leadership in a local manufacturing company. He would only fly with Kaelen. The two men had shared many a conversation, which usually led to discussing favourite Bible passages.

Four hours later, Mark watched as Kaelen and the mechanic moved the helicopter into the hangar and then closed and locked the doors. Kaelen trudged towards him, Joshua at his side. Joshua shared a look with Mark before he reached for Kaelen's keys.

"I'm driving you home, Kaelen. This flight has taken a lot from you. You're still recovering from your beating." Joshua walked away, not giving Kaelen an opportunity to refuse. Not that he would have any ways.

"He's taking care of you, Kaelen. You need that." Mark turned Kaelen towards where the vehicles were parked. "I was here all the time that you were away. No one had a chance to get to your vehicle."

Kaelen's feet slowed before he came to a halt. His eyes slid closed. Mark was right. If he had been on his own and left the truck, someone could well have tampered with something.

"Thank you, Mark. I am going to owe you so much."

Mark's hand rested on Kaelen's shoulder for a moment.

"That's not how we do it, is it, Kaelen? You're our friend. We never charge friends for anything. Let's get you home to Keller. She was working today?"

"She was. The studio has tightened up security for her. No one has complained. The artists are actually glad for that, given that they sometimes have fans who can be a little too intense." Kaelen gave a brief grin as Mark laughed.

"I can see that. Off you go, Kaelen. I'll follow you." Mark watched as Joshua drove away before he scanned the area around him and then drove off after them. This was when it could become very dangerous for Kaelen. And none of them wanted to see that happen.

Keller turned as she heard the door open and then close, the lock clicking into place. She stepped to the hallway, her eyes on Kaelen as he struggled to take off his sneakers and then rested for a moment with a hand on the wall. She simply walked up to him and was swept to his heart, a kiss delivered at the same time. The couple stood, grateful and happy to be together but still sensing the growing danger around them.

Chapter 32

Two weeks later, Keller walked towards the music studio, a frown on her face. There should be cars there at that time of the morning and there were none. Her steps slowed before she turned and was running for her car. She locked herself inside it before reaching for her phone.

"Aidan? Where are you?" Kaelen hated the quiver of fear that shook her voice.

"Keller? Where are you? And what is wrong?" Kaelen headed for his car, his take-out cup of coffee into the cupholder in his car.

"I'm at the studio. There should be people here, and there aren't. I locked myself into my car." Keller was frantically searching the area, looking for anyone who belonged to the studio. "I was to be here to work with a huge country star. And no one is here."

"Stay in your car, Keller." Aidan reached to activate his emergency lights and sirens. "I'll call in in. Patrol officers should be there in just a few moments."

Keller watched as the cars flew into the parking lot and slammed to a halt before the officers were out and heading for the building. Some went inside while others searched outside. Aidan had appeared as well and headed into the building. His hand had been raised to acknowledge Keller.

Keller sat with her phone clutched in her hand. A scream came from her as it rang. Fear shone on her face and in her eyes as she stared at it before she calmed herself. It was only Delanie.

"Delanie?"

"Keller? Where are you? And are you okay?" Delanie could hear the fear in Keller's voice.

"No, I'm not. I'm at work but no one else is here. Aidan is here looking around." Keller could not control her fear. "Something is wrong."

"Where are you, though?" Delanie turned as Don approached her, a frown on his face. "Don? There's something going on at Keller's work."

Don nodded. He had expected something like that. With a security team in for training, he could not pull his full team. He looked around and motioned to Caleb and Paul.

"With me, guys. Delanie's on the phone with Keller. Something's off at her work." Don ran for his truck, the other two men on his heels. He sped through town as fast as he could before he parked near the studio. He was out of his vehicle and waiting for one of the officers to acknowledge him.

Keller was out of her vehicle, her purse and phone in her hand, as she ran towards Don. Delanie had told her that he was on her way. Aidan had sent her a text to let her know that once Don arrived, she was to go with him, leaving her car in the lot.

Don swept an arm around her and into his truck. The three men then stood with their back to the truck, on guard for their friend's lady. They had expected something like this but not so soon.

———

Aidan stepped away from the studio. Keller had been correct. There was no one inside even though the door was unlocked and they could see evidence of people being there. He frowned at the parking lot. With the evidence inside, there should be vehicles in the lot and there weren't any at all.

Walking across the parking lot at last, Aidan watched Don and his two team members. He was well aware that they knew he was approaching them by their attitude but they did not move from how they were watching the area.

"Don?" Aidan stopped beside him, scanning the area himself.

"Yeah? What's going on? Keller didn't say much other than what she said to Delanie."

"She didn't go into the building, did she?" Don shook his head at Aidan's question. "There is no one inside but the building is unlocked. And that is unusual from what we can determine. We haven't been able to raise anyone who should be there." He moved to the truck door, opening it to face Keller. "Keller?"

"Aidan? Can I go inside?" Keller reached for her purse, her motions stilling as he shook his head. "Aidan? Why can't I?"

"It's a crime scene right now, Keller. There is no one inside. Should there be?" Aidan watched her intently.

"There should be. We had a full day booked." Keller looked more scared than she had. "Where are they?"

"I don't know, Keller. I really don't. Do you know?" Aidan watched her closely but he was still frustrated.

"No, I don't." Keller glared at him and then at the studio. She sighed. "I'm guessing that I'm not working today."

"Not likely. Don and his guys will watch out for you. You can't add anything?"

"No. I can't." Keller frowned at him. "Can I go home now?"

"You can. Don will take you there and he will search your home before you enter it. Kaelen is away today?"

"He is. He had a flight up north but will be back late this afternoon." Keller sighed once more. "You're telling me that everyone has disappeared and you have no idea where they are."

"That's about it. We'll find them, Keller. Have no doubt about that." Aidan walked away, anger on his face. This should not have happened, he decided.

Don nodded at the other two men before they were into the truck and driving off. Keller was quiet, not sure what to say. Caleb watched her closely but didn't say anything. Once at Keller's home, Don and Paul walked towards the house, keys in hand. They searched both inside and outside the house but didn't find anything out of the ordinary. They were all puzzled by what had happened.

Keller paced her home that day, unable to settle down to anything. Her phone was in her hand and she was constantly checking her messages, not finding one from her boss. That troubled her deeply. Hearing the door open and then close with the lock sounding, she almost ran towards Kaelen.

Kaelen stood for a moment, puzzled at Keller's manner before he wrapped her into his arms. He had not spoken to anyone that day and had no idea what was going on. He moved Keller to the living room and sat, gathering her close to him. He could only pray for her. Keller was sobbing as he held her, unable to control her weeping.

"Keller? Sweetheart? What's happened?" Kaelen's voice finally broke through Keller's distraught crying.

"The studio. Everyone disappeared from it." Keller's arms tightened around Kaelen's neck, almost strangling him.

"What? What are you talking about?" Kaelen was shocked to say the least.

"Everyone is missing. Even their cars are. Aidan can't explain it." Keller's sobs lessened as she leaned against her groom and then slept.

Kaelen could only hold his lady, not sure what had happened or why. He began to pray for her and then the ones from the studio. He would follow up with Aidan as soon as he was able to.

Chapter 33

Aidan tapped quietly at Kaelen's door that evening. He was there to interview Keller. He just didn't know if she would speak with him. He turned back to the door as it opened and Kaelen beckoned him in.

"Aidan? You're here?" Kaelen moved back towards the kitchen. He had been tidying it up from their meal.

"I am. I do need to speak with her. Where would I find her?" Aidan looked around, not sure what to say past that.

"She's having a shower, I think. She's devastated, Aidan. She's at a loss to know why or who. Now, she's more than worried about the people from the studio." Kaelen looked at his friend before he heard the soft sounds of Keller walking their way. He reached to wrap her in his arms.

Keller frowned at Aidan before she nodded.

"You need to talk?"

"I do, Keller. I need to find out what you know about the people who work with you and who might have been in the studio that day." Aidan pointed towards the table. "We need to sit, Keller."

Keller glared at them before she reached into the fridge for a bottle of juice. She stared at it, not sure that was what she really wanted but it would do. She sat with Kaelen beside her, his arm tight around her.

She was more than grateful for his support and thanked God for that.

"What do you want or need to know, Aidan?" She was not backing down from him. She had found freedom in the last few weeks, especially since marrying Kaelen. He backed her decisions even when he didn't totally agree with her. That had given her the confidence that she had needed. Fairley had merely grinned at her and told her that she was becoming so much like her mother. Keller had to admit that she had cried a bit at that, not knowing the lady who Fairley had loved so much and who had loved Keller that much as well.

"Talk to me, Keller. Tell me about your work, what you do. Tell me about who you work with. We have their names and their relatives and friends but that doesn't tell us about how you know them. Give me your impressions of them. Does one of them strike you as being suspicious? I know that you can't name who comes in to the studio. Only the studio owner or manager should do that. Does one of them strike you as being off in any way?" Aidan waited patiently for Keller to think through what he had asked. It would take time, he knew, and likely more than one interview with her.

Keller nodded before she reached for the pad of paper and pen that Aidan was shoving at her. It would help her to write it down, she knew. That way, she could go back over it and then make any changes or updates that she could. It seemed as if she had been writing for hours, her hand cramping as she set the pen aside.

Kaelen was on his feet, gathering up her papers and heading for the office to make copies. He kept the original for Keller, shoving a copy over to Aidan. Aidan stared at him for a moment and then nodded. Kaelen had done the correct thing. He would have taken the original. That was not what Keller needed right now. She needed to control what he was given, even though he was the investigator. He would and could grant her that.

"That's it for now, Aidan." Keller was exhausted, leaning back on Kaelen. "Will it do?"

"It will more than do. Thank you, Keller. This has taken a lot from you to do this. I'll go over it and then come back and question you."

"I know that you will. But will I go over it with you?" Keller was grumpy and it showed. The two men simply grinned at her. "Have you talked with Dad? Does this go back to him?"

Aidan nodded. He had spent a long time with Fairley a few days ago, just asking what his life had been like and if he had any enemies. Fairley had frowned at that before he shook his head. Other than the babysitter, he wasn't aware of any enemies. Aidan had taken what Fairley could tell him and then reached out to his friend, Emma, to research the names that he had been given.

Kaelen watched as Keller shuffled the papers later that night. He reached for them before he wrapped her into his arms. He felt the sobs that shook her body. All Kaelen could do was pray for her and beg God to keep her safe. He felt the gathering storm that was surrounding them and the growing danger that they were facing.

Don turned as Delanie approached him that night, wrapping an arm around her. He waited patiently for her to speak.

"How's Keller?" Don finally spoke.

"She's hurting, Don. I don't know how to help her other than to pray for her." Delanie was sober as she thought through the conversation that she had had earlier with Keller. "I can't imagine what her life was like."

"She had a hard life, that much we can agree on. She's changing, growing more confident. That has come from having friends but it is also coming from Kaelen. His support of and love for her has given her that ability to rise about her past. That sounds odd but it's true."

"It is. What can we do for them?"

"For now, we pray for them. We're around them as much as they will allow. Emma is looking into it but she's having trouble finding any information. That's odd for her." Don paused, a thought coming to his mind. "What if someone has given us the wrong names?"

"That's possible. How do we find that out?" Delanie watched as Don sent a text off to Emma, who responded that she had thought of that and had found the correct names. She would be in touch with Keller over the next day or so.

Keller watched as Kaelen slept. He had not gone to bed, instead curling up under a blanket on the couch. She dropped a kiss on his cheek and then walked to the office, staring down at the pile of papers. She shoved them aside for the night and instead reached for her Bible. She needed some God time and that had to be at that particular time.

Chapter 34

The next day, Keller headed back for the studio, Delanie volunteering to drive her there. Keller was not aware that two of Don's men followed them, on the alert for anything that was off. Keller stood for a moment beside her car, staring at the studio, seeing the police tape moving slightly in the soft breeze. She could not go inside and wanted to.

Delanie waited beside her, hesitant to let Keller enter her car.

"Keller? Don't get in your car." Delanie drew her away, waving at Thomas to approach. "Thomas, can you check out Keller's car? I think that there is something off about it."

Thomas nodded, waving at Paul to stay with the ladies. Paul moved them away from the car and towards his truck. He watched carefully as Thomas inspected the car before his attention went to the area around him. He could feel the eyes on him but not seeing anyone who stood out.

Thomas dusted off the knees of his jeans and then walked away from the car. His phone was out. He had found a bomb up under the motor and that needed to be dealt with right away.

Paul shoved Keller towards the door of the truck and then inside. Delanie jumped up to sit on the seat beside her before he was driving away from the lot and parking down the street. He was out of the truck and walking around it, watching intently for anyone who meant harm to Keller.

Thomas finally walked towards him, frustration on his face. The bomb squad had removed the bomb but had suggested that Keller's car be towed to the police garage for the techs and mechanics to go over it more thoroughly. He had agreed, knowing that Keller would have said to do that.

"Thomas?" Paul kept his voice quiet, his eyes on Keller as she stared out at them.

"A bomb, Paul. The car will go to the police garage. They don't want her driving it yet." Thomas opened the truck door, finding Keller shaking with fear. "Keller, there was a bomb on your car. They've towed it to the police garage. Whoever is after you has just stepped up their fight with you."

"I know that they have." Keller handed over her phone. "These messages need to go to Aidan. They're threatening Kaelen with death. How do we keep him safe? I don't want him to crash somewhere he can't be found."

"We understand that, Keller. David has brought in security to be in and around Kaelen's hangar. The mechanic goes over his helicopter every morning before Kaelen takes off." Thomas had spoken with David and confirmed that.

"He has done that? That's a relief. But there's still getting him to work and back home again." Keller chewed at her lip, trying to come up with a way to do that without putting herself at risk.

Paul gave a grim smile. He had spoken with Don and then with Richard, a friend of Don's who had a security team as well. They had made arrangements for at least two of the team members to be with Kaelen every day and then the same with Keller.

"We've made arrangements with our team and another team to be with both Kaelen and yourself every day. We also have another team who will move into help if we need them." Paul's hand went up. "And there is no charge. We don't charge our friends. Kaelen has been there for us so many times. And now it's our turn to repay him."

Keller blinked at him before she nodded. Kaelen had already warned her that the teams would likely move in and protect them. She just worried about them.

"What about Dad?" Keller worried about her father. She frowned suddenly. Something had seemed off the last couple of days. "Paul? Have we looked into my Dad and what he's said?"

Paul shared a look with Thomas. They had suspected something was off and had asked Emma to look into him. They were waiting for her report.

"Emma is doing that, Keller. It's what she does. She looks into everyone around a person and then just keeps expanding who she looks at. She has trained her staff well to look outside of the box as we say to find information. Emma thought that she might have a preliminary report today."

"That fast?" Keller was in awe before she frowned as she saw Aidan walking towards him. "I don't want to talk to him." She reached and shut the door, looking away from where Aidan had come to a stop.

Aidan shared a grin with the other two men, knowing exactly what Keller was doing. He would speak with her, that was a given. He reached to open the door, leaning on it as Keller tried to close it again. He could see the wide grin on Delanie's face.

"Keller? What can you tell me?" Aidan waited for her to speak. He was not prepared for her to leap from the truck past him and then run towards Kaelen. "Did she just do that?"

"She did. Kaelen's here and he's her safety spot right now just as she is his." Thomas shook his head at Aidan. "Let her be, Aidan. Her car has been parked here overnight without any security around it. It could have been tampered with at any time. Keller would not know about it."

"And people will say that she did it herself." Aidan was frustrated and it showed. He walked away, needing to be elsewhere.

Kaelen held Keller, feeling her body shaking with her deep emotions. He had finished what he needed to do at the hangar, not having any flights booked, and then had decided to surprise Keller at her work. He had not expected to see police activity there for a second day but not seeing any other usual vehicles.

"Keller? What happened, love?" Kaelen had to repeat his question before Keller raised her head from where she had buried it against him.

"My car, Kaelen. Someone put a bomb on it." Keller was too shaken to say much more. With her head against him, she didn't see the shocked look that crossed his face or the anger that followed it.

Kaelen looked up as Thomas approached him, seeing Paul waiting by his truck. He frowned at Delanie as she walked towards her car and drove away.

"Thomas? Is that true? A bomb?"

"It is. We found it before Keller could even get close to her car. Aidan's been around. He'll want to speak with her. She refused right now." Thomas was frustrated. They had no answers all the while the danger around their friends was growing.

"I see. And we now have you guys with us, correct?" Kaelen had been expecting that.

"You do. Don's on board and Abe will be as well. We have people with you when you're out and about. A security team will be around your home at night. Toryn has officers volunteering to do that." Thomas walked away, not satisfied that they could keep their friend safe.

Chapter 35

Keller walked through the backyard that evening. She was still highly troubled by the events of the last few days and had told Kaelen that she needed some alone time. He had nodded, saddened that she would not speak with him but understanding that her upbringing had led to that. He had kissed her and then sent her outside. Kaelen, however, did not move from the back door, a hand on the door knob, the other hand on the door itself.

Unsure what to think or even pray, Keller just paced. Her thoughts were too muddled for her to make sense of anything. She finally walked back into the house, not finding Kaelen waiting for her as she expected. She found him in the living room, his head bowed in prayer. She simply sat beside him, an arm wrapping around his.

Kaelen raised his head at last and reached to kiss his bride. This was not how he expected to start married life, being in danger and fearing for her.

"Okay, love?" Kaelen's voice was low.

"I am, now, I think, Kaelen. How do we do this? How do we walk forward and not bring harm to anyone?"

"Keller, we can't keep everyone safe. It's just not possible. We have to accept that. It's hard, I know. However, that being said, we walk forward, hand in hand with one another and hand in hand with God. He is the One who is in control. He is the One who will protect us. We may not like what we have to go through, but we can trust that He has only our best in mind. He does not want harm to come to us. It's hard being human."

"It is. I want this over." Keller snuggled down under his arm. "It's preventing us from living life."

Kaelen began to shake his head. There was no way that he would let that happen. He had a beautiful bride who he wanted to be out and about with. That would change, starting tomorrow. He planned to take her out for meals, for walks, and whatever else they decided to do.

"We're not hiding any more, love. We're going to do what we should be doing as newlyweds. We are going to be out there. Tomorrow, I am taking you out for a meal. A dress-up meal. I loved how you looked on our wedding day. I want to do this with you." Kaelen kissed her. "I love you, Keller. I don't want to see you harmed but we can't prevent what may well happen. Even hiding at home or somewhere else is not going to keep us safe."

Keller nodded. Those were her thoughts too. She was ready to face whoever it was. Keller looked up at Kaelen, seeing the determination on his face.

"We'll do that, Kaelen. And we will have guards, won't we?" Her voice was plaintive at that.

"We will, unfortunately. That's part of what we deal with right now." Kaelen paused for a moment. "Have you spoken with your dad today?"

Keller frowned. She had not and he had promised to call her.

"No, and he was to call. What is going on, Kaelen?" Keller looked up at him to find him frowning as he stared across the room.

"I don't know, love. I really don't know." He was on his feet, pulling her with him. A finger rubbed at his temple. He still has some residual headaches at times and this was one time that he had one. "Let's look through our paperwork and then check our emails. Neither of us is working tomorrow. We can take all night if we have to."

Keller sighed. She didn't want to spend any more time on this, whatever this was. She wanted to put it behind her and walk forward. God was not allowing that, she knew. She had to trust and wait on Him. It was just so hard waiting on His timing.

Four hours later, Keller was on her feet, heading for the kitchen. She needed a hot drink and food. Kaelen had not roused from his reading when she walked away. He looked around a few moments later, not seeing Keller, and then rose to follow her. He had been following a train on information that made sense at last.

Keller turned as he approached, handing over the mug of coffee.

"What did you discover?" Keller was certain that he had found something.

"I have a trail that I'm following. It goes back to your mother. I need to clarify something with your father. And I can't reach him." Kaelen was troubled at that.

"No, we can't. I don't like it. Can we drive out there this morning?" Keller yawned before she leaned against her groom.

"You're asleep on your feet, love." The mug of coffee was set down before Kaelen swept her into his arms and carried her back to the office. He tucked her under a blanket on the couch before he was back to the kitchen and returning with his mug of coffee. Kaelen wanted to follow the track that he was on before he lost the threat of it.

The chiming of his email notification brought him back to the present three hours later. He yawned as he looked over to where Keller was still asleep. He pulled up the email. It was from Emma with the information that he had asked for. She had been able to confirm what he thought and that pleased him. He had confirmation that neither Keller's mother or father were involved in what had happened to her as a baby. Emma had confirmed who it had been and forwarded that to Aidan.

Kaelen rose and stretched. He was happy with what he had found but also disturbed. He had forwarded his findings on to Aidan. He knew full well that Aidan would be around that day to question him.

"Kaelen?" Keller had sat up, pushing at the hair covering her face. "What did you discover? And you let me sleep." She frowned at him as he grinned before he was sitting beside her and kissing her.

———

184

"I found out that your parents are not responsible for what we're going through or why you were taken as an infant. Emma has confirmed that. I sent our findings on to Aidan."

"And he'll be around today, won't he?" Keller sighed. "I apologize for my attitude. I have to keep going back and asking for forgiveness for that."

"God understands, love. He really does understand. He takes any and all emotions that we throw at him. He wants only the best for us but He also takes us at our low points."

"And that is what this is. A low point for sure." Keller was lost in thought at that, wonder in her heart at how God worked in their lives.

Chapter 36

Aidan stared at the email that Kaelen had sent him and then pulled up the one from Emma. How they had arrived at their conclusions, he had no idea. Now that he had this information, he would need to work through it. The only thing was that he was in court that morning. He sent off an email to Kaelen, confirming that he had received the information and would be in touch later that day. Would the both of them please stay safe?

Keller had snorted when Kaelen told her that, causing him to laugh. He wrapped her into a hug and then asked what she wanted to do for that day. Keller had shrugged and asked what he wanted to do.

Kaelen had rushed Keller to change into something casual. He wanted to spend the day in a nearby town and told her that. She had frowned at him before she shrugged. They were beginning to live their lives and who would stop them.

Keller stared at the shops in the town that they had arrived at. She had never been to Riverville before and looked forward to exploring the town. Kaelen grinned at her, seeing the relaxed attitude that she had developed over the last few moments. He loved that and wanted to see her keep that.

Walking hand in hand towards a local diner, Kaelen turned as he heard someone calling his name. He drew Keller to a halt, waiting for the couple to approach them.

"Kaelen? You're in our town?" Murphy O'Brien grinned at them. "And this is Keller?"

"This is indeed Keller. Keller, this is Murphy O'Brien and his wife, Adriel. He's co-owner of a security team here in Riverville." Kaelen grinned as Keller scowled at Murphy.

"We don't want security today."

Murphy began to laugh, watching as Adriel linked her arm with Keller.

"No, you don't, and you don't have. Not unless it's necessary." Murphy watched as the two ladies headed into Mac's diner. "Kaelen? Abe has told us what's happening. What can we do for you?"

"I really don't know, Murphy. I know what you all went through. I just don't want to lose her or see her hurt." Kaelen paused before he walked into the diner.

"We understand that, Kaelen. We're coming up with plans that may or may not work. I understand that there are some people missing."

"There are. The ones from the studio. We don't know if there are any singers who are missing. Aidan hasn't shared that. And then there's Fairley, Keller's father. We can't contact him. We stopped by his home but he wasn't there. I didn't say anything to Aidan yet. We need to find him." Kaelen thought through what he had determined. "We came up with a name but we're not sure if it's correct."

"Does Emma have it?" Murphy slid onto the bench seat beside Adriel.

"She does." Kaelen reached for Keller's hand. "Let's set this aside for now. What else is fun to do here in town?"

Murphy grinned. He and Adriel would make sure that this couple had a fun, relaxing day, including stopping at the Irish bakeshop owned by friends of theirs.

Keller looked out of the back window of the truck late that afternoon as they headed for home. They had needed that time away. God had provided friends to spend the day with and that had been a blessing for them. Murphy had spoken sternly with them, telling them what they could expect and how they could best prepare themselves. Keller and Kaelen had shared a look before they had nodded.

"This was a good day, love." Kaelen's eyes were on the move, searching for anything that was out of order. He couldn't see anything. He also didn't see the two trucks that were tailing them. Murphy was in one. His teammate, Matt and his wife, Sarah, were in the other one. They would ensure that the couple got home safe.

The next morning, a Saturday, Keller was on the move. She had left Kaelen at home, working through their mystery, as she headed for the grocery store. She knew that they really didn't need a lot but she wanted to buy some fresh fruits and vegetables.

Pausing as she shut her car trunk, Keller looked around. Someone was out there and close to her. She almost ran to lock herself inside her car before driving off. She didn't see the car that pulled out and followed her before a patrol car pulled inbetween Keller and that vehicle, slowing to a stop. The officer walked back to the car and then pulled the man from it, clapping handcuffs on him and arresting him. They had been looking for him for a while. Keller had led him straight into their hands.

Kaelen was on his feet as he heard the garage door and walked towards the door that led out to the garage. He reached to help with the bags, a kiss delivered before he waited for Keller to enter the house. He dropped the bags on the table before Keller turned to him.

"Are you okay, love?" Kaelen watched her closely as she moved around putting away the food.

"I don't know, Kaelen. I was driving home and a patrol officer pulled over the vehicle that had followed me from the grocery store. I was ready to head for somewhere safe when that happened. Someone was following me." Keller was angry. She knew that she had to turn that anger over to God but didn't want to. She wanted to hold on to it and let it fester.

"You're angry." Kaelen had no doubt that he had pegged her feelings.

"I am. I want this over. I want to go on with life. What is God doing in all this? What are we supposed to be learning?" Keller's words were spit at Kaelen.

Kaelen let her talk, knowing that she needed to. He sighed to himself. He prayed for God to relieve their situation, to bring an end to their fight. He also prayed that they would have peace in the situation and that they would be the witness for Him in everything.

Keller finally was quiet. She had vented and Kaelen had let her. She had needed that. Keller's eyes studied her groom, seeing the steadiness of him. She was thankful for him.

The couple had taken time to go our for a meal, trying to be positive for one another but still struggling with their fear and doubts. Kaelen turned towards their home, slowing as he approached it. He didn't stop, however. He kept on driving, causing Keller to stare at him and then turn and stare behind them.

"Kaelen? You just drove by our home."

"I know. I couldn't stop. Call it in, please?" Kaelen turned around and then parked where he could see their home. "Something is wrong there, Keller."

Chapter 37

Aidan walked towards Kaelen's house, not sure what he was walking into. He reached to unlock the door, keying in a code to the security system. The officers followed him into the house. They all stopped in surprise as they reached the living room. All those sets of eyes staring back at him were disconcerting.

The officers worked to untie and remove the gags from the people who were tied up there. They were the ones who had disappeared from the music studio. Fairley was the last one untied. He was on his feet, rubbing at his wrists, before he turned to Aidan and motioned with his head. He knew that it would take time to sort out what happened and to get everyone's statement.

"Aidan? Let me tell you what happened to me. Where's my girl?" Fairley was deeply afraid for her.

"She's safe with Kaelen. They're parked down the street with officers around them. He drove by here a while ago but wouldn't stop." Aidan was puzzled by the

"It's a good thing that they didn't. The men who brought us here had a police scanner. They left when they heard the call to come here." Fairley was angry. "I was at home, working in the yard when I was knocked out. I woke up in a warehouse not far from here, bound and gagged. All those people were there as well. Are they from the studio? We couldn't communicate at all. And don't ask if I saw anyone. I didn't. Anyone who approached us was masked."

"That's about what we thought." Aidan moved Fairley from the house and called for an officer. "Here. Get Fairley down to Kaelen."

Keller saw her father walking rapidly towards her. Before anyone could stop her, she was out of Kaelen's truck and running towards him. He caught her into a tight hug and then forced her back to the truck, her reluctance to let go of him obvious. Shoving her into the truck, he jumped into the back seat.

Kaelen turned to him slightly, catching the shake of his head. He sighed before he reached for Keller's hand. Hers was cold to his touch, fear making it so.

"Dad? Where were you?" Keller twisted to look at her father.

"We were held in a warehouse and then moved here today. Whoever it was, Kaelen, had a key to your home and the passcode to your system." Fairley was angrier than he had been. "We weren't harmed, just keep out of sight. And before you ask, they were the ones from the studio."

"Oh, no! I'll never be able to go back there and work!" Keller blinked back her tears. "How can I ever do that?"

"We'll work it out, love." Kaelen watched the activity at his home. "We're not going back in there tonight."

"No, you're not. Head for your friend, Don's place. See if he can put us up somewhere." Fairley was adamant about that. "We need to get you two out of sight."

———

"No, he's away for a couple of days with his team." Kaelen tried to think of who he could contact or where he could take them. He frowned as he saw the tall man walking towards him. "Richard?"

Richard paused by the truck, his eyes on the area around him. His team was also there. Don had reached out to him when he left that morning, asking for Richard to come that afternoon.

"Kaelen? Don was worried about you. Where do you want to go?"

"I have no idea." Kaelen shared a look with Keller. "We can't go home. Where can we go?"

Richard nodded. It was about what he figured. They needed to hide somewhere for a day or so.

"Hop out of your truck and lock it up. We'll take over getting you three somewhere." Richard had them inside his vehicles and leaving the area before anyone could move in on them. And he knew that men were waiting to do just that. Stephen had seen them and had called in their location. He watched the activity behind him as they drove away.

"Richard? Where are we heading?" Keller was exhausted all of a sudden. She wanted to go home and wasn't being allowed to do that.

"Somewhere we can keep you safe at least overnight. Aidan will call me." Richard refused to say any more than that.

Fairley paced the house that they had been taken to. He had not expected a house that seemed to be rundown but he shrugged. He was not the one who found these places after all. He just had to trust Richard. And he was not sure that he could. Richard was a stranger to him. Fairley turned to watch Kaelen, seeing him deep in discussion with Richard. Keller was with the two ladies on the team. That left him on his own. He walked to the door and then stepped outside. He had disappeared by the time that anyone realized that he was gone.

Richard was angry at that. Fairley had just compromised their safe house. Bundling the couple back into a vehicle, the team drove away, heading for somewhere else. Richard wasn't sure what was going on with Fairley. His conversation with Aidan was heated.

Aidan was surprised but not surprised, he decided, that Fairley had walked away. That man had depended on himself for too long and didn't trust easily. That could very well get his daughter and her groom killed. He paused to pull out his phone, a frown in place before he was running for his car and the office. He sent a text off to Richard, warning him that the Fairley who had been there that day was not Keller's father. That Fairley had been found in the warehouse where the group had been secluded. He had been hurt. The Fairley that had spoken to him was an imposter.

Kaelen turned from speaking with Richard at the new home. Richard had told him what Aidan had discovered. He was devastated at the news. He approached Keller and drew her to one side. His words had her staring at him and then shaking her head.

"It was Dad. It had to be." Keller was adamant about that.

"It wasn't, Keller. He was made up to look like him. He was close enough to your Dad not to raise our alarm at first. That's why he disappeared. He couldn't continue to be around you." Kaelen swept her into his arms, holding her as she sobbed.

Chapter 38

Sounds outside of the house drew Richard to the window before he was running for his team and then shoving Kaelen and Keller from the house into the darkness. Naomi led them on a run from there and towards the houses behind them. Richard waited for a moment, hearing the sound of the house door being broken in. His feet picked up their pace as he followed the others ahead of them. Their vehicles were not accessible.

Stephen dropped back to stand and watch the house. Richard paused beside him.

"What happened, Richard? Are we not safe there?"

"No, we're not. That man who we thought was Fairley? He was an imposter. Aidan let me know that just before that broke loose." Richard pointed towards the house. "We can't go back there. Let's get on the move."

The two men moved rapidly towards where the group had disappeared. They paused in the shadows as a car passed by, driven very slowly. They exchanged a look before they were on the move again. They knew where the team would be heading and they needed to get there as well.

Timothy appeared briefly and waved before he was gone from sight. Richard and Paul headed that way, disappearing into the darkness before the car reappeared. Richard turned to watch it, knowing that his team was heading for shelter. He would not call for help, not yet. He was afraid that there was someone close to the investigation letting the enemy know where they were.

"Richard?" Timothy appeared beside him. "We have them under cover but we can't stay here for more than a few hours. What happened?"

"Fairley. It wasn't Keller's dad. He was a plant." Richard was angry and frustrated. He turned to pace towards Keller and Kaelen. Kaelen was waiting for him. He left Keller in the darkness.

"Richard? What just happened?" Kaelen's words were bit towards Richard.

"Fairley. That was one of your abductors. Aidan let me know that they found the real Fairley and have him secluded somewhere. He's not saying where. For now? We need to find somewhere to hide you two. I just don't know where." Richard walked away, angry but also praying for the situation and the couple. He did not want to let them out of his sight but that might be necessary, he was well aware. His phone was out as he called Don. "Don? Richard. What is your team up to right now?"

"We're training ourselves for the next few days." Don rose from where he had been sitting at his desk. "You need us."

"We do. We have Keller and Kaelen with us but our security was breached by an impostor. He was posing as Fairley. We've had to run from our safe house. Right now, we're on the move without vehicles." Richard paused and looked around. "We need to get them under cover somewhere."

"We do. Let me call the guys and we'll head your way. Meet us at Ben's." Don's phone clicked off before he was sending out a group text. Delanie had approached, worried about the tone of the conversation. "Delanie? The team's heading for Richard. He needs our help." He simply hugged his wife, kissed her, and then ran for the packs that were always kept ready.

Delanie watched him move before her own phone was out, sending a text to the ladies. They would meet shortly at her place to spend the night in prayer for their fellows and the others.

Richard walked quietly back to his group, pointing towards the next street. He had no compunction about walking through people's yards. He was well known in town and had never had any issues if he had to do that. The group headed for the downtown area and to a deserted building. Kaelen and Keller was shoved into an inside room where they found chairs, a bed, and food and water. They looked at one another and then at Richard. He simply shrugged before he walked away.

Keller leaned against Kaelen, exhausted. He turned to the bed, making her lie down and then pulling a surprisingly clean blanket over her. Someone had prepared this room and he was grateful for that. He thanked God for those provisions.

Silver stood just outside of the door, watching Kaelen as he paced the room. He was worried, that she

———

had to acknowledge. Her head turned as she heard footsteps. Naomi had approached her.

"Silver? They're okay?" Naomi peeked into the room, seeing that Kaelen had dropped to the floor and sat with his back to the couch, his head bowed. "Is he sleeping?"

"Praying, I think." Silver looked around. "Don's on the way?"

"He is. I pray that we don't have to separate them but we might need to." Richard was worried about that. He didn't want that to happen. He knew exactly how he would have felt had it been Raleigh and himself.

Don approached the diner, not sure if Richard would be there. He was dismayed that his team had been away and unable to help until now. He looked around in the dim, early morning light. His head turned as he heard a slight noise and Richard appeared and then disappeared. Don nodded. He walked away, taking a circuitous path to reach Richard. A simple nod from Richard had Don following him.

Coming to a stop, Richard's head was twisting and turning as he searched for anyone who should not be there and who would present harm to the teams and also the couple.

"Richard? What's going on?" Don kept his voice to barely a whisper.

"Keller and Kaelen. We need to keep them out of sight. Aidan's team went into their home and found the people from the studio. A man pretending to be

Fairley was there. We took him with us but he walked away from our safe house. It was compromised not that long afterwards. We had to run and leave our vehicles." Richard was frustrated at that. He needed to move the couple quickly and didn't have the means to do that.

Don nodded. This had to be their worst fear, he acknowledged, having people in their car and not having the means to properly protect them. He looked around, frowning. There were usually people around here and today there wasn't. Don caught a slight movement and frowned as his eyes narrowed. He nodded. The street people were watching out for them and would help to protect Kaelen and Keller.

"Where do you want to go, Richard?" Don waited for his friend to speak. They had been friends since childhood and could almost read each other's minds.

"For now, we'll stay where we are. With your team and mine, we should be safe. I'll see what I can do about finding vehicles." Richard waited as Don's hand was on his arm. "Don?"

"We have both of our big vehicles. I spoke with Aidan. He's sending a transport van this way that isn't connected with either of us or the police. Someone reached out to him and asked him to use it. He didn't say who but he says he trusts this person." Don looked towards the parking lot as he heard a vehicle and began to laugh quietly. "There you go, Richard. The church van. Gideon's on top of this."

"That he is. He gets those nudges from God and just follows them." Richard disappeared into the darkness of the alleyways, Don following closely.

Chapter 40

Kaelen was on his feet, intent on the doorway. Keller was still sleeping and he would not awaken her until he had to. He paced to the door, standing beside Silver.

"What's going on, Silver? Something is." Kaelen would not back down from getting an answer.

"Don's team is here. Richard called him in. We're trying to come up with somewhere to tuck you two away." Silver didn't look at Kaelen. Instead, she watched the area and the team members who were moving around them. She heard Kaelen give a sigh.

"How long are we going to have to hide, Silver? Hiding will not end this. I want to go home." He felt Keller's arm around him and gathered her close to his side. "Just take us home, Silver. I want this over and that is the only way to accomplish that."

Richard and Don had approached without Kaelen seeing them. They exchanged a glance and nodded, resigned to that. Richard appeared in front of Kaelen, Don just behind him.

"You understand what that means?" Richard's voice was stern as he asked the question. He could hear the team members moving around them. He brushed at a cobweb that suddenly dropped in front of his face.

"We know that, Richard. I want to go home." Keller turned and walked back into the room. She

<hr>

stood with her arms wrapped around her, her back to the door.

Kaelen had turned and watched her. He spoke once more without turning.

"Take us home. We'll manage. And we want you two teams to go about your own work. I know what the ramifications are of that but we will not take you away from that. Richard, you have a team coming in tomorrow. Don? I'm sure that you have something or someone to train."

Richard and Don shared a look before Don shrugged. They would do what the couple asked but they would not be too far away from them.

"We'll do that, Keller, Kaelen. Come on then. Let's get you two back to your home." Richard walked away, a somewhat defeated slump to his shoulders. He could get why they wanted to leave. He just feared that this step would mean their deaths. His phone was out as he sent a text message off to Aidan to explain what was happening.

Aidan stared at the text message, shaking his head. He needed to head that way at some point, to speak with Kaelen and Keller. It was not happening at the present time. Aidan was on the scene of a triple murder and that would take most of his night and well into the day. He sighed. There were just too many crimes at present, he decided.

Keller moved through their house, searching for anything that seemed off. She stared at the dust from the crime scene team and sighed. That would be her first priority, she decided, before she headed to change into grubby clothes that would not be harmed by her cleaning.

Kaelen locked the door behind Richard and stood with his hand against it. He was exhausted and needed to sleep. That was not happening, he knew. Keller would need help cleaning and he would work through the hours to clean their home.

Three hours later, Keller leaned against Kaelen. She was exhausted as was he. Their house was clean at last. Kaelen hugged her, his chin resting on the top of her head.

"Go and get cleaned up, love. I'll find something for us to eat." Kaelen didn't move as Keller gripped his hands. "Keller?"

"We can't eat whatever is in the house. They may have tampered with it." Keller was afraid, almost running to the kitchen and beginning to throw out the food and what ever was in the fridge and freezer.

Kaelen's head dropped for a moment. Keller was correct, he knew. They would have to replace everything that was edible. He desperately wanted a cup of coffee but knew better than to even suggest that.

A tap at the front door had him pausing and then walking that way. He peeked out to see Don and Richard standing there, bags in their hands. He unlocked the door and opened it, stepping back to let them in.

"What do you have there, Don?" Kaelen pointed towards the kitchen. "Keller throwing out all of our food."

"That's what we wondered, Kaelen." Richard gave a grim smile. "Silver asked if anyone had checked the food. She and Naomi went on a shopping trip for you."

Keller turned as she heard the footsteps, frowning at the two men. Her eyes caught the bags of food and her face lit up.

"Someone brought us fresh food? How did you know?" She reached for the bags, her hands stopping at the two men shook their head and just put the food away.

"Silver. She and Naomi made the trip to buy food for you. We didn't think that you would be eating anything that is left here." Don grinned at her. "Now, what can we do for you two? Besides getting rid of the bags of garbage here."

"I don't know, Don." Kaelen moved up beside him. "What do you suggest?"

"Don't hide. That's what they expect you to do. Be out and about. You're newlyweds. Do what a newlywed couple would do. Go on walks, out for dinner, for lunch. Shop. Wander the downtown area and window shop." Don was thinking through what he and Delanie had done as newlyweds. "Be present at church, the Bible studies that you go to. Work. Your work will be different now, Keller. I'm not sure how comfortable you will be going back there."

"I'm not. Not when I'm responsible for what happened." Keller sighed. "I spoke with the owner and quit. He was sorry to see me go but he understood. He will call me if anyone specifically requests me to sing on an album. I'm fine with that. I just have to decide what I want to do."

"You have your music diploma?" Richard was positive that she had.

"I do. When I got it, my plan was to teach voice and singing. That's a possibility I'll think more about once we have found the ones responsible for this." Keller shuddered. The storm clouds were moving in. Even though she knew that God was in control and would calm the storms around them and within them, they would still face whatever danger that was out there. Keller just prayed that they survived.

Chapter 41

Keller paused before she entered a small gift shop the next day. She was out on her own, Kaelen having a trip that morning. He stated that he should be back by early afternoon, he had informed her before he kissed her and walked away. She had been afraid that day, afraid that he would not return to her.

Looking around at the front of the shop, Keller finally walked through the shop. She was looking for something for Kaelen. She just didn't know what. Then, she saw it, a mug with the photo of a helicopter on it. The helicopter was almost identical to Kaelen's new one. She reached for it, cradling it to her. Then she continued to walk around.

A framed photo caught her attention. She leaned forward to study the clouds over an angry lake with sunbeams breaking through them. She had to have that one, she decided. It reminded her of how God was there for them.

The clerk nodded at her before wrapping the gifts and slipping them into a paper shopping bag. Keller headed back towards her home. She had walked that day, secretly wishing that whoever it was after them would appear and she could defeat them. Keller shook with fear for a moment, sensing that someone was following her. She knew that she was alone and vulnerable.

Running up the steps to her home, her keys shook in her hand as she reached to unlock the door. She slammed it behind her, locking it and then walking to the office. She felt uneasy, as if God was warning her that something was about to happen. She had learned to trust those instincts. She had had to over her life.

Kaelen paused as he approached the house mid-afternoon. He was afraid for his bride, not sure why. Entering the house, he searched for Keller and grew more fearful as he could not find her. His heart was racing as he almost ran for the backyard. His steps stopped as he found Keller, kneeling in front of a flowerbed as she worked in it.

His steps were rapid as he walked towards her and dropped to his knees beside her. A quick hug and kiss had her leaning against him.

"Have a good day, love?" Kaelen's eyes were searching the area. He could feel the storm moving in on them as well. "Working in the gardens?"

"I am. They're in good shape but I just felt like doing this. I was never allowed to and always wanted to." Keller leaned back on her hands. "This is a nice yard, Kaelen."

"It is. It was what drew me here. I love the outdoors but didn't want to live outside of town." Kaelen drew Keller to her feet.

"I feel the same way. My foster parents had a show garden but never worked in it themselves." Keller bit at her lip. "Are they the ones behind all this? They would dress me up and show me off in public but were monsters behind closed doors."

"I know, love. I get that." Kaelen stopped her. "Are we ready to put our plans into play?"

Keller nodded. She was more than ready to go on the offensive and draw out whoever it was.

"I am. I started this morning, just like we talked." She handed him the small box. "I found this for you."

"What is this?" Kaelen's face had a look of interest as he accepted it. He opened the box, shooting looks towards Keller, a grin on his face. His hands stopped as he stared at the mug but he could not speak. He simply reached for Keller and hugged her. "This is so like mine."

"It is. That's why I chose it." She bit at her lip. "I also found a beautiful photo." She pointed to the wall in the kitchen that had never had a photo or picture on it. "That one."

Kaelen's eyes found the photo and he became motionless. He could feel the warmth from the sun and then the fury of the storm. His arms tightened around Keller as he quoted what verses that he could remember about storms.

"You like it?" Keller thought that he did.

"I do. It's perfect, Keller. And you have put it where we'll see it all the time. We need that reminder." Kaelen kissed her temple. "Now, how be we go out for dinner?"

Late that evening, Keller paused at Kaelen's truck. They had finished their meal and then gone for a long walk along the river. They were heading home.

Kaelen helped her into the truck and then climbed into the truck himself. He paused before he drove away, not heading for their home but for the other side of town. They had talked and were in agreement on their next move.

Kaelen pulled into the garage of a secluded home, shutting them in. Keller reached for his hand. This was part of their plan, to go somewhere they could not be found easily. At least, that was their hope. Kaelen had reached out to Abe Finlay, another man with a security team, who had arranged for this house for the next few days. He had been glad to. Abe's wife, Emma, was working through the volume of information that she had found and would be in touch tomorrow to go over it with them. He prayed that they stayed safe.

Keller only turned on a few lights, keeping the lighting as soft and low as possible. They were trying to stay out of sight. Neither one felt that they would be totally able to do that but they would do their best.

Kaelen walked away from the hangar the next afternoon. He knew that Keller was waiting inside the business office for him. They were going out again that night. Kaelen was afraid that day. He felt as if the adventure was about to end and he didn't want to see Keller injured in any way. Aidan had reached out to him that day, letting him know that they were close to arresting the ones responsible. Could the couple just stay safe? Kaelen had given a grim laugh, promising to do their best.

Keller and Kaelen had spent time the night before in prayer before they reached for the material that they had gathered and spent the night going through it. They had come to a consensus of who it was. Keller's face had paled as she realized the name was related to her foster parents. She reached out to her father, just asking if he knew the man. Fairley had been quiet for a moment, before he had acknowledged that he did. He had known him since they were children. Why was Keller asking? She told him, hearing the indrawn breath from her father. Fairley begged his daughter to stay safe.

Chapter 42

A hand to her throat, Keller backed away from the front door of their home. They had stayed away for a week, letting Aidan finish his plans and then had moved back home. She knew that Kaelen would be due home soon. She just didn't think that he would reach her in time.

The heavyset man stared at her, a sneer on his face. She had been outdoors and working in the front flower beds when her arm had been grasped tightly and she was pulled roughly to her feet. Fear had shown briefly on Keller's face before she shook her head. These men would not defeat her. They may kill her and Kaelen would grieve, but the cameras that had been set up would catch everything that they did.

Keller was shoved into a chair, the roughness of how she was handled bringing a whimper from her. Her hands were tied behind her back and a gag slapped harshly across her face, the cloth feeling as if it was rubbing her flesh raw. She waited, eyes watchful, as the man paced. She knew him.

"Well, Keller, you didn't expect to see me, did you? I've been following you for far too many years." Jack Moyne sneered at her. "You're now in my hands. It's been many years that I've been planning this. Be prepared to leave here and never see anyone again."

The two men with him shared a look, a puzzled look. What he was saying was not what he usually said to victims. He usually asked for money or jewelry or something along those lines. This was different. Was he really implying what they thought he was? They would not be party to that. Robbery and assaults were one thing. To separate someone like that from their families? That was not what they would be party to.

Keller carefully twisted her wrists, finding the rope loosening. She snorted to herself. Whoever had tied her up didn't know his knots. She would be loose soon but would wait until the opportunity came to run. She knew exactly where to head for. Kaelen had shown her a hideaway spot that morning, warning her to use it if she had to.

One of the men headed outside, stretching as he did so. He shrugged his jacket back into place, covering the holster that held his weapon. He walked towards the large luxury car that his employer owned. His steps halted suddenly as he felt a gun barrel against his face and then nodded. The police had arrived and he was under arrest. In some ways, he was relieved. He could and would turn evidence against his employer, hoping for a lighter sentence.

Aidan crouched down behind his car, his eyes on the house. He had no way of knowing how many men were inside the house. The patrol officer who had crept close enough to peek in had said that there were still two inside as well as Keller. One of them was the man that they were scouring the town for.

Kaelen stood near a patrol vehicle, his focus on the house. Keller was in there and alone. He wanted to be with her. He turned and walked away, making his way to the back of the house. He didn't see the officer who reached out to stop him from entering the house.

———

Closing the door behind him, Kaelen whistled as he dropped his keys to the counter. He was trying to act as normally as possible and as much as he would when he returned home.

The men spun and stomped towards the kitchen. Keller was on her feet, moving as silently as she could and heading for the hiding spot in the office. She closed herself in, praying that Kaelen would be safe.

Moyne stared at Kaelen, not believing that Kaelen was standing there in front of him. He pointed to him, motioning the man with him to bring Kaelen into the living room. The man didn't move, his eyes on Kaelen, seeing the calmness on the younger man's face. He frowned at him before he stepped backwards. He kept moving backwards until he felt the front door behind him and opened it, to step outside into an officer's custody. He nodded. This was over, as far as he was concerned.

Kaelen watched him walk away before his attention went back to Moyne. This was the man who Keller and he had determined was behind it all. He was brother to her foster father.

"Why?" Kaelen's single word split the silence.

"Why?" Moyne was frowning at him, not sure what Kaelen was asking.

"Yes, why. Why Keller? What did she or her family do to you? We know that her foster father is your brother. You didn't really hide your relationship all that well. It's all over town by now." Kaelen had made sure that the street people spread word. He had also gone to a friend on the local newspaper and given him an exclusive story about what Keller and he had faced. That had come out in the paper that morning.

"Why Keller? Because I could. Her father was nothing. I offered to take his daughter when her mother died. He refused. The babysitter was a cousin of mine. She helped to get Keller to me and then I left her with my brother." Moyne was boasting.

"That doesn't explain why." Kaelen saw Aidan and the officers moving in behind Moyne.

"Why? Because I could. And I have made arrangements for her to disappear overseas. She will not be returning. That has been my plan all along. I was waiting for her to grow up. I saw her as a baby and realized how much money that she could bring to me. Only, there were no opportunities to take her until now." Moyne was puzzled at that. "Someone always got in our way."

"God. God prevented it. And now, He has prevented you once more." Kaelen stepped backwards as patrol officers reached to restrain Moyne.

Moyne struggled as his arms were jerked behind his back and shiny silver handcuffs snapped around his wrists. Aidan stood and watched as the man struggled to escape. He then turned his attention to Kaelen.

"You just had to, didn't you?" Aidan rubbed at his cheek before he gave a tired smile. "It's over, Kaelen. It's all over. You two faced danger just because of a man's greed. He focused on you because he thought that you were a couple. We don't know where he came up with that." Aidan looked around. "Now, where is Keller?"

Kaelen ran from the kitchen and didn't find Keller. His steps paused for a moment before he was running for the office and on his knees in front of the hiding spot. His fingers could not open it and he began to pound at him, his voice calling for Keller.

Keller froze for a moment as she heard hands clawing at the door and then the pounding. She surged forward, unlocking the door and shoving it open, launching herself at Kaelen. Kaelen caught her close, not hearing Aidan exclamation at her hiding place.

"It's okay, love. It's okay. He's under arrest. It's all over." Kaelen's arms tightened about her and held her as she wept. His tears wet her hair.

Aidan walked away, leaving them to their privacy. They were breaking down in relief but also grief. He knew that only too well. He would be back to get their statements later but for now? He would let them have time.

Six months later, Kaelen walked away from the hangar. He had had to be away on an overnight flight and was eager to be home. His arms opened as Keller ran towards him. He hugged her to him and kissed her, setting her back on her feet.

"Okay, love? You didn't have any problems overnight?" Kaelen studied the face turned up to him.

"I had a wonderful day. The students are just so eager to learn. I wish that I had started teaching earlier. God's timing is right, isn't it?" Keller hugged him tighter.

"It always is. The trip went fine as well. It is a relief to be able to move around without being afraid." Kaelen turned them towards his truck.

"It is." Keller bit at her lip for a moment. "I talked to Dad last night. He's not doing well, Kaelen."

Kaelen reached for Keller's hand. Fairley had been diagnosed with a lung disease and was struggling each day. He had refused to move in with them. He wanted to stay in his own home. They had not pushed it with him, knowing that he was correct. Kaelen had held Keller more than once as she had sobbed out her sorrow.

Walking towards Keller later that afternoon, Kaelen watched her closely. Something was different about her. He would wait for her to speak unless his curiosity got the better of him.

Keller turned and walked into his hug. She had grown accustomed to his hugs and welcomed them. She laid her head against his chest, hearing the beating of his heart.

"Are you sure that you're okay?" Kaelen waited for her to speak. "I love you, Keller, more and more each day."

"I love you too, sweetheart." Keller leaned back to look up at him. "Aidan called this morning. He said that the trials are all over. Moyne died last night from a heart attack. He's gone on to face a higher Judge."

"He did? That's a relief in a way, love. I wouldn't have wanted to face him or his lawyers."

"Nor did I, but we would have gotten through it. God would have seen to that." Keller moved restlessly, not willing to leave Kaelen but not quite sure if she should stay. "I spoke with the studio owner. None of them blame me. They were worried about me. He asked if I would consider coming back. I told him that I wouldn't. I had found teaching was more in line with what I wanted to do."

"And he understood. But you will go back if you're requested by a particular artist?" Kaelen thought that she would.

Keller shook her head. She had prayed that through and knew that God didn't want her there any more.

"No, I don't think so. That part of my life is over. Where I am now? That's where God wants me. He provided for us, Kaelen, in so many ways."

———

"He did. He was our shelter in the storm and our protector. I feel as if I am walking on holy ground when I approach Him, more so than ever before." He hugged her tighter before turning them back into the kitchen and seating Keller.

"It is, isn't it? We need to reach out to others, don't we? Can we set up a charity or something to do that?" Keller shoved a letter across to him. "Barnabas Carey has sent this letter. He wants us to take on leadership for a charity that helps victims of crime, given what we went through."

"He does? We've been praying that way, haven't we? I know that they pray over any charity or whatever it is that they want to set up and then pray for a couple. It is always unanimous when they come to an agreement. Then they ask the couple to pray it over for however long it takes to find God's place for them."

"I have heard that. I think we'll be saying yes. I could run it and you would be around when you're not flying. You're not giving that up."

"No, I don't think that I would. It's where God wants me, the same as with your teaching. We'll pray it through and then go back to them. But I think that you're correct. We'll be taking it on."

The couple grew quiet, each lost in their own thoughts. Keller turned to Kaelen, watching him, falling more in love with her husband. Kaelen turned at that point and simply reached to draw her to him, his prayer of thanks whispering through the stillness of the room.

Dear Readers:

Thank you for choosing to read the story of Kaelen and his love, Keller. I never know how a story will play out. The characters always play out their own stories, just letting me know what the story is as it goes along.

I had no idea that human trafficking would be part of why Keller was taken from her father. It is a huge issue now all over and sometimes it does creep into my stories.

God was there for Keller and Kaelen each step of the way. He was their Shelter and Protector and led them along a path that He had already predetermined for them. Their faith was shaken and yet stood firm.

The characters who came into the story? Richard and his team are in *His Defenders*. Don and his team are in *His Protectors*. Abe and his team are in *His Guardians*. Toryn and Slaney are in *Toryn*. Aidan and Artis are in *Aidan*. Burnie and Muir are part of *The Barnabas Chronicles*. My characters don't stay in their own stories. They walk back and forth between them, adding that much more to the story.

Once more thank you for choosing the story of Kaelen and Keller. Kaelen first appeared in Caleb's story. As I find, minor characters demand a story of their own.

Trust God to shelter you in the storms of life. He will be your Protector and guide you on the path that He has chosen for you.

God bless.

Ronna